Dissonance

A Novel of Music & Murder

Barbara Burt

Bent Tree Press

For all the readers who love music
and all the musicians
who love books,
I'm right there with you.

"Virtually every writer I know would rather be a musician."   —*Kurt Vonnegut*

One

"When I am making music, there are no questions and no need for answers." —*Gustav Mahler*

Allegra Brewster surveyed the conference room. Three plastic pitchers filled with ice water were evenly spaced along the table. She set a ruled tablet at each seat and positioned a pen exactly parallel to the top, adding a plastic cup about four inches to the right of the pen. She didn't bother to leave a cup for the seat at the head of the table. Allie rolled her eyes at the thought of Dr. Sylvia Abbott, the board chair. Persnickety old bag, she thought, not a description I use often, but it describes Dr. Abbott.

The meeting room's rough white-washed walls were evidence of the building's former life as a milking barn. The edges of the long table's pine boards were also rough, contrasting with its silky varnished top. Spaced around the table were colorful plastic chairs, their contemporary style adding a bit of whimsy. Allie made sure they were all set at the same precise distance from the table. A series of framed posters marching along the walls provided additional shots of color, each celebrating a year from the Kenni-mac SummerFest Symphony's past seasons. Interspersed among the posters on one wall were three square windows, their panes slightly frosted in the corners. A trace of wood smoke scented the air.

Allie regarded the posters with affection as she tweaked each to make sure it was hanging straight. From about 1990 on, their images were imprinted in her memory. Each was illustrated in a different style; every year a different local graphic artist was invited to design that season's poster. Highlights from the summer's repertoire were listed on each. Allie remembered the first time she heard Tchaikovsky's *Serenade for Strings*[2], Stravinsky's *Firebird*[3], and Handel's *Water Music*[4]. In 1993, she heard Elgar's Cello Concerto[5], and that's when she fell in love with the cello.

Back to work. Was everything set for the board meeting? Allie moved one chair away from the table against the wall. She would sit there, taking notes. As the assistant executive director, she wasn't welcome to take a place at the table with the trustees. Her boss, George Park, was the only staff person allowed to sit at the table. She placed her chair so that she'd be able to see George's face, in case he had any instructions for her. She also hoped she'd be able to see her father's face as well.

Allie liked to think she got her much-needed job as George's assistant through her own credentials and hard work (last year's master's degree in arts management, for example) and her long association growing up as a volunteer, music student, and avid supporter of the SummerFest Symphony. But she had to admit that it probably didn't hurt to have her dad on the board, especially as he was one of the SummerFest's founders.

Lately, though, her father seemed less interested in the festival. Less interested in everything, actually. Something was bothering him, beyond his usual anxiety. Allie wanted to keep an eye on him during the meeting.

Since moving back home to take the SummerFest job, Allie saw how isolated her dad was. Of course, he knew practically everyone in the small town, but he didn't enjoy much of a social life. He spent most evenings stoned in his chair in the living room, a symphony by Mahler or Bruckner blasting from the speakers. He used to have musician friends—classical, jazz, Celtic, and bluegrass—who played gigs with him on weekends, but that activity had waned. Allie tried to interest him in playing duets with her, he on violin and she on cello, but what was a joy for him five years ago was now more like a chore. They'd stopped practicing together, she claiming that she was too busy, but they both knew his heart wasn't in it.

The lower her father sank, the higher her mother seemed to rise. Remarried and living in Europe, Allie's mother poured all her energy into her career. Funny how two such different people got together, thought Allie, not for the first time. Her dad liked to say Allegra inherited the best traits of each of her parents: creativity and musical ability from him; organizational skills and business acumen from her mother. Although, unlike her parents' differing ways of thinking, Allie's weren't in conflict within her own psyche.

"Allie, are we ready to go?" Her boss, George, stuck his head through the conference room doorway. "Looks good," he said, looking over the table.

"It feels weird not to have a printed agenda," Allie replied. "What's up with that?"

"Ah, yes, well, I guess it will soon become clear why Sylvia didn't want to release the agenda ahead of time." George shook his head as if to clear a troubling thought. "Let's hope the snow holds off until the meeting is over."

Allie looked out the windows. "Looks fine for now. Hey, here comes the first car. Guess we're starting. I'd better go put another log in the wood stove."

Two

"Works of art make rules; rules do not make works
of art."   —*Claude Debussy*

I ce cubes splashed from the plastic pitcher as board chair Sylvia
Abbott refilled her glass. She had brought the cut crystal glass
from home when she ascended to the chairmanship, choosing not
to use one of the plastic cups from the Kennimac SummerFest
Symphony's kitchen cabinet.

"In the first place," she stated, setting the pitcher down with a
thump and narrowing her eyes, "due to our financial situation, we
cannot afford to pay the musicians what they have received in the
past." She looked around the long oak plank table, willing each of
the 13 other board members to meet her gaze.

"In the second place," she said, lowering her voice, "this is our
best chance to break the damn musicians' union."

Allie lifted her fingers from the laptop's keyboard in surprise
and listened expectantly. Nothing. Not a word of protest, not even
from her father.

"I need to be sure that each of you is with me on this," continued
Dr. Abbott. "We must present a united front."

George Park raised his hand. "Ah, Sylvia," he said, "Are you
starting with option number one that you outlined to me this
morning?" He cleared his throat and straightened his tie. "That's
going to be met with a lot of resistance."

"Fuck the resistance." An electric shock ran through the room at the board chair's uncharacteristic profanity.

Allie suppressed a smile. "Do you want that in the meeting notes, Dr. Abbott?"

"For God's sake, Allegra, no notes on any of this until I tell you. Understood?"

Allie nodded, looked down, and pressed a button on her phone.

"So," said George Park, "I want to make sure we all understand. We're asking for a 35 percent pay cut..."

"Yes, yes," interrupted Dr. Abbott, "And we'll ask them to do some free pops and children's concerts. They also need to write an essay describing their commitment to the SummerFest. I want to weed out the uncommitted and the troublemakers. I also think they should re-audition every year."

"Sylvia." David Brewster interrupted. "As I told you earlier, this will seem like an attack on the orchestra. They'll never go for this. I just don't see..." He dawdled for a moment, tapping his pen on the pad of paper. "Have you talked with Anthony Bainbridge about this?"

Dr. Abbott exhaled loudly in a show of impatience. "I have not talked to our music director. But there's no need to. He's not in charge; we are. He works for us, remember? Face it, David, the musicians' union has been running the show here for far too long. Running it into the ground, that is. They must be stopped."

"She's right, you know," the board member in the Chanel jacket said in her faux Boston Brahmin accent. "There's absolutely no reason the musicians here need a union. Unions always create a wall between workers and their employers." She frowned slightly. "We take good care of our musicians here. For example, I always invite them to The Point for a cocktail party at the beginning of the summer. And they can bring their spouses and what-evers—significant others..."

Another board member leaned forward and placed his tanned and manicured hands on the table deliberately, as if to claim the space. "Helen has hit the nail on the head. We would rather deal directly with our musicians. And in the event their expectations are too high, well, we can adjust them." He looked around at the other board members. "I must admit it galls me to think some of my not inconsiderable financial donation is going to the musicians' union, even if indirectly. It simply galls me. It's the same way I feel about food stamp recipients buying soda and candy."

George Park looked as if he were about to say something, then thought better of it. David Brewster groaned.

"So," said Dr. Abbott, "Let's go around the table. I want each of you to give your support to this. Can someone make a motion? Allegra, get this down."

"Ok," said a banker who'd retired to Kennimac and still wore a suit with a pocket square to board meetings. "I move we accept the chair's proposal to require the musicians to take a 35 percent cut in pay, perform some free concerts, and... what were the other things?"

"Write an essay demonstrating their commitment to the Kennimac SummerFest Symphony and re-audition each year," Dr. Abbott rattled off.

George Park raised his hand again. "That last thing, Sylvia, the re-auditioning, there's no way we could do that. For one thing, that means more than 60 auditions each spring. It would take months. And it would be incredibly expensive." He cleared his throat. "It's just not feasible."

"Hmmm. Well, maybe that has to go. Can we get back to the motion? Does anyone second?" Another board member glanced at Dr. Abbott and raised her hand, with a wrist encircled by a twinkling tennis bracelet.

"Thank you, Alice. Now, I want to know who's on board with this."

"Sylvia, this is much too hasty. It'll tear the festival apart," said David Brewster.

"Don't be a fool, David. We must present a united front." Dr. Abbott drummed her fingers on the table. "Allie, get this down: Ron Osbourne made the motion and Alice Vogel seconded it. John? Helen? Great, add John Campbell and Helen Davis. Arnold? Add Professor Arnold Schimler. And I know Ken Henson was in favor, but he couldn't be here today. Don't write him down, though, Allie. Okay, everybody else, raise your hand if you agree."

All but two of the board members raised their hands, some timidly, some reluctantly, some with conviction. Allie entered the names as quickly as she could.

Honing in on a small older woman, Dr. Abbott said, "Esther, aren't you with me?"

Esther Swift looked at the Chair, her eyes enormous through thick glasses. "Did I hear correctly?" she asked, her voice quavering. "You are asking the orchestra to take a pay cut? Is it necessary?"

"It is. Absolutely." said Dr. Abbott. "We went all over the financials at the last meeting. Are you with me?"

"I don't know... I suppose so, if you're right about this, but I..." said Esther.

"Add Esther Swift, Allegra. And now, David." Dr. Abbott turned once again to David Brewster.

"David?"

He shook his head slightly and looked out the window. "I vote no, Sylvia," he said. "You already knew I would."

"If you must," said Sylvia Abbott, with a brittle smile. "But, as a member of the board, you cannot speak against this to anyone. Confidentiality is absolutely critical. Especially since you are the vice chair of this board."

David Brewster nodded. He looked at his daughter, who met his gaze with a questioning look, then he set his pen down and folded his hands.

"Allegra, that's all in favor with one absence and one abstention. The motion passes. Board meeting adjourned. Now, I've got to run." Dr. Abbott closed her leather portfolio, rose from her seat, and stalked out of the room. The rest of the board filed out in silence.

Allie snapped her laptop shut, clicked off the recording feature on her phone, and followed George to their shared office.

"Holy shit, this is Armageddon," George muttered to himself. "Allie, you know that none of this can go beyond these walls," he said to her with a sharp look.

"Hmmmm," said Allie, nodding.

"This is a disaster," said George. "The musicians will never agree to this. They'll strike. And here it is March; the season starts in four months." He rubbed the furrows in his forehead. "Christ!"

"Shall I type up the meeting notes? Or is there something else you want me to do first?"

"No, let's get those notes done and distributed. Please put 'Confidential: For Board Eyes Only' at the top. Email them to me and I'll check them over and send them around. I'm going on an errand. I have to get out of here." George grabbed his wool coat from its hook and rushed out the door.

Allie sat at her rickety desk and opened her laptop. She pulled up the template for board meeting notes and began to type.

Three

"Music gives a soul to the universe, wings to the
mind, flight to the imagination,
and life to everything." —*Plato*

The Kennimac SummerFest Symphony was located at the site
of a former dairy farm. Its offices were housed in one end
of the milking barn, a low cement block building with a concrete
floor. It had been modernized somewhat: there was no central
trough and the milking stalls were gone, for example; the walls
inside had been insulated and sheet-rocked; and windows had
replaced most of the barn doors. But it still was drafty and somewhat shabby. Because most of the organization's activity took
place in the summer, there was little attention paid to heating. A
woodstove occupied one wall. Allie noticed she would need to
feed it shortly.

On her laptop screen, an icon popped up, showing that the
recording of the meeting had migrated from her phone. Allie
quickly labeled it "March Development" and saved it to a file on
her laptop.

Gotta type the notes, gotta type the notes. First some wood,
then some music, she said to herself. Just outside the office door
was a neat stack of wood. It was warmer outdoors than it had
been a month earlier, but March in Maine could still be chilly.
Allie grabbed two pieces of wood and carried them in by the

woodstove. She opened the stove's door with an oven mitt and pushed the logs inside.

She knew something had been brewing on the board. Her father had seemed distracted lately, and George had been twitching with anxiety before the meeting. But Allie had no idea Dr. Abbott was planning such an assault on the musicians. It made no sense. The musicians, who came from all over the country to play together for six weeks in the summer, provided the center of gravity for the festival. Board members rotated on and off, music directors came and went, but many of the musicians had come for so many summers that they were considered part of the community.

Like many others in Kennimac, Allie had grown up attending the festival orchestra's concerts and taking lessons from its members. But the friendship extended beyond the professional—the locals invited musicians and their families for boat rides, lobster bakes, blueberry picking, and more—all the activities that made spending the summer in Maine worthwhile.

Allie could foresee that Dr. Abbott's antagonism toward the musicians was going to cause a terrible reaction. This wouldn't be accepted, not by the musicians or by the audience members who revered them.

And I'm going to be stuck right in the middle, she thought. I need music. "Mars," she decided, "the Bringer of War," from Holst's *The Planets*, Op. 32.[6] James Levine conducting the Chicago Symphony. Perfect.

The ominous percussion and growling low brass on the YouTube recording filled the room.

Four

"This looks fine, Allegra. Go ahead and send it to the board." George handed back the hard copy of the notes.

"I wasn't sure about including that part about the goal being to break the union," said Allie.

"Leave it."

———ell———

The next morning, Allie emailed the meeting notes to the board members. No one responded, except for Dr. Abbott, who texted

George:

Why did you let her include the part about breaking the union, damn it all! You are useless.

Five

"Some people come into our lives, leave footprints
on our hearts, and we are never the same."
—*Franz Schubert*

D avid Brewster was a former violinist, now mostly a fiddler,
farmer, and tinkerer. He came to fiddling via an unusual
route—strict classical training. He spent his childhood master-
ing the violin and graduated from Juilliard. After several years
as a semi-successful freelancer, disillusioned by the cut-throat
nature of the classical music business and the anxiety of living
hand-to-mouth in New York, he took a trip to Canada to check on
possibilities for escape there. On the way home, he took a detour
to Maine and fell in love. Twice. Once with an old farm begging for
someone to nurture it back to productivity, and once with Melissa
Sewell, a local Maine girl with a personality bigger than the small
town she grew up in.

Class valedictorian, star of all local theater productions, broad
shouldered, hazel-eyed Melissa waited on David at the local sandwich shop. David studied the placemat menu much longer than
most of Melissa's customers. Finally, she interrupted his reverie.
"Can't you find something you like?"

David looked up and smiled. "No, I like most everything. Just
trying to stretch my dollars the farthest they can go. Recommend
anything?"

Melissa smiled back. This guy, though sporting several-days-old stubble, was clearly not from Maine. That was a plus. He looked at her as if she were an intelligent person, not a pair of boobs and a long blond braid. The two struck up a conversation, then met after Melissa got off work. David decided to stay longer, and on his third day in Kennimac Melissa brought him home to her parents' farm.

Hidden down a side road just off one of the main roads in Kennimac, Robinson Farm was nestled in a small valley of some thirty acres of fields made up of variegated green patches bounded by barbed wire fences. A swale lined with spindly alders ran through the bottom. Woods surrounded the fields, and several logging roads, long unused, trailed off into the dense fringe. Between the main road and the farmhouse lay a marsh of several acres.

The farmhouse's white clapboards were peeling; a porch sagged off the north side. Melissa took David into the kitchen and introduced him to her parents, who seemed surprisingly old. Later he learned they weren't as old as they looked; they'd just had a hard life of subsistence farming and chain-smoking.

Arlene and Roger Sewall welcomed David, glad Melissa seemed to have met her match. The young man spoke softly and didn't brag. Hearing his quest for a healthier lifestyle, they invited him to stay for the rest of the summer and offered him the use of their small cabin down by the shore of the bay. David cleared out the spider webs and mouse droppings, fixed the broken chairs and table, and replaced the missing cedar shakes on the roof. He got the pump working again and whitewashed the interior of the outhouse. He liked the work, the feeling of accomplishment when each project was finished. And he liked practicing the violin by the light of the kerosene lantern; the logs of the cabin created a warm acoustic and, in the half of the cabin open to the rafters, the sound rose up and then poured back down like maple syrup. Weeks passed and the gigs he would have played in New York were assigned to others. One day he realized it had been two months since he'd arrived in Kennimac. And he was happy.

Melissa joined him at the cabin most nights. When she returned to classes as a senior at Bowdoin College that fall, a mere hour away from Kennimac, she came home frequently, or at least returned to the cabin—often her parents didn't know she'd come home. After the weather got colder and the unheated cottage became uninhabitable, David rented a studio apartment near the college and they moved in together. He'd begun teaching violin and playing with any groups that needed a good violin. That's how he turned to fiddling: there was a greater call for a bluegrass or Celtic fiddler than for classical violinist, and David found he loved the freedom of the less formal music. He also enjoyed the camaraderie of the groups, riffing off one another's performance, the unspoken challenge to play faster or better or to change key in mid-chart. New York and his classical career receded in his mind—to Melissa's chagrin—though he continued to love symphonic literature and earned a spot in the first violin section of the Portland and Bangor symphonies, both part-time commitments.

Staying in Maine, however, wasn't Melissa's goal. She ignored the signs that David was becoming rooted in coastal Maine. Surely he would grow as bored with it as she had, she reasoned. After all, if gigging and teaching were his career goals, he could do that as easily in New York or Boston as in Maine. Somehow, though, the two of them refrained from discussing their future plans in any detail. Each thought the other understood what they wanted: Melissa was confident that David knew she was heading for the city—and not just Portland!—and David assumed that Melissa could tell he loved the life he was building in Maine.

They married two weeks after Melissa's graduation, and that summer they lived in the cabin. As the weeks passed, Melissa urged David to begin auditioning for orchestra jobs around the country, but he wasn't interested. Then Melissa discovered she was pregnant. They moved in with her parents for the winter (who were thrilled to have them), then back to the cottage—newly fitted out with a small woodstove—in April. In late June, Allegra Sewall Brewster, soon known as Allie, was born.

When fall came, the three of them moved to an apartment in Portland. It was as close to urban-living as Melissa could get David to agree to. After twiddling her thumbs, bored and unhappy, through Allie's first two years of life, Melissa got a job at the branch office of a large bank. By then, her long blond braid had been converted to a pert wedge cut, and her blue jeans were transformed into a navy blue pantsuit. Melissa loved the job and was good at it, rising to a new level each time an opportunity opened up. And David was happy taking care of Allie during the day, as most of his gigs were in the evening. Their opposing schedules were hard on their marriage, though, and the distance between the couple slowly morphed into a chasm.

—ele—

When Allie was five, Melissa's parents, Roger and Arlene, died within several months of each other—Roger of cancer and Arlene of heart disease. That seemed to loosen a knot within Melissa; in six months, she announced she was taking a new job and moving to Chicago, and she thought divorce was the best solution for their marriage problem. David and Allie could stay in the Sewall farm in Kennimac. She promised to visit often. It was all civilized and amicable. Each person got what they wanted, except for Allie, who would have preferred a mommy and daddy who lived together.

In the first two years after the divorce, Melissa flew to Maine to bring Allie back with her to Chicago for summer vacation. But Allie wasn't happy in Chicago. While she visited, Melissa was still working long hours, so Allie would rotate through a series of day camps with kids she didn't know. She and her mom would take weekend trips to resorts on Lake Michigan, but sometimes Melissa had to work on weekends, too.

The same year as the Brewsters' divorce, a group of music lovers started the Kennimac SummerFest Symphony. David was involved from the start. He served in many capacities, not the least of which, in the beginning, was as concertmaster of the orchestra and a recruiter of other musicians. Recruiting talent wasn't difficult; a six-week position in a festival orchestra in a beautiful summer place was an irresistible enticement to his friends from music school who'd been living in small city apartments around the country. And as the years went by, while some of the festival personnel changed from year to year, many became regulars. Winter jobs changed, children grew, marriages failed or new ones began, but one constant in their fluid lives was that annual six-week festival in Kennimac, Maine.

Once Allie hit the age of eight, she refused to leave Maine for a summer with her mother. She loved sailing, swimming, hiking—long days outdoors—but the strongest pull came from the music. Although beginning on violin at five with the local Suzuki teacher, from the age of eight she studied cello with the Summer-Fest's principal cellist, Anne Kirschner, every summer.

Anne was an inventive teacher, as full of delight in the cello as when she was a kid, and her enthusiasm was infectious. Her playful attitude helped loosen Allie's reserve, for Allie had become a rather solemn child after her parents' divorce. She'd inherited her father's love of music and her mother's clear hazel eyes. Those eyes could level an unnerving gaze without flinching, often cowing the adults who attempted to disagree with her. She brooked no nonsense and set high standards for herself, as well as for those around her. But with Anne she could be silly. They took their cellos to unexpected places, like the canopy in front of the Red Barn Grocery or on the hiking path along the bay, and they played unexpected music, like duets based on Beatles[7] or Carole King tunes, which Anne arranged.

As the years went by, Allie's connection to her mother grew more and more tenuous. Melissa rose in the ranks, was head-hunted by other corporations, and by the time Allie was in high school, Melissa was posted to the Swiss office of a multinational bank. She sent fat checks that paid for Allie's undergraduate education, but she couldn't attend recitals or graduations. That was ok with Allie; by then, she and her mother didn't have much in common. Their Skype sessions were less and less frequent and filled with awkward patches of silence. Melissa always signed off with, "You know I'm always here for you, Allie," but somehow that didn't seem true to her daughter.

Besides, a neighbor, Kate Zeller, had become a significant figure in Allie's life, perhaps more an aunt than a mother, but a female caregiver and guide, nonetheless.

Six

"As a musician I tell you that if you were to suppress
adultery, fanaticism, crime, evil, the supernatural,
there would no longer be the means
for writing one note."
—*George Bizet*

C onductor Anthony Bainbridge noticed he had a voicemail from the Kennimac SummerFest Symphony office. "Maestro," said the harried voice of George Park, "I think you should schedule a visit to the SummerFest office. We need to talk about some of this summer's soloists. And, Tony," George paused for a few beats, "There are some developments here I think you should know about."

Bainbridge grimaced. Maine in March was not a pleasant prospect, especially when he was in the midst of conducting the Sarasota Opera Company's *Marriage of Figaro* in balmy Florida. And why was George calling him directly? Usually, he dealt with scheduling and travel issues through Tony's assistant, Ted.

"Call Ted," Bainbridge ordered his smartphone. His assistant picked up on the first ring. "Maestro?"

"Ted, George Park thinks I need to plan a quick trip to Maine. I would much prefer to simply do a Zoom. Could you contact him and find out why he thinks a visit is necessary?"

A few minutes later, Ted was back on the line. "Sorry, Mr. Bainbridge. Evidently there's some sort of problem with the board and the musicians? Mr. Park was insistent that an in-person meeting was essential. I told him..."

"Oh, bloody hell. Maine is the last place I want to be in right now." Bainbridge paused. "Do you think he's over-reacting? George doesn't usually go in for drama."

"He seemed quite insistent."

"Ok. Can you get him on the phone for me? I'll try to find out what's going on. In the meantime, in case I have to go, what's my schedule like for the next few weeks?"

"Let me check... Well, you're in Florida through April, then to Houston for the master classes at Rice, then a week in Baltimore, then home to England for a long weekend with your mom in mid-May..."

"What a bother. Get George for me, would you please."

———ℓℓ———

"Hello, George. What the hell is going on up there?"

George cleared his throat. "Look, I'm sorry, Tony, but the board is about to start a fight with the musicians. It could be bad."

"What do you mean? A fight? Why?"

"Sylvia Abbott has it in her head that the musicians' pay needs to be cut. I know, I know," George said as Bainbridge started to interrupt. "She thinks we are facing a financial shortfall. I'm not sure where she gets that idea." He paused. "And I believe she also would like to get rid of the union."

"Well that's a non-starter." Bainbridge thought for a moment. "I suppose you want me in person to confront Sylvia. Throw some of my own histrionics into the mix, as it were."

"It would be helpful, yes."

"I'll see what I can do. Expect a call from Ted with the details."

Bainbridge called Ted again. "Do I have any days that are free in the near future? I think it'll take just a flight up to Portland and back in the same day."

"You have no rehearsals on Wednesday, a week from tomorrow. March 15th. There is an interview but I could reschedule that."

"Brilliant. Book me a flight, and call George Park and let him know when I need to be picked up at the airport." Bainbridge ran his hand through his hair. To himself he muttered, "Beware the Ides of March, what?"

Seven

"Where words leave off, music begins."
—*Heinrich Heine*

Allie collected the empty coffee cups and water bottles from the backseat of her aged Volvo wagon and dumped them into the recycling bin at the car wash. As she sprayed the faded blue wagon with hot water, she thought about the task ahead. Number one, she was excited to be chosen to pick up Anthony Bainbridge at the Portland Jetport but, number two, what on earth would they talk about during the hour-long drive back to Kennimac? George had instructed her not to talk about the draconian board decision in detail; he wanted to do that himself.

Allie despaired of her small talk skills. Lately she hadn't been playing her cello as much as she should—what if he asked what she was working on these days? Bainbridge was pretty decent, as conductors go, not too pompous or self-absorbed. But that British accent and that crop of spiky platinum hair, it was all a bit awe-inspiring.

Allie drove out of the carwash, the windshield wipers sweeping sheets of water in her wake and the car speakers blasting Yo-Yo Ma playing the Bach *Cello Suites*[8]. Ever a source of calm and inspiration, the *Cello Suites* had drawn Allie closer to her instrument; her attempts to master them had deepened her love of its rich sound and the physicality needed to make it sing.

She didn't see how she could keep from discussing the Board's decision with Bainbridge. He was bound to be curious. In two weeks, their offer would be presented to the musicians' union rep, and there was bound to be a huge explosion. Dr. Abbott was evil. Allie thought about her friends in the symphony, musicians who had been in the orchestra summer after summer, whose kids had grown up with Allie sailing and swimming in the bay. How would they take this? What would Mari Tashimi, the concertmaster, do? She could get a position in just about any summer orchestra, but she came back to Kennimac because she loved the atmosphere.

Where had Dr. Abbott—not a "people doctor" but an oil company PhD geologist who insisted on being called "Dr."—come from, anyway? Why was she even on the board—did she care about music? Allie couldn't remember seeing her at many concerts before she joined the board. She bought her way on, Allie decided.

A wealthy summer person with family roots in Maine, Sylvia Abbott was true to type: big old summer "cottage" on the water, all Martha-Stewart-ish inside; a graceful wooden yacht "varnished with her wallet" (as Seth at the boatyard would put it) floating on a mooring out front; weekend lobster bakes on the rocks for her Texas friends.

Actually, Abbott was not so bad for Kennimac, Allie had to admit. Several of her high school classmates worked on the Abbotts' place, and *Windrider*, the 45-foot yacht, along with *Osprey*, Dr. Abbott's small racing boat, kept Seth busy at the boatyard over the winter. Abbott was an avid racer. She sponsored the Wednesday night race series and also supported the kids' sailing program. Allie had heard stories about Dr. Abbott's daring on the water. She believed the races should always take place, even in the case of high winds and rain or hail. Of course, she was a fearsome competitor herself. Allie giggled as she recalled how her former boyfriend, Luke, had described crewing for Abbott. A tyrant, she remembered him saying, with the mouth of a pirate. Captain Ahab Abbott, he had called her. She went through a new set of crew members every summer and usually had to bribe them to stay for the entire season.

It was because of people like Dr. Abbott that the main street of Kennimac was becoming cluttered with little shops selling expensive tchotchkes and designer clothes instead of groceries and hardware. One good side effect, though, thought Allie, was the increase in decent places to eat and drink. Kennimac was certainly more lively in the summer, thanks to the influx of people like Dr. Abbott and their money.

Eight

"Do you know that our soul is
composed of harmony?"
—*Leonardo DaVinci*

"Well, this is a pleasant surprise." Tony Bainbridge opened
the car door. "I much prefer your fresh face to George's
melancholy one." He stowed his bulging leather briefcase in the
backseat and took his place in the front.

"How are you, Mr. Bainbridge?" Allie asked.

"Tony to you, Allegra. You're old enough now to be on a
first-name basis with me. After all, you've even played in my orchestra. And now you're my chauffeur." He unwound a brightly
colored wool scarf from his neck. "How has your job as assistant
executive director been going? Rather well, I would imagine, for
someone of your capabilities."

"You can call me Allie... if I call you Tony, Tony," Allie said.
"It's getting pretty busy, I guess. There's the big fundraising gala
concert in April to plan, and we're getting the programs all set for
the summer. Ads, posters. And soon we'll have to finish up all the
rooming stuff for the musicians. You know how it goes."

"Indeed I do. But what's all this hullabaloo about asking the
musicians to take a big pay cut? What do you know about it,
Allegra? Allie, I mean." Tony smiled.

"Do you mind the music?" Allie asked. "I'll turn it down." The music had shifted to the Dvorak *Cello Concerto*[9], with Rostropovich as soloist.

"No, no. I adore the Dvorak. And, of course, Rostropovich. Is this the Deutsche Grammophone recording with the Tchaikovsky *Rococo Variations*[10]? Berlin Phil with von Karajan? Sounds like it."

Allie looked at him in wonder. "How could you tell that?"

"You wouldn't believe how many times I've listened to this recording. Let's see, I think it was released just before I was a conducting student at Tanglewood. I was scheduled to conduct the concerto with the student orchestra, so to prepare, I listened to the recording over and over. Then it turned out that Rostropovich was in Lenox that week to solo with the BSO. The Shostokovich, I think. He heard we were going to work on the Dvorak and came and sat in for the first movement. What a thrill that was. For all of us. Though I was terrified, I must admit."

"Wow. What a great experience."

"Well, you know, the bigger the artist—it's often been my experience—the more generous and unassuming. Maybe because there's nothing to prove."

Allie nodded. She was thinking of all the idiosyncrasies and special demands from the upcoming summer's soloists she had dealt with over the past few months. One vocalist's contract required that nine pillows be on the hotel bed, another soloist could have no ambient noise whatsoever...

"Well, enough about Rostropovich," Tony said. "What is going on with the SummerFest board? What's this George has been telling me about cutting the musicians' salaries and all?"

Allie flashed back to the text she'd received from Dr. Abbott just before she'd left for the airport:

If he asks about the recent board decision, play dumb.

Sorry, she thought, no way.

"I think it's all about busting the union. For some reason—I don't know why. It all came from Dr. Abbott, and she had it all worked out ahead of time. My dad is the only one who voted no. Oh, and Ken Henson wasn't present, but she said he agreed, too."

"What does your father say about it?"

"He seems kind of at a loss of what to do. And really mad. I think he had tried to talk Dr. Abbott out of it beforehand, but he thinks Dr. Abbott had lined up some of the other board members before the meeting. He says he had a feeling she was doing some political dirty work."

"So, what's the actual decision?"

"It's unbelievable," Allie said. "They approved a 35 percent cut in pay, some ridiculous essay requirement... Abbott wanted the entire orchestra to re-audition every year!"

Bainbridge closed his eyes. "Good God! Does that woman have any idea what that would mean? It would be utterly impossible!"

"No worries there," Allie quickly reassured him. "At least George was able to convince her it was not only impractical but also too expensive."

"Not to mention demeaning." Bainbridge reached forward and turned down the music. "Speaking of expensive, why this focus on cutting the musicians' pay? I knew we were a bit short from last year but I didn't think it was desperate by any measure."

"I know." Allie shrugged her shoulders. "That's what my father says, too. As far as I've seen and heard in other meetings, our development work is going well, and Esther Swift made up the money that had to be borrowed from the endowment."

"It makes no sense. And when the musicians get wind of this, there will be hell to pay." He turned the music back up again. "Ah, well. No use worrying about it until I get there." He leaned back and closed his eyes, moving his hands in small conducting motions.

Nine

"The word "listen" contains the same letters as the word 'silent.'"   —*Alfred Brendel*

G eorge Park, Anthony Bainbridge, and Sylvia Abbott sat in silence while Allie passed around cups of coffee. "Here's black, black, and a little cream and sugar."

"Thank you, Allegra. You may go now." Sylvia Abbott dismissed her with a wave of her hand.

Allie walked toward the conference room door. Should she mention to Dr. Abbott that there was a heating register, basically a hole in the wall, between this room and the main office? Allie decided not.

The voices coming through the wall were faint but easily distinguishable. George's was placating and mild, Dr. Abbott's was sharp and unwavering, and Anthony Bainbridge's was civilized outrage.

"Tony, you know full well I've been talking about our financial concerns for several years now. And last year was worse than the year before. We cannot ignore a downward trend. It's not responsible management."

"Sylvia, love, you know why last year's income was down. We played three fewer concerts."

"And, Tony, the ones we did play were not as well attended as they used to be."

George broke in, "Well, only one week's concerts were low. And that's the week of the hurricane. No one could have..."

"George, never use bad weather as an excuse. You told me the ticket sales were already down for that week."

"Yes, but I also said advance sales are always down for that week. People like to be spontaneous in the first week of August, for some reason."

"Why penalize the musicians?" asked Bainbridge. "Why the drastic cut, with no warning? They'll never accept it. You know that."

"Perhaps not. And then the union will strike. And that will give us an excuse to clean house and start over, free of union demands." The volume of Dr. Abbott's voice rose with emphasis.

"Sylvia," said Bainbridge. "You and I have a fundamental disagreement here. And I don't know where you stand on this, George, I truly don't. Basically, Sylvia, you think we'll save money by diminishing our artistic offering, whereas I wanted to hire some top tier soloists, like soprano Heather Johanssen. Yes, I'll grant you she's expensive, but she also brings in enthusiastic crowds."

"But Tony," Dr. Abbott replied, "We can attract those same enthusiastic crowds by offering performers like 'The Beatles on Classical'—and our out-of-pocket expenses are much less, with only a few musicians required."

There was a loud thud. "That is outrageous! It is an insult. To music, to me, to our players, to the mission of this organization."

"Well, the rest of the board agrees with me."

George tentatively spoke up, "Not entirely..."

"Oh, shut up, George. Who cares if David Brewster isn't enough of a man to agree. He's half out of it most of the time, anyway."

Allie stiffened in her chair. She felt a flush of heat creep up her throat to her cheeks.

"Sylvia Abbott," said George with uncharacteristic strength. "You know as well as anybody that David Brewster has given more than two decades of service to the SummerFest. Without his tireless work, we wouldn't even be here."

"And he understands what this organization is all about," added Bainbridge. "Now tell me about these drastic steps you've been plotting."

"First, we need to ascertain the musicians' dedication. I proposed they write an essay describing their commitment to the organization."

"That's the most preposterous thing I've ever heard. Who's going to read the bloody things?" Allie thought it sounded as if Tony was foaming at the mouth.

"You, naturally."

"Bloody hell! Over my dead body. You don't pay me half enough to spend my leisure hours reading the forced blathering of orchestra members. I care about how they play, not if they can write. It would be a supreme waste of time."

George cleared his throat. "So, can we knock that one off the list, Sylvia?"

"I suppose so. But I thought it would be a good way to gauge the true level of interest."

"That, my dear woman, is in the hearing, not the reading. It's about the music and the audience's appreciation thereof."

"The other major piece I insist we institute is the cut in pay. We simply cannot afford to pay these musicians at the rate we have been paying them."

"Since when?" asked Bainbridge. "Is there a financial debacle looming that you haven't told me about?"

George jumped in. "She's concerned because the revenue was down last year."

"But we played three fewer concerts! Of course it's down!"

"I know. I've tried to make that clear..."

Dr. Abbott interrupted. "So many excuses. The fact is, we need to trim expenses. Our biggest expense is personnel. Therefore..."

"You've got your knickers on backwards! The orchestra is our biggest asset. It's why we exist!"

"Oh, piffle. You sound like David Brewster. The fact is, we have buildings, waterfront property, a name, a reputation..."

"For fine orchestral concerts..."

"For cultural programming. There's more in the world than simply Beethoven and Mozart, for Christ's sake. And some of those other things—yes, interspersed with symphony concerts—could bring in much more money. And right now, our hands are tied because of the damn musicians' union."

Allie heard a fist hit the table. "I've had enough of this conversation," said Bainbridge in a cold voice. "I will fight you, Sylvia. Make no mistake about that. Your actions have painted disaster on the horizon, and you shall be blamed for whatever results." There was silence. For many seconds.

"Now, George," Bainbridge finally continued in a calmer voice, "I think you wanted to talk about some issue with the soloists this summer?"

The door to the conference room opened and Sylvia Abbott stalked by Allie's desk, her mouth pressed in a thin line. Cold wind ruffled Allie's hair as Dr. Abbott left the building, slamming the door behind her.

Allie got up and went to the conference room. "I saw that Dr. Abbott left. Do you need more coffee or anything?"

"You heard the whole thing, didn't you." George stated, rather than asked. He knew about the heating register. "Allie, I..."

"No worries," interrupted Allie, pretending she didn't know he was referring to the statement about David. Her father. Her father who suffered from time to time with paralyzing bouts of depression and anxiety.

"No worries," she repeated. "I won't repeat a thing she said. Or anything you said, either. So, coffee refills?"

"Yes," Bainbridge replied, as George said, "Not for me."

"I'll need to leave for Portland in about an hour and a half," said Bainbridge.

"I'll drive you back, Tony," said George. "I know Allie has a lot of work to do on the database, don't you, Allie."

"True," she answered. But I would rather come back tonight and work on it after driving Tony to the airport, she thought. Oh, well. She started work on the member file, but the murmur of the two voices coming through the register distracted her. I need music, she said to herself. Satie. *Gymnopédies*. She put on her headphones and the soothing piano of *Gymnopédie No.1*[11] floated into her ears.

Ten

"Playing lifts you out of yourself
into a delirious place." —*Jacqueline du Pré*

That evening, inspired by her conversation with Tony Bainbridge but still worried about the fate of the SummerFest, Allie decided it was time to practice her cello, something she had been neglecting.

The glossy fire-engine red fiberglass case stood in the corner of her bedroom. She set the case down on its back and snapped open its latches. As always, the beauty of her instrument swept her away—its voluptuous curves, the graceful cutouts on its face known as the f holes, and the sculptural arch of the bridge. The cello's color was a burnished amber, close to Allie's own hair color. She breathed in the scent of varnish mingled with rosin, aged wood, and a faint tinge of metal from the steel strings.

First, Allie retrieved the bow from the case. The cello's bow was a long swoop of pernambuco wood fitted with an ebony frog, which held one end of the horsehairs. When pulled across the cello's steel strings, the friction of the taut hairs created the musical sound.

Slowly, she turned the knob at the bow's frog, tensioning the hairs. Back and forth, back and forth, she rubbed the cube of rosin across the horse hairs, coating them with the light stickiness that would help them grab the steel strings and make her instrument sing, howl, dance, weep—whatever the music called for.

That finished, Allie set the bow on her music stand. She gathered her long hair into a ponytail and wound it around itself, making a loose knot. Gently she lifted the cello itself from the velvet-lined case. The wood of the neck was satiny beneath her fingers. She fitted the cello's end pin into its anchor at her feet and let the cello rest between her legs and across her chest. It was a full-blown love affair, she thought. Not only could she express the deepest, verbally unreachable emotions throughout the sound of the cello, but she adored the physical nature of her instrument. She played it with her whole body. Some people might assume that playing the cello was a sexual experience, but to Allie's mind, the rapture was more arid, intellectual—more to do with texture and beauty, history and pleasure.

She clicked on the electronic tuning app on her phone and one by one, then together, tuned the four strings. She slid her left hand up and down the steel strings, feeling their tiny ridges, the muscles in her fingers instinctively remembering the positions for various notes. Then, picking up her bow in her right hand, she drew it across the strings, starting the sound. For the next two hours, Allie was lost to the outside world as she practiced her scales and études.

Eleven

"Music is the mediator between the spiritual
and the sensual life." —*Ludwig van Beethoven*

I t turned out that Tony Bainbridge spent the night in Kennimac.
The discussion about the upcoming season and how to cir-
cumvent the board's decision had lasted too long. George drafted
Allie to drive Tony to the Portland Jetport early the next morning
after all, as George already had an appointment.

Allie stopped at the local bakery to pick up a pastry and coffee.
Then she headed out to the Kennimac Inn to pick him up. As she
pulled up, he hustled out the front door.

"Christ, that woman can talk," he said, as he settled into the front
passenger seat."I don't know how her guests can stand it."

"I think most of them love it," Allie replied. "She knows everything about the area—gossip and all. It seems like the inn is
always full, at least during the summer season. Sorry you felt
overwhelmed."

"It was a deluge of mindless chatter. All I wanted was to drink
my coffee and catch up on my emails."

Allegra gestured to the cup of coffee in the holder and the pastry
on the armrest. "I brought you some coffee and something to eat
from the Barn Loft Bakery."

"Hmmm," mumbled Tony, as he bit into the flaky crust. "I must
say, Allegra, you are marvelous. You anticipate my every need!" He

smiled, his lips decorated with sugary flakes. "That reminds me," he added, licking his lips, "I meant to bring this up with George, but I got distracted by all the fireworks yesterday. I've found the perfect assistant conductor for this season."

"I thought..."

"Yes, I know. The budget is 'too tight' for an assistant this year." Tony used air quotes as he said "too tight." "But this fellow is too damn good to pass up. And I don't think he'll be expensive."

"Should I talk with George about it? Like, how to present the idea to Sylvia and the board?"

"That would be terrific." Tony continued to consume coffee and pastry between his words as he spoke. "I think you'll like this young man. He's about your age, I believe, and from Los Angeles. A protégé of Dudamel's program there. Not quite the precocious talent that Gustavo was, but still a fiery athletic conductor, and natural leader. I think he'll go far."

"What's his name?"

"Thomas Ramirez. He's about 28, I think. I met him at the Young Conductors Retreat in San Juan, Puerto Rico, last December and was impressed. We've been corresponding since then, and he's confirmed his interest in working with me here in Maine this summer."

Allie thought through the list of accommodations. The festival had a hard time finding enough places to house the musicians last summer, and this summer was proving to be equally difficult. "When will you know for sure?"

"Well, actually it's pretty well firmed up. Thomas has turned down some other offers, in fact. He's only asking for room and board, he's that committed to coming. So I can't see how there will be any problem with having him join us, can you?"

"When would he start?"

"I assume he'd come when I do. I'll have him send you his professional details—head shot, bio, that sort of thing. And I'll have a chat with George while I'm waiting to board my flight. In the meantime, I'd better get back to this email. Ted really should do a better job of weeding out the extraneous drivel," he muttered to himself.

Allie thought Thomas Ramirez sounded like a good prospect, but she had no idea where she was going to be able to house him. And there were sure to be fireworks when the board (Sylvia, at least) found out. Not to mention George, who had already done much organizing of the publicity for the summer without the mention of an assistant conductor, of course.

This summer's festival was promising to be one challenge after another, she thought.

———ℓℓ———

By the time Allie returned from the airport an hour and a half later, George had already spoken with his music director. As Allie walked in the door, George was pacing.

"It's going to complicate things, right when we're in the middle of a crisis!" he said. "What did Tony say to you about this guy?"

"Not too much. He's a protégé of Dudamel and talented, I guess. Doesn't want to get paid — just room and board."

"I'm not sure we can even do that," countered George. "We're not allowed to employ slave labor."

"Could it be considered an internship?"

"No unpaid internships, either." George shook his head. "This is a problem. And I can't wait until Sylvia hears about it. I'm sure Tony delayed telling me because he knew she would meet it with opposition. One more thing for Sylvia to..." George resumed his pacing.

Allie's phone pinged. She glanced at it and saw she had a new email from cramirez@SFA.edu. Opening it, she saw a photo of an extravagantly good looking man with dark wavy hair and a serious expression that looked as though it might break into a dazzling smile.

"George, take a look." She passed her phone to George.

"Huh," he said. "That may help our audience turnout. But before I plaster his gorgeous face all over our publicity posters, I'd better get the board's approval."

— ℓℓ —

George came into the main office where Allie was working at the computer.

"You'll never guess," he said.

"Sylvia went for it?"

"Yes, well, sort of. It was the weirdest thing." George shook his head. "She started off extremely negative. No way. But after I sent his headshot, she said something like he would liven up the atmosphere, and people might forget that the regular musicians weren't there. Something like that."

"Do you think she expects the orchestra to walk out?"

"Sounds like it." He stopped pacing for a moment. "I think she's wrong. But we still have the question of what and how to pay him. That's a tough one."

"How much do we need to raise?"

"I'd say we need $10,000, at a minimum." George frowned. "Where on Earth will we get that?"

"Maybe we could have a special donation opportunity at the April fundraiser concert? Perhaps he could even come."

"Great idea. I read his bio—he's an accomplished cellist. Maybe he could even play..."

Allie had forwarded Thomas's email to George without reading the bio. A cellist! Thomas sounded more and more interesting.

"I'll get in touch with him," said George, "and we'll see what we can do."

Twelve

"To play without passion is inexcusable!"
—*Ludwig van Beethoven*

to: Karin Anders <corenfa@gmail.com>
from: Sylvia Abbott, PhD <sabbott@xcav84oil.com>
date: March 19 at 4:25 PM
subject: negotiations

As you know, the Kennimac SummerFest Symphony is currently under extreme financial duress. This will impact the upcoming discussions between the musicians' union—which you represent—and the management as we set terms for future contracts. We do anticipate difficult negotiations ahead and will be prepared to explain our basis for the dire predictions.

sylvia

Sylvia Abbott, PhD
Board Chair, Kennimac SummerFest Symphony

———ele———

Another day, another snowstorm. It's almost April, for Pete's sake, thought Allie. Enough! She grabbed a couple of logs for the wood-stove as she opened the door to the office. Just as she lit the match to get the stove going, the phone rang. Her cell phone, not the office phone. The phone screen lit up: "Karin Anders, cor-en-fa" spelled out the caller ID. Karin had explained to Allie that "cor en fa" was Italian for "horn in F"—Karin's instrument.

Uh oh, looks like the word about the board decision has gotten out, thought Allie.

"Hi, Karin. How are you?" Allie waited for the inevitable volatile response.

"What the fuck is going on up there, Allie? Do you know? I got a strange email from Lady Stick-up-her-ass Abbott yesterday. Something about the 'extreme financial duress' and 'difficult negotiations ahead.' What the hell is she talking about?"

"Maybe you should ask George, Karin. He knows way more about it than I do."

"I tried to call him last night and this morning. He's not answering any phones." Karin took a breath. "And that makes me even more worried."

Allie paused for a moment. "Well, here's what I know. But, please, please, *please* don't quote me, ok?" I'll probably lose my job over what I'm about to do, she thought.

"The board has asked the musicians to take a 35 percent pay cut, provide some free services (I think, like a children's concert or something). And they wanted all the musicians to re-apply for their position, including writing an essay explaining what their commitment to the SummerFest is. Or how strong it is. Something like that. But Tony Bainbridge got Dr. Abbott to drop that last part."

"What! Are they out of their fucking minds? Un-fucking-believable!"

Allie held her phone away from her head to protect her ears from Karin's shrieks.

"It's all Abbott's idea, isn't it. Oh my God, wait until everyone hears about this. Doesn't she know we're already at the god-damned low end of the pay scale?"

"Wait, Karin, I don't think you should tell anyone about this until you talk to George. I mean, you don't want to get everyone upset until you have the facts from him."

"Shit, George—it's hopeless if we need to count on him. He'll just march in line with the board. The whole goddamn board, Allie? Did they all agree? Your dad, even?"

"No, he voted no. I think he's… well, not happy about it but he doesn't quite know what to do."

A blast of wind and snow followed George as he entered the office. Noticing Allie was on the phone, he pointed at it and gave her a questioning look. Then he silently mouthed the name, K-a-r-i-n, while mimicking holding a French horn. Allie nodded.

George drew his finger across his throat, meaning "cut it short" and pointed at himself, then at the phone.

"Karin," said Allie, "I have to go. But I'll make sure George calls you right away. I'm really sorry about all this." As she hung up, the sound of a string of expletives spewed from her phone.

"Ok, fill me in," said George. "What does Karin know?"

"Evidently, Dr. Abbott sent an email telling her the orchestra was in dire financial straits and mentioned something about difficult negotiations."

George sat down at his desk and rubbed his forehead. "Why on earth did she do that? Is she trying to make trouble before it's even begun?" His phone lit up and vibrated. "I guess I should talk to Karin," he said.

"Watch out," said Allie. "She's not happy."

"Is she ever happy?" George sighed and picked up his phone.

That wasn't a fair statement about Karin, Allie thought. Karin could be an invincible advocate for the musicians, but she was also a tireless supporter of the SummerFest.

Allie opened her laptop and looked at her to-do list for the day. As she decided what to tackle first, the door opened once again and a head with straggly blond curls sprinkled with snow looked in. "George available?" asked Lucas O'Donnell, his black-rimmed glasses fogging in the office's warmth.

Allie motioned toward the open door to George's office, where George was engaged in a heated phone conversation with Karin. Her caustic voice emanated from the earpiece of George's phone.

"Oh, sounds like Karin Anders is on the warpath," said Luke, wiping his lenses with his t-shirt. He leaned against the corner of Allie's desk but stood up when she glared at him as she wiped melting snow from its surface. Then she returned to her laptop screen.

"I need to talk with George about the risers for the chorus this summer," he explained. "I know he said we needed another row, since the chorus is going to be bigger. But he never gave me the dimensions. You wouldn't know anything about that, would you?"

Allie didn't look up from the computer. "Nope."

"Guess I'll have to come back later."

"Yup."

"Ok, well, I'll be in the shop. Have George buzz me when he gets off the phone." Luke headed toward the door, then stopped and turned around. "How about lunch, Al? You busy?"

Allie gave him a clear-eyed look. "I am," she said.

"Oh," said Luke. "Another time, maybe?"

"Doubtful."

Luke shuffled toward the door in his bulky snow boots. As he opened it, a gust of snow whirled in, bringing with it Sylvia Abbott. She hung up her fur-collared black wool coat on a hook and, motioning toward George, asked Allie, "Karin Anders?"

Allie nodded.

"I thought she'd call him as soon as she got my email. I wonder what took her so long."

Allie decided that the best course was to remain silent.

"Yes, Karin, I know, I know," said George. "Yes, I'll talk to her. Yes, I'll find out more. And, please, Karin, don't fly off the handle and go calling people. Let's stay calm; there may be nothing to get upset about. Nothing's written in stone. I'll let you know more as soon as I know." He set his phone down on his desk and turned to Dr. Abbott. "Sylvia, how nice of you to drop by."

Dr. Abbott looked around the office. "Allegra, is there any fresh coffee?"

"Uh, no. We ran out yesterday. Would you like me to make a run to Dunkin' Donuts?"

"That would be lovely."

That's one way to get me out of the office so you can talk privately to George, thought Allie. "I'm on my way," she said, in simulated cheerfulness.

As she closed the door, she heard George say, "Sylvia, I'm wondering why you sent out that email without letting me know?" Dr. Abbott responded, but Allie couldn't make out what she said.

Thirteen

"When I hear music, I fear no danger.
I am invulnerable. I see no foe.
I am related to the earliest times,
and to the latest. —*Henry David*
Thoreau

K arin Anders picked up her horn mouthpiece and started
her warm-up routine. As she made the buzzing sound, she
envisioned steam coming out her ears. She had to focus on practicing—she had a challenging part in an upcoming concert, playing
the horn obligato part in Mahler 5^{12}. But Jesus! How was she going
to concentrate, knowing all hell was about to break loose with her
summer gig at the Kennimac Festival?

Not for the first time, she thought about the awkward relationship between artists, management, and boards in nonprofit arts
groups. When it worked, it was lovely. Yeah, right, she thought,
whenever the hell that was. In Karin's experience, the paternalistic
nature of the board of these groups—the bad ones were composed
mainly of wealthy status-seekers, with a few music-lovers added
for window dressing—caused more trouble than they were worth.
Except, she had to admit, their donations were important. But this
latest news...

Karin inserted the mouthpiece into her horn, blew a loud blast,
then set her horn down again. She fought the temptation to call

some of her friends in the festival orchestra. No use ruining their peace of mind just yet. And anyway, if what Allie told her was true, better to bring them the news along with a plan of action.

Karin was good at action. She didn't mind taking risks—you can't be a horn player and play it safe. And she'd fought to get where she was. There weren't many women in major symphony horn sections when she was a conservatory student; her female role models had been few but strong. Hell, there still weren't many women, especially considering that more girls than boys started on horn these days, and more girls stuck with the unforgiving instrument through those formative years of high school.

That's gonna change, especially if I have anything to do with it, she thought. She had an active studio of both male and female students, high school age through college, and she worked hard to inculcate a sense of fearlessness in all of them. If you miss a note, she told them, if you enter on a pianissimo high A and split it, if you aim for a E but hit an G instead, act as though nothing happened and go on with confidence. Clams happen! Mistakes occur! Musicality isn't about perfection; it's about expression. It's about what you feel inside and what you're trying to communicate to your fellow players and the audience.

When she was a student, Karin had received mixed messages from her teachers. Her first teacher, Jane, had been a supportive teacher who was a fine orchestral horn player. Discouraged because she didn't get jobs at the level she deserved, Jane finally gave up trying to make it professionally and became a wildlife naturalist instead. Karin wasn't sure what message that gave her, an ambitious young player. Her second teacher, the famous principal horn in a major symphony, was a much better player than teacher. Karin thought back to those lessons. If he had simply played and let her play along, matching his tone and pitch, she might have learned something. But instead he subjected her to his perfectionism, turning each lesson into an hourlong litany of her playing faults, gradually diminishing her confidence and stifling her enthusiasm. What she learned from him was how *not* to teach, and how much influence—positive or negative—a teacher could have.

She had stuck it out. Finally discovering another teacher while also regaining a love of playing and a sense of her own abilities, she had risen through the ranks of the various orchestras in New York. She practiced like a fiend, not always easy in small apartments with roommates who didn't appreciate the incessant scales and arpeggios. And the work had paid off. Now she played with several groups of differing sizes and repertoires, all of which she enjoyed, had a full studio of students, spent six weeks every summer in a beautiful vacation-like setting, and earned an adequate living. Many, many good friends but no permanent partner or children. In her late forties, she knew the latter were no longer possible and doubted whether the former would come along.

But, hey, she had a full life! She loved it. She could afford her own place in the city (which she sublet in the summer), got lots of great gigs, and generally enjoyed her life. No complaints. Until maybe now. Well, she was damned if she was going to let something or someone take away her cherished Maine summers.

She picked up her horn and moistened her lips. Centering the cool silver ring of the mouthpiece on her mouth, she began practicing long tones. Starting as softly as possible on middle C, she held the note and slowly counted to four while gradually increasing her volume to a double forte (extra loud). Then, without taking a breath, she counted another four beats, smoothly returning to pianissimo (very soft).

Fourteen

"To achieve great things, two things are needed: a plan, and not quite enough time."
—*Leonard Bernstein*

L uke intercepted Allie as she headed out to Dunkin' Donuts.
"Al, is George off the phone now?"
"Yes, but Dr. Abbott is in there with him. I wouldn't go in if I
were you."
"Why not?"
"Well, she got rid of me on the pretext of sending me for coffee.
Want any?"
"No, but why kick you out? What's going on?"
Allie realized Luke didn't know about the board's decision. It
made sense; no one was supposed to know. He would definitely
side with the musicians—he'd known many of them for years. He,
like Allie, had spent childhood summers at the SummerFest. He
wasn't a musician himself, but his family had a summer place next
door to the festival, and he'd taken many of the festival regulars
sailing in the bay every summer.
As the stage manager for the last two years, Luke knew almost
everything that went on behind the scenes at the SummerFest.
Allie hesitated, should she tell him about the conflict, would he

keep his knowledge a secret? But it didn't seem fair to keep him in the dark.

"Why don't you come with me to get coffee? I'll fill you in on the way." Allie and Luke got into the old blue car, and Allie tried to start the engine. "Come on, Pablo," she coaxed the car. "You can do it." After several coughs and grinding noises, the engine caught on.

"So, what's up, Al? I thought I caught some weird vibes lately," Luke said as he brushed the snow from his hair. Allie noticed there were a few wood shavings mixed in.

"Ok, so, get ready for this." Allie paused. "Dr. Abbott is trying to change the orchestra. She's got the board to agree to ask for a 35 percent pay cut..."

"What! How? That's impossible! She can't do that, can she?" Luke's usual sleepy expression looked almost sharp and alert.

"Hang on; let me tell you." Allie said. "She's convinced the board to agree to ask for a 35 percent pay cut from the musicians, but her real goal is to get rid of the union and bring in more pops-y types of music. She also had this weird idea of making the musicians re-apply for their jobs by writing an essay, but luckily, Tony Bainbridge talked her out of that. It's bizarre. She even wanted to make them all re-audition each year, but George killed that idea based on budget considerations."

"Didn't anyone stand up to her? How did she get the board to agree? What does Bainbridge think?" The outrage in Luke's voice rose higher with each question.

"The board pretty much rolled over."

"Those lapdogs! Even your dad?"

"He voted no, but he didn't really fight it." Allie frowned. Her father had seemed particularly unfocused over the last few days.

"Bainbridge must have made a fuss. I can't imagine he'll let this happen."

"He can't do too much about it, but, yeah, he doesn't like it. And that's why Karin was calling—Abbott sent her an email." Allie pulled into the Dunkin Donuts drive-up lane. "You sure you don't want any coffee?" Luke shook his head and pulled his phone out of his pocket while she prepared to order.

"Hold on, Luke, don't tell anyone. Not yet. Don't do anything—wait until I get past the pickup window. There's more."

———ℓℓ———

It turned to sleet as Allie reached out for the tray of coffees. She turned on the windshield wipers and slowly drove out of the parking lot, thinking about what the next steps should be.

"Luke, I think her plan is to get the musicians mad enough that they go on strike. I'm guessing she thinks that will make them look bad and they'll lose the support of the public. Then she can eventually toss them out and start over."

"Yeah," said Luke slowly. "So... "

"So, the thing to do is to let them know that. And hopefully help to keep them from falling for her plan." Allie started to see the outlines of a strategy. "Karin Anders called this morning, looking for George. I talked with her for a few minutes. She'd gotten an ominous but vague email from Dr. Abbott and was already smelling a rat."

"I bet she was," said Luke. "And, as the union representative, and a pretty volatile personality, she's the one Abbott wants to rile up. Abbott's hoping Karin will whip the rest of the orchestra into a frenzy and they'll all walk out."

"I'm sure it's something like that," agreed Allie. "When Karin called, I told her what I know. But she also spoke to George. I'll see if he told her about the idea of breaking the union. When I find that out, we can figure out where to go from there."

Luke looked unhappy. Allie figured he was itching to send out a few texts to his friends in the orchestra to let them know what was coming. "Luke," she said earnestly, "Hold off on contacting anyone until we have a plan, alright? Please?"

Luke held her gaze for a few seconds. "Ok. But we can't wait long." His face lit up. "So, we'll have to have lunch together, after all."

Allie rolled her eyes. "Ok. You win. But let me find out from George what he told Karin. We have to go slowly and do this right. I don't want to get in trouble. I know you aren't thinking of your job as a major career move but I didn't get a master's in nonprofit arts management for nothing. I want this job on my resume. And I can't afford to get fired. I've got graduate school loans to pay."

"I thought your mother paid for your education. Isn't that what you told me?"

"Yes, well, she paid for Bowdoin, but she didn't think a master's degree in arts management was a good investment. She wanted me to do an MBA in corporate finance or something." Allie smiled ruefully. "She thought music could be a pleasant little hobby on the side. When time permitted, of course. She doesn't want me to end up like my father..."

"That sucks. So you had to pay for the whole thing yourself? That's a lot of money."

"I got some scholarships and a teaching fellowship, so I didn't have to come up with the whole thing. But it's still a big amount for a not-very-high-paying profession." She brightened. "But, hey, it's worth it. I'm a big girl. I made the right decision."

Fifteen

"I was obliged to be industrious. Whoever
is equally industrious will succeed
equally well."
—*Johann Sebastian Bach*

When Allie got back with the coffee, George and Dr. Abbott were sitting in the conference room. Luke went back to the wood shop, his question about the risers' dimensions unanswered. Allie delivered a cup of coffee to each of them, then resumed her work at her desk. As before, George and Sylvia's voices came through the register.

"George, it's important that this goes well," said Dr. Abbott. "I have a lot riding on it. And I'm afraid you're going to botch it up."

"Why would you say that?"

"To be frank, George, I think you don't know which side you're on. You're always the inscrutable Oriental. I can't read you. I'm just not sensing the sort of enthusiasm and support I was hoping to get from you."

"What more do you want? I've done everything you've asked. This isn't going to be easy, you know. And I'm American, not 'Oriental.'"

"I thought you were Korean."

"My grandparents came to the U.S. from Korea. A long time ago."

"Oh, let's not split hairs. What I need to know is, are you for or against the board's wishes? And it doesn't help to have that little snoop, Allegra Brewster, sitting in the next office. I think we both know how dangerous that could be. In fact, I think maybe you should let her go. Maybe you can think of some pretext."

"Sylvia! You've gone too far." Allie heard a chair push back, and George strode through the conference room doorway.

"George Park, get back in here," Dr. Abbott called from the conference room, where she still sat at the table. "I'm not finished yet."

"I have another meeting in ten minutes," said George, returning to the table.

"Ok, I'll grant that last item was a non-starter," said Dr. Abbott. "And I didn't mean to insult you. But we can't have any leaks from this office. Can you impress that upon her? Threaten her with losing her job, if that will help."

Allie heard George mutter something in return, but she couldn't make it out. Then Dr. Abbott's voice rang out.

"George, your job's on the line, too, you know."

The conference door opened. Allie scrambled to look like she had been obliviously working away on her computer.

"Thank you for the coffee, Allegra," said Dr. Abbott. "I'll be on my way." Her high heels tapped across the concrete floor. George held her coat for her and opened the door for her as she left. Then he turned around to Allie.

"You heard, didn't you?" he said.

Allie nodded.

"Well," George continued. "We both have to be careful. God knows I need this job."

And I have those school loans, thought Allie, as she nodded her head.

"It will not be easy when the word gets out around here." George rubbed his forehead. "You know that, right? Karin will probably kill us all with her bare hands. I think she was calling Tony Bain-bridge next."

"How much did you tell her?" asked Allie.

"I outlined the new proposal. But not much more than that. She was furious, as you might expect."

Sixteen

"I haven't understood a bar of music in my life, but
I have felt it." —*Igor Stravinsky*

L unch was a couple of sandwiches from The Green Reaper,
the local food coop, eaten in the SummerFest wood shop,
while *The Suburbs* by Arcade Fire[13] played on the shop speakers.
Although she thought him an ally in this business, Allie didn't trust
Luke much beyond that. Besides, she couldn't afford to go out to
lunch at a place like the Kennimac Grill, and she didn't want him
paying for her. She didn't want to be in his debt, ever.

"So, let's fill Karin in on the whole story and let her know the
musicians should not strike." Luke was raring to go.

"Wait. We need to think this through. First of all, if she's talked
to Bainbridge, then she already knows about the hidden goal to
break the union." Allie cleared her throat. "So we don't need to be
the ones to tell her."

"Ok. Well, then, we can give her some advice about how to
thwart Abbott's ulterior motive."

"Maybe it would be better to just listen at this point. Karin may
have her own ideas." Allie took a sip of her kombucha.

"I want to do something." Luke shook his head and pushed his
black-framed glasses back up his nose. "I don't want to sit around
and watch something I care about be destroyed by a rich summer
person who has no real stake in this organization."

Allie smiled. "Spoken like a rich summer person, Luke."

"A former rich summer person. But now I'm living here year round and earning my keep—somewhat, anyway. I'm practically a local."

"Whatever." Allie gathered up her hair and secured it into a bun. "You're a little sensitive about that, you know."

"Well, I'm loving it here." He stopped for a moment, then continued. "And that's why I don't want it to change. If I lose this job, I'll be heading back to some city, most likely. I doubt I could find anything else here."

"I get it. But promise me one thing. Let's not rush into anything. Let's find out what Karin knows and plans to do. We can help her. But we have to be smart about it. Ok?"

"If I could just get my hands on that fucking Abbott. I'd like to wring her stringy little neck."

"Luke, promise."

"Yes, yes, I'll hold off. For a few days. Not much longer, though."

"By the way," Allie said, "Tony Bainbridge is bringing in an assistant conductor this summer. From L.A."

Luke wasn't particularly excited. "Yeah?" he muttered through a mouthful of sandwich.

"He's a cellist, too. His name is Thomas Ramirez."

"Thomas the cellist."

"Cellist *and* conductor."

"Yeah, yeah. How did Bainbridge ever get the board to agree to that?"

"I guess Sylvia liked his looks." Allie smiled at the memory of Thomas's photo.

―――*ℓℓ*―――

Back in the office, Allie considered her music list. Something somber but not too overbearing. She decided to play the LA Guitar Quartet's rendition of "Farewell to Stromness" by Peter Maxwell

Davies[14]. The elegiac tones filled her earphones, and she got to work.

It was so awkward, having to work in the same place as Luke. She couldn't very well order him to leave—he seemed as enamored of his job as she was of hers. But after their acrimonious breakup two summers ago, she didn't quite know how to behave with him. Should they be friends? How? How can you be friends with someone you loved, someone who hurt you so badly? Face it, she would never trust Luke. Not after the way he had betrayed her.

Halfway through the Peter Maxwell Davies piece, a message popped up on her screen.

Any chance you could come by this evening?

Kate Zeller lived by the harbor. Almost on the harbor, for her house was a converted canning factory. Kate was a sailmaker and an avid sailor and had taught all the local kids to sail during the summers. She had three kids of her own, and Allie had been their primary babysitter when they were younger. But now the oldest was 14 and could be in charge when needed.

Kate had been a surrogate mom to Allie in lots of ways: teaching Allie how to cook, so Allie and David didn't have to eat fried rice for every meal; taking Allie shopping for a bra when that time came; and filling her in on the finer points of dealing with her period. She was Allie's confidant when Allie and Luke had become more than friends. Allie supposed she was the daughter Kate didn't have, or maybe more like Kate's younger sister.

Recently though, tragedy had struck Kate. Her middle son, Toby, drowned in a sailing accident two summers ago. He had gone out when the wind was rising in front of an oncoming storm. His small sailing dinghy overturned, and those on shore who witnessed the accident couldn't reach him in time.

Allie tried to return the favor of support and caring as much as she could, though away at graduate school during the winters, but the accident had altered Kate. Her sunny disposition disappeared, understandably. But Kate seemed unable to get beyond her overpowering grief. She and her husband, Paul, divorced a year later, much to Allie's dismay, for she was close to Paul, too. She hoped Kate was finally getting some of her old liveliness back.

Allie responded to Kate's text:

no plans. what time?

Via text, they agreed upon seven o'clock.

Seventeen

"Music is about the only thing left that people
don't fight over." —*Ray Charles*

Lucas O'Donnell was the youngest son of a wealthy hedge
fund manager from Westport, Connecticut. His two older
brothers preceded him at Groton, excelling in all ways. Not so with
Luke. He preferred building things in the school's shop rather than
sitting at a desk or charging ahead on a playing field.

Luckily, his effervescent personality helped smooth over the
differences between himself and the rest of his family. He rebelled
unobtrusively, never confrontationally. Enduring the long months
of school in patient silent dissension, he reveled in the freedom
of his family's Maine summer house. Eleanor O'Donnell was a
school psychologist in the Westport schools, so every year, as soon
as summer vacation began, she packed up the three boys and
decamped for Maine.

The O'Donnells' summer house was originally part of the dairy
farm that had become the Kennimac SummerFest campus. Theirs
was the original house built by the family in 1793 and was sited near
the bay, as water was the main mode of transportation in those
days. More recently, it had been the home where grandparents
and elder aunts and uncles retired when they no longer needed to
work on the farm. As the SummerFest was getting started in 1995,
the founding group couldn't raise enough money to buy the entire

farm property, including both houses. So, Sean O'Donnell, Luke's father, already an investment whiz, bought the whole parcel and donated the bulk of it to the festival, with the proviso that nothing could ever be built in the 20 acres of waterfront fields separating his house from the rest of the campus. In this way he secured the favor of the town and his neighbors, while preserving the privacy of his family's summer refuge.

When they bought it, the O'Donnell house was a simple two story saltbox, but it had morphed over time into a bigger, grander place not visible from the road. There was a tennis court discretely hidden from view in a grove of cedars and a saltwater pool in the rose garden. The lawn rolled down to the bay, where a long wooden dock marked one edge of a small beach (for which they trucked in sand every spring) that shrank and expanded, depending on the tide. Tall grasses that became cattails and then marsh bounded the other edge of the beach. Because of the entreaties of little Lucas, who loved to listen to the croaking frogs and the boundary-marking calls of the red-winged blackbirds, his parents had resisted the idea of pulling up the marsh plants to expand the beach. Nowadays, that would be illegal, so the marsh was there to stay.

Usually summer people as wealthy as the O'Donnells had a fancy boat—power or sail or one of each—moored off their summer house. But Sean suffered from seasickness, so the only watercraft at the O'Donnells' were kayaks and small day sailboats. Two of the sailboats were of the class that raced in the Wednesday series on the bay. It was a unique class of sailing skiffs that had raced on summer Wednesday evenings for decades. Though many of the boats were now made of fiberglass, the oldest boats were of wood and lovingly restored each year by their now second- and third- and even fourth-generation owners.

Much to his brothers' surprise, Luke loved racing, and by the time he was thirteen, he regularly beat his brothers and most of the rest of the fleet in the boat he claimed, Redwing.

Allie often crewed with him. She'd learned to sail with her father in their old boat, Calliope. But her father cared more about varnishing and painting Calliope—one of the original wooden versions of the class—than racing her.

When they first started sailing together, Luke was put off by Allegra's apparent solemnity. She was so damned serious. So, he began deliberately to try to make her smile. Soon he discovered she did have a sense of humor, a silly side, and even a sardonic streak, but she dispensed them parsimoniously.

As they spent more time together on the water, Allie and Luke discovered they had compatible racing styles. She could read the sometimes flukey winds of the bay, often predicting a shift in direction before it was apparent to anyone else. He understood how the boat would respond to a tug on the tiller and how to correct for the pull of the current or tide. Allie knew how to finesse the spinnaker so the colorful parachute-like sail would carry them over the finish line; Luke was a master tactician.

But the most fun they had was when they spent a lazy afternoon on either Calliope or Redwing. When they were teens, they would raid the always well stocked O'Donnell kitchen for a couple of sandwiches, two cans of soda, and a handful of cookies. Then they'd spend the afternoon trying to catch the breeze. Allie loved nothing more than sitting high on the windward gunnel as the boat heeled in the wind, water foaming over its leeward rail. "Rail under!" one would shout, and the other would answer back, "Rail under!" Sometimes, if the tide was right, they'd stop at Happy Island, a tiny knob of green rising above a ring of granite boulders. They'd drop the sails, pull the boat up on the tiny gravel beach, and lie on their backs on the grassy hill, watching the osprey and seagulls gliding overhead.

As they grew older, their friendship became something more. They didn't spend as many afternoons together because Luke was teaching sailing at the sailing club and Allie was busy with her cello, but the time they did spend together was more intense. Lying side by side in the field on Happy Island, Luke might tickle Allie's cheek with a strand of grass, she might retaliate with a seagull feather, and soon they'd be making out. Luke attended concerts to watch Allie play, and Allie helped when his sailing classes held their end-of-session picnics. Everyone who knew them generally recognized that Luke and Allie were a couple. Luke's parents were happy their nonconformist son had found such a lovely summer girlfriend, David Brewster thought Luke was a decent boy, and Melissa Brewster (from a far distance) secretly cheered that Luke would be a ticket out of Maine for Allie if they stayed together. Kate and Paul Zeller thought the two kids were made for each other.

College raised a dilemma. Allie got into Bowdoin College, much to her mother's delight. David Brewster was happy, too, that Allie wouldn't be going far away to school. Although the college's music department was small, Allie knew she'd have lots of opportunities to play her cello and learn more about music, while also taking a variety of other courses. But Luke didn't have the grades for Bowdoin and besides, he had no interest in trying to survive in a rigorous academic environment. Finally, he decided on the University of New Hampshire, which had a Bachelor of Fine Arts program in sculpture.

The two continued to see each other as much as possible during college, and they still spent summers together in Kennimac. Luke continued to teach sailing, but he also started volunteering to do some work in the SummerFest wood shop. Allie helped out in the SummerFest office, as well as occasionally playing in the orchestra when extra cellos were needed. She began to think she'd like to make a career of working around and ultimately managing music organizations. Luke supported her ambition, even though it meant Allie would be going to school far away for two years to get her masters. As it worked out, Allie didn't have to go so far—only to Boston University, about three hours away from Kennimac. And, although they didn't talk about it, they, along with everyone else, assumed they'd eventually be reunited, get married, and live happily ever after.

And it was working out that way. Until Toby Zeller's tragic accident.

Eighteen

"Mournful and yet grand is the destiny of the artist."
— *Franz Liszt*

A llie left the office at 5:30 and headed home. She still wasn't used to the idea of living with her father. When summer came, she would stay in the little guest cottage (shack, really) down by the shore, but it was too cold during most of the fall, winter, and spring. So now, having returned to take the job at the SummerFest, she was back in her old bedroom. At least it was rent free, even if she had to listen to her father's snoring down the hall every night.

Allie noticed that the driveway hadn't been plowed. She gunned Pablo and swerved in, just missing the granite post that marked the walkway. Smoke was rising from the chimney, so at least her dad was home and had started the woodstove. The house was dark, however. The ominous strains of the opening bars of Mozart's *Requiem*[15] were blasting through the house as she opened the door, and the faint scent of marijuana lingered in the air.

Archie, their ancient but still exuberant Westie, bounded up to Allie as she came in. He obviously needed to be let out. Allie opened the door again and followed Archie out and back in. Finally, she took off her boots and hung up her coat.

"Dad?" Allie walked through the cold kitchen into the dark living room. "Dad? What's up?"

David Brewster lifted his head from his hands as the soprano began. An ashtray with the remains of a joint was on the side table.

"Uh, oh, Dad. Anxiety again?"

Her father looked into the distance and nodded.

"Did you call your doctor?"

"No." He shrugged his shoulders and sighed. "What good will it do? The pot didn't even help."

"Dad. You know you need to call Dr. Hudson."

"I don't know. Nothing works."

"You'll feel better. This will pass." She took his hands to pull him up out of the worn chair. "Come. Let's make some dinner. I have to go visit Kate at 7:00."

Her father looked up at her. "That poor woman. Poor sad Kate. She was so bright and happy once, before the accident."

"Come on." Allie half dragged her father into the kitchen. "How about we make some vegetable soup? We've got all the ingredients."

Allie set her father to chopping carrots and celery. He seemed to perk up a bit; his voice took on more energy.

"Allie, I've been thinking about this horrible plan Sylvia Abbott has put in motion. We've got to do something drastic to stop her. Any ideas? Short of murder, I haven't got a clue."

Allie stopped stirring the onions and garlic for a moment and laughed. "That would do it, for sure." She became thoughtful again. "I actually think the musicians can outlast her. I mean, they'll have tons of community support. I don't think she has many friends here in Kennimac, do you?"

"Not unless she's paying them." Her father stopped chopping and looked down at his hands. "It seems intractable, though. I'm afraid it's going to tear the Kennimac SummerFest apart." He looked at Allie. "It'll ruin this coming season, that's for sure."

"It certainly will cause damage," agreed Allie. "We'll have to work our butts off to minimize it."

"I don't understand why Sylvia feels compelled to do this now..."

"She says the financial picture is grim." Allie gathered the chopped vegetables and dumped them into the pot, stirring them with a wooden spoon in a bit of chicken stock.

"Have you looked at the financials, Allie? Things are not that bad. Certainly no worse than many other years. We've always pulled through."

Allie put down the spoon. "You know, I haven't taken a close look at them. In comparison, that is. That's a good point, Dad. Why didn't you bring it up at the board meeting?"

David Brewster looked down at the empty cutting board. "Don't know. I don't know. My brain just was on hold or something. Maybe because I was so shocked. I never really thought she'd go through with it."

"We all were," Allie said, stirring. "But don't let it get you down, Dad. I'm sure something will come along to make things right. I know I'll do whatever I can."

"Allie, don't take any risks with this. As I well know, Sylvia can be vindictive. I'd hate for you to get a black mark on your career just as you're starting out." He glanced at her. "You haven't been doing any plotting, have you? Like with the musicians, or with Lucas?"

"Archie! Do you want some carrot?" Allie avoided her father's eyes as Archie bounded over. She put the carrot pieces in Archie's bowl and bent to scratch his ears.

"Dad, don't worry about me. I'll be careful and I know what I'm up against. But you, I don't want you getting anxious. You worry enough as it is."

As they sat down to eat, David Brewster clasped his daughter's hand. "You're so like your mother that way. Capable."

Allie raised her eyebrows but said nothing.

Nineteen

"When you're drowning, you don't say 'I would be incredibly pleased if someone would have the foresight to notice me drowning and come and help me,' you just scream."
                                                    —*John Lennon*

When Kate greeted her at the door, Allie was shocked at her appearance. Kate looked haggard and grim. She was wearing a heavy canvas gray tunic that looked several sizes too large and her pants were splattered with mud and bagged out at the seat and knees. Her hair was a tangled mess—it obviously hadn't been brushed in days.

"Oh, Allie," she said, hugging her. "I'm so glad you could come. I need to talk to you. I just don't know what to do."

Allie followed her into the house. The Zeller's house was a brick warehouse—at one time a factory where crabmeat and lobster were canned—overlooking the water. They had remodeled it, adding walls and plumbing. It had been a multi-year project, with Kate and her then-husband Paul equally sharing the work. Allie could remember when their three little boys slept in ships' berths in an area cordoned off with curtains made of old sails, the numbers and insignias still decorating the stiff dirty-white fabric.

Kate headed down the stairs to the basement, which was finished as a sailmaker's loft. A damaged sail from one of the fleet of boats used in the local sailing lessons covered the large worktable.

Kate's sailmaking tools were arrayed along a side table: the sail-maker's leather palm; a marlin spike; a sewing awl; the hot knife; a pack of giant needles; a Swedish fid; and huge spools of heavy polyester thread. Joni Mitchell's album, *Blue*[16], was playing on the large speakers. Allie remembered the upbeat music Kate used to play while she sewed: Marvin Gaye, Vivaldi, the Beach Boys... She wondered if she would ever hear those tunes booming from Kate's speakers again.

"Allie," said Kate, "I have to talk with you about Harris. He's telling me he wants to live with his father. I don't know what to do about it. I mean, he's 14, but I can't imagine him living in Boston. He'd go crazy." She looked at Allie. "Really, what I mean is I'll go crazy, if he's gone." Her eyes filled with tears. "You know Harris better than anyone. What can I say to him to make him stay?"

Allie thought back to the Harris she had babysat. He had been a cheerful little boy, sweeter than most. She could picture him running around the yard, singing at the top of his lungs. He was so gentle and protective of his brothers; Toby's death had hit him hard. Allie had seen little of him lately, though she'd run across him in the back parking lot in town a few weeks ago, smoking cigarettes with some other boys behind the dumpsters. She'd waved hello on her way to her car, but he pretended not to see her. Allie decided not to mention it to Kate; it would only add to her distress.

"It's so tough... Being 14 is bad enough. And with Toby's..." Allie stopped, not sure if she should continue.

"I know, I know," agreed Kate. "But he won't let me help him. He blames me for the accident. I told him I wasn't the one who said Toby should go out in that blow. But I think Harris still holds me responsible."

"Where would he go to school if he moved to Paul's in Boston?" Allie asked.

"Oh, Paul says if Harris moves in with him, there are lots of good schools he could go to. I don't know... Kennimac High is so comfortable. He can walk to school. I can't imagine him in a big school..."

"There might be some advantages," Allie said. "There might be more courses he's interested in. Kennimac's pretty small. There'd be more kids to choose from for friends. Kids who share his interests. Maybe."

Kate shrugged her shoulders. "Maybe," she echoed. "I don't know, Allie. Could you talk with him? He might open up to you. He won't even discuss it with me. Everything's come through Paul. And I don't know if I can trust Paul to tell it straight, if you know what I mean. I'm just beside myself—I feel so helpless."

Allie thought about Harris's youngest brother. "What does Chris say?"

"Harris doesn't want Chris to find out until it's all settled. I know it will destroy Chris. Probably worse than it will hurt me. Oh, Allie, what if Chris wants to move in with Paul, too?" Kate's eyes filled with tears.

Allie gave Kate a quick hug. "Kate, let's not imagine the worst yet. I'll try to talk with Harris. Maybe I can get him an after-school job at the festival—would that convince him to stick around?"

"It might. It would be worth a try, anyway. And it wouldn't have to be a paying job, just something with responsibility, you know? Something to make him feel needed. He's still playing horn—and I know he's looking forward to studying with Karin again this summer." Kate smiled ruefully. "If we ever get summer..."

Allie matched her smile, thinking about other problems besides the weather.

—ееe

When she got back home after sharing a couple of glasses of Pemaquid Ale with Kate and cheering her up a bit, Allie decided to practice her cello. She pulled out the cello part for the second movement, the "Allegretto," of Beethoven's *Symphony No. 7*[17]. It was on the program for the last concert of the SummerFest season and Allie was hoping she'd be invited to play. She hadn't dared to ask Tony Bainbridge if he needed Allie in the cello section for that concert. The symphony ran the gamut from mournful to exuberant, and Allie hoped its joyous conclusion would be heard that summer. She decided to play along with the old Leonard Bernstein recording, imagining she was performing with the SummerFest orchestra.

Twenty

"Actually, you never eyeball a horn player. That's
one of the real rules. You just don't. They're stuntm
en... You don't eyeball stuntmen just before they're
about to go near death..."
—*Simon Rattle*

Over the weekend, Karin Anders practically had to sit on her
hands to keep herself from calling various friends in the
SummerFest orchestra. So, she was especially pleased to get a text
from Allegra Brewster on Sunday evening, asking if she'd be willing
to be on a conference call early the following morning. Maybe
something was finally going to happen.

She knew it was dangerous, talking about this situation with
other people without knowing exactly where they stood. On the
other hand, there would be no question about her own perspec-
tive on the mess, so it didn't matter who knew how she felt about
the way the musicians and their union were being trashed.

Besides, she trusted Allie. She'd known her since Allie was a kid
taking cello lessons and hanging around the orchestra's rehearsals.
Karin thought about that kid, with the jean cut-offs, crooked
braids, and serious hazel gaze that made you take a ten-year-old
seriously. As one to laugh uproariously, scowl furiously, tear up at
the slightest sense of melancholy, and generally wear her emotions
on her sleeve, Karin was a bit mystified and in awe of the kid who

doled out smiles infrequently. When a smile appeared on Allie's face, it lit up all those in its path with a burst of joy and the thrill of rarity.

Karin finished her cup of morning espresso just as her cell phone rang.

"Karin? This is Allie Brewster. And Luke O'Donnell is with me. We have you on speakerphone. Is that ok?" Allie sounded slightly breathless.

"Ok, where are you two calling from?" Karin asked.

"We're actually in my kitchen. Dad's gone and Luke and I don't need to be at work for a half-hour. No one's around. So we have a few minutes to talk."

"How are things in Maine? Is everything I heard about still going forward? Abbott still pulling the frigging strings?"

"Yes. That's what we wanted to talk about with you."

Luke jumped in. "Karin, we need a plan to deal with these goons. We need to take them down and hurt them bad enough that they never get up!"

Karin laughed. "Luke, you've watched too many episodes of something... maybe "The Sopranos" or some other mob show. But you're right; we need to make sure we win this god-damned fight."

"I was thinking about what's at stake, and what the musicians' assets are," said Allie. "First and most importantly, people in Kennimac kind of think of you all as family. I mean, there are some deep longtime friendships here."

"Not to mention at least two town-orchestra marriages," added Karin.

"Right," said Allie. "So I think we should play to that strength."

"Don't you think the town will automatically side with the musicians?" asked Luke. "Nobody likes Abbott, except her own little entourage."

"Well, that's the tough part," said Allie. "I think if the orchestra went on strike, the feelings of the town might change. After all, having no orchestra in residence would cause financial hardship for a lot of businesses. And there might not be a lot of sympathy for unions in general around here."

"So," said Karin slowly, "you're saying going on strike would make us the bad guys in the eyes of the town."

"Exactly," said Luke and Allie together.

"In fact," added Allie, "that's what Dr. Abbott and her supporters are hoping you do. I actually heard Dr. Abbott say the point was to get you to call a strike."

"So, to beat them, we need to show them up as the assholes they are... Hmmm. Well, one thing we would need to do is make sure people know and understand what the hell's going on. I haven't spoken about this to anyone—although I sure have been tempted. Does anyone in Kennimac know about this besides the board?"

"No," replied Allie. "The board's been sworn to secrecy. And George and I have been threatened with losing our jobs if we tell. So it's hard to know how to get the word out."

"Look," said Luke. "It'll be common knowledge as soon as the letters go out to musicians about their contracts. I don't think the board can expect it to stay secret after that."

"Do you know when that's supposed to happen, Allie?" asked Karin.

"I haven't heard. But that's a good point. So what would we do then, leak it to the Kennimac Weekly?"

"I actually think it would make bigger news than just the local weekly paper," said Karin. "I would think the Portland Press Herald and the Bangor Daily News might cover it. TV stations, Maine public radio. After all, it's a shitty attempt to break a union that has had good relations with the community for years."

"Let's create a communications plan, then," said Allie. "I'll know when the letter is being mailed because I'm likely the person who has to send it. I can alert you, Karin, and maybe you can write a follow-up letter to the musicians."

"Yes, something to the effect that this is heart-breaking mind-fucking news; we can't sign the contract as it stands but we're working on a counter offer; we want to ensure the continued health and success of the SummerFest, etc., etc. Something that, if it's leaked, will not put us in a bad light but will expose the harm the board's actions are causing."

"I can set up a social media site," added Luke. "And a text group, so we can share news immediately."

"Sounds great. Allie, let me know as soon as possible when that letter's coming out. I'll start working on my response today—after all, we know what the damn board letter will say. I think we have the beginnings of a plan. Hey, thanks, you two. I'm feeling more hopeful now. We're going to win this, damn it all."

"You bet!" said Luke.

"Remember, though," cautioned Allie, "we have to be patient and calm. We are not the ones causing trouble here. Oh, and I almost forgot—Dad and I were talking about the finances. I'm going to do some research and see if I can figure out where Dr. Abbott's financials are coming from. Dad thinks they don't make any sense, and George was surprised at all the talk of so-called dire straits."

"That would be fucking excellent, Allie," Karin said. "We'll eventually need all the ammunition we can find to fight their arguments. Let me know how it goes and what you discover."

"We're on it," said Luke.

Allie shot him a look. "Yes," she said, "I'll see what I can find out."

Twenty-One

"All that counts in life is intention."
—*Andrea Bocelli*

G eorge met Allie's entrance into the office with a smile. "I have good news," he announced.

"Really?"

"Especially for you, I think." He motioned to his laptop on the desk in his office. "I just heard from our friend Thomas. He's willing to come to the April benefit concert and help raise the funds for his position."

"Oh, that's great."

"Even better, I told him about you, that you're a fine cellist, too." George could barely keep from dancing, he was so excited by his news. "And here's the thing—he suggested that you and he play a cello duet at the concert."

Allie felt her heart drop into her boots.

George continued, "He said he'd give you a call later this morning to talk it over."

—ee—

Allie saw her phone light up with an incoming call. Caller ID showed a number starting with (310). She inhaled and hit the green button.

"Hello? This is Allegra Brewster."

"Allegra, so nice to talk to you. This is Thomas Ramirez. I'm looking forward to working with you and Tony Bainbridge and the orchestra at the Kenni... Kennimac Orchestra this summer."

His voice was warm and friendly, not a bit pompous or formal.

"Yes," said Allie. "The Kennimac SummerFest Symphony. We're glad you are coming. Um... and George says you're planning to come to the April benefit concert, right?"

"Absolutely. I was talking it over with Mr. Park this morning—it fits right in with my schedule. That's what I want to discuss with you. It seems we have something in common." Allie could hear the smile in his voice. "Cello!"

"I guess so. I'm a little out of practice these days, working in the office here..."

"Well, so am I. I bring my poor cello everywhere with me, but I don't get to practice too often. I'm going from being cellist to conductor, and I'm finding that conductors have a lot to learn. At least I do. Every night I am studying scores in my hotel room and not playing my sweet cello." He laughed, undercutting the sorrow of his words.

"That's understandable," said Allie.

"But I hear this fundraising event in April is a concert. And I thought, well, Thomas, maybe you aren't in A-1 shape on the cello, so if you find a partner to play with, the audience won't notice so much. What do you think, Allegra?"

"Oh, everyone calls me Allie."

"Ok, Allie."

Allie paused before responding. "It sounds like a good idea, but I'm just not sure I'm up to it, Thomas. What piece do you have in mind?" Thoughts of a virtuoso composition loomed.

"Ok, don't laugh. When I was in middle school, I played the Vivaldi *Concerto for Two Cellos*[18] at a school talent show. So, it's not too hard—we could put it together quickly."

"I think I worked on that with my teacher years ago. G minor, right? But there won't be an orchestra available..."

"No problem. The Adagio movement is only accompanied by continuo. Do you think we could find a harpsichord player to join us?"

"Maybe... I can ask around."

"Ok, it sounds like we might have something going here. I'll download the music and email you a copy. Do you want the first or second part? Nevermind, I'll decide. And you try to find a harpsichordist. You have my email address, right?"

"I'll let you know if there's someone who can play the continuo. Yes, I have your email." Allie mentally counted the days she'd have for practicing before the concert. "Oh, Thomas," she added, "Will you be able to get here a day or two early so we can rehearse?"

"I can come the day before. That should be fine. Thanks for saying yes, Allie. I'm glad to have a reason to play my cello for the next few weeks."

"You're welcome," she answered. You may not thank me once we rehearse, she thought to herself. "I'll be in touch."

"Great. Talk to you soon."

It turned out that there was a fine harpsichordist in their midst, none other than Sylvia Abbott. George explained to Allie that he'd heard Sylvia play at a Baroque concert in Portland several winters ago, when Allie was away at graduate school. He said that Sylvia accompanied a recorder trio in some Handel transcriptions and had kept the group tootling along in fine rhythm, just as the continuo was supposed to do. He said that Sylvia actually seemed to enjoy it, and the recorder players had a good time, too. Though he noted a sense of relief on their part when they finished the performance.

"I'll call Sylvia," he offered. "This might be a good way to create some goodwill. God knows we'll need it."

He called Sylvia and got a prompt assent. "*If* they are prepared to rehearse for a few hours," she added. He assured her Thomas and Allie would want to be well-prepared.

—ℓℓ—

How ironic, thought Allie, that Sylvia would be performing in the same concert as Karin and her woodwind quintet.

Twenty-Two

Kennimac Summerfest
PO Box 2100
Kennimac, Maine 04533
www.KennimacSummerfest.org

Ms. Karin Anders
corenfa@gmail.com

<u>Via Internet March 26</u>

Dear Ms. Anders:

Due to grave financial problems besetting our non-profit organization, the Board of Directors has decided to take some serious steps in hopes of putting the Kennimac Summerfest on a more secure financial footing. Personnel expenses are by far and away the largest part of the budget and as such, must be the first in line to receive cuts. As the local representative of the musicians' union, you are receiving this notification of the proposal for the upcoming seasons two-year contract between the management of the Kennimac Summerfest and the musicians we employ.

The new contract has several key features, which although perhaps painful are necessary:

1. 35 percent reduction in pay compared to the 2013-2014 contract.
2. Requirement that musicians play three additional services pro bono.
3. Requirement that all musicians submit a 250-word essay describing their allegiance to the Kennimac Summerfest.

Please notify your current union members of this proposal. We ask that the new contract be signed by the first of May so the summer season can proceed as planned.

Yours truly,

sa

Sylvia Abbott, Ph.D., Chair
Kennimac Summerfest Board of Directors

CC: Board members & staff members

to: Summerfest Musicians
from: Karin Anders <corenfa@gmail.com>
March 26 at 1:24 PM
Subject: Contract proposal from the board

Greetings, friends,

Attached to this email is a letter from Sylvia Abbott, the chair of the board of directors of the Kennimac Summerfest, outlining their new proposed 2015 & 2016 contract. When you read the proposal, you will not be happy, trust me! But please don't over-react. It is simply the first offer from the board. We will negotiate a better one.

I believe this is an attempt by Dr. Abbott and the board to kill the union. But we don't want that to happen -- without union representation, we each will have to negotiate our contracts separately with Abbott and the board, and that could be disastrous.

Let's keep our cool and present a united front. Please don't talk to the press or any friends outside the orchestra unless you talk with me first. We will be coming up with a communications plan in a few days. In the meantime, don't hesitate to email me or call me if you have any questions.

Have faith it will all work out!

Karin Anders, Representative
AFL-CIO American Federation of Musicians, Local 9-535
March 30

Sylvia Abbott, Chair
Board of Directors
Kennimac Summerfest

<u>Via Email</u>

Dear Dr. Abbott:

Please be advised that the proposal as outlined by you in a letter to me dated March 26th is not acceptable to the musicians of the Kennimac SummerFest. We are in process of preparing a counterproposal but would first request to see the financial reports that have caused the board to propose these draconian cuts.

The members of the orchestra want to stress that we have a deep respect and love for the SummerFest organization and don't want to do anything to harm it, financially or artistically. But we believe the proposal as it stands would make it financially impossible for many of our players to continue with the festival. Therefore, we will seek to offer a proposal that benefits both the organization and the musicians who are such a critical part of that organization.

Sincerely,

Karin Anders

Karin Anders, Union Representative
Musicians of the Kennimac Summerfest Symphony

The press picks up the story:

SUMMERFEST BOARD TO MUSICIANS: HARSH CUTS AHEAD

What's Behind the SummerFest's Untenable Offer?

SummerFest Called a Lucrative Linchpin by Local Businesses

Kennimac Residents Fear the Breakup of SummerFest
Residents Rally Behind Beleaguered Musicians

To the Editor:

Why is the SummerFest board of directors treating its musicians, many of whom are longtime summer residents, with disrespect? They shop on Main Street, eat in our restaurants, and draw crowds to their concerts. They teach our children and liven the summer atmosphere with impromptu music performances. Kennimac would be a boring place without the SummerFest Symphony. I urge the board to reconsider its attack on the musicians.

Sincerely, Mary Montgomery, Kennimac

To the Editor:

We want your readers to know that we are mad about what is happening to the SummerFest musicians. We are students of many of the musicians. Every summer we have fun learning with them.

They really care about music, about us, and about Kennimac. Please don't force them to go away.

Signed, Harris Zeller, Maryellen Marston, Sarah Small, Clary Treats, Jasper Yeoman, Sherman Tucker, Peter Nussbaum, Grace Wallace, Madeline Weeks, Bobby Olsen, Zander Bensen, Ella Smith, Hanna Nielson, Nathan Lockwood

To the Editor:

It is understandable that a nonprofit arts organization must be a careful steward of its finances. However, in recognition of the tremendous value of the Kennimac SummerFest to the town of Kennimac, we would like to recommend to the SummerFest board of directors that they do all they can to ensure the continued maintenance of the orchestra. In addition, we would like to offer our assistance in working to find a solution to the current impasse between the orchestra members and the board. In closing, we'd like to point out that an arts venue, as opposed to a resident orchestra, would not offer the same benefits to Kennimac, while most likely exacerbating those problems, such as traffic jams, that come with one-night performances.

Yours truly, RuthEllen Cox, owner of the Kennimac Inn, and president of the Kennimac Business Association

———*ele*———

Text from Luke to Allie:
RAIL UNDER!
Text from Allie to Luke:
YUP

Twenty-Three

"I'm hitting my head against the walls,
but the walls are giving way."
—*Gustav Mahler*

Karin Anders <corenfa@gmail.com>
April 1 at 5:03 PM
to: SAbbott@xcav84oil.com
RE: Contract proposal from the board

Dear Sylvia,

As you undoubtedly know, the Summermusic Woodwind Quintet has long been scheduled to play at the benefit gala for the Summerfest on the afternoon of Sunday, April 19th.

I would like to meet with you after that concert to present the musicians' counterproposal to the board's offer.

Please let me know if this is acceptable to you. Any other members of the board you wish to be present are welcome. I will be alone.

Karin

from: Sylvia Abbott, PhD <sabbott@xcav84oil.com>
to: Karin Anders <corenfa@gmail.com>
date: Thurs, April 2 at 4:25 PM
re: negotiations

VIA EMAIL

After the concert is fine. We can meet in the conference room at
the festival office.

Let's hope your counterproposal is something worth listening to.

sa

P.S. You might be surprised to learn that I'll be performing in the
second half of the April benefit, with Thomas and Allegra.

———ℓℓ———

What the...? Good God, thought Karin. Now she's a musician? And
who the fuck is Thomas? Whatever.

Twenty-Four

"With the truth, all given facts harmonize; but with
what is false, the truth soon hits a wrong note."
—*Aristotle*

The reporter from Maine Public Radio clicked on her recorder
and thrust the microphone in front of George's face. He recoiled,
then cleared his throat.

"Tell us, Mr. Park," she began. "What would you characterize as
the rationale behind the Kennimac SummerFest board's actions?"
She waited while George blinked.

"There's no doubt," he finally said, "that they are concerned
about the SummerFest's sustainability. This is something all arts
organizations face. We can't cater exclusively to a small group of
enthusiasts. We need to develop a broad base. We... ah..."

"But by all accounts, the SummerFest's annual offerings were
popular. I've read all the recent letters to the editor—not just in the
local paper but in the state-wide papers, too. With all that community support, why would the sustainability of the organization
be in doubt? Was there financial mismanagement?"

"No!" George recoiled. "What I mean is, there's no question of
impropriety. We did have a slight loss last year, but it..."

"It must have rattled the board members," finished the reporter.

"I guess so."

"Where do you stand in all of this? You've been the executive director of the festival for almost a decade. Where do you stand—with the board or with the musicians?"

George seemed astonished at the question. "I... I have good relations with most of the musicians," he said, "but I am employed by the board. It's my job to implement the board's decisions. I can advise them, but they don't have to take my counsel."

"It sounds as though perhaps you sympathize with the musicians?"

"I wouldn't say that. No. I mean, as I said, I have long-term friendships with many of them. But that's not relevant. I also have a job to do." George wiped his hand across his forehead.

The reporter gave him a skeptical look. "What do you think will happen next? Is there a way to break the logjam?"

"Well, we have a meeting between the musicians' union representative, Karin Anders, and the board's executive committee coming up in a couple of weeks. I am hopeful we'll be able to reach a compromise everyone can agree on. Oh, and we have a benefit concert that same weekend."

"Might that not turn into a protest scene if the problems aren't settled by then?"

"I don't think so. This is classical music, after all. We're not talking about a declaration of war or something."

The reporter laughed. "From what I hear, some people do think of it as a declaration of war. Well, thank you for your time, Mr. Park."

As she folded up the microphone cord, the reporter eyed George speculatively. "I think you've underestimated the community response," she said. "I wouldn't be surprised if I'm not back here in a few weeks covering a demonstration."

"Really? I disagree. But thank you for your interest. When do you think you'll run the story?"

"It's scheduled for tonight's 'Maine Things Considered.' It probably will run around 5:15. As you know, I've already interviewed

Dr. Abbott. I'm hoping to catch Karin Anders by phone for a comment, as well."

"Oh," said George, wondering what Karin would come up with.

Matching silk-shaded lamps glowed, creating pools of light in Silvia Abbott's cherry-paneled study. Her scowl contrasted with the elegant surroundings as she switched off the radio with an impatient snap.

Christ, George, she said to herself. If only we could have replaced you before we started this fight. Having you as a spokesperson is like having one hand tied behind our backs.

Her phone rang. "Sylvia Abbott," she said, answering the call. "Hi, yes, John, I heard it. Thank you; I thought it important to lay out our position clearly... I know, he was pretty weak... Oh, I'm glad you didn't think he was too bad. As long as he doesn't harm our cause, I guess we'll get by... Yes, it was good that the reporter never was able to reach Anders. Although, perhaps she might have made a fool of herself with that big mouth of hers!" Sylvia trilled a false little laugh, and then signed off the phone call.

At the SummerFest office, Luke, Allie, and George sighed in unison as the broadcast turned to other news.

"Cringe-worthy," said George.

"Not too bad," disagreed Allie. "At least, not your part. I thought Dr. Abbott sounded pretty shrill."

"What a bitch!" said Luke. "You could tell her nose was in the air as she spoke to the reporter. I bet she lost a bunch more supporters after that."

"We can only hope," agreed Allie.

"I can only hope," added George, "that she didn't take offense at what I said."

Twenty-Five

"Life is for the living. Death is for the dead.
Let life be like music. And death a note unsaid."
—*Langston Hughes*

D avid Brewster's therapist had officially diagnosed him with obsessive/compulsive disorder, but he didn't think that was a particular descriptive label. He just liked things to be carefully crafted, beautifully tended, wholly realized—to be right.

He surveyed the small sailboat he'd turned upside-down on the sawhorses. The barn doors were open, and the sun was bright outside. Even so, the interior of the barn was in shadow except for the work lights he'd strung around. Strains of classical music came from the dented and paint-spattered radio on his workbench, and the smell of the muddy yard permeated the barn. David was glad those nasty biting black flies hadn't yet appeared. Even with the sun, it was still a chilly April afternoon, but in his dark green chamois shirt, David was comfortable enough.

The wooden planks of Calliope showed cracks between them, where the dry wood had shrunk and left a gap. David was in the process of filling those gaps by stuffing strips of cotton between the planks. Only about a fifth of the way into the job, he had laid his tools on the bench and seemed lost in thought.

"Dad?" David looked up as Allie and Archie came through the open barn doors. "How's it coming?"

"Well, I've still got quite a lot to do before we can paint her. But we'll get there. Eventually. May not be in time to race, at least not in June." He bent down to scratch Archie between the ears. "Remember how the jib had a slight tear in the clew? I thought maybe you could take it to Kate and see if she'd have time to do a patch job."

"Good idea." Allie ran her hands along the portions of the hull her father had already caulked. "This looks beautiful, Dad. You are turning into a pro." She laughed. "Remember the first time you and I tried to do this? We stuffed too much cotton batting between the planks..."

"And after we launched her, one of them popped off when the wood began to swell? How could I forget—we watched from shore as she dipped lower and lower in the water."

"I rescued good ole Calliope."

David smiled. "You sure did. Twelve years old. Just swam out to the mooring and dragged her back to shore, half full of water and sinking fast."

"So, Dad, where's the sail I should take to Kate's?" Allie looked around the barn but didn't see a sail bag. She walked over to the workbench and fiddled with the mallet and iron her father had been using to press the cotton into the open seams between the planks. Picking up a long sharp pointed tool with a hole at one end, she asked, "What's this? It looks like a needle."

"Oh, I keep forgetting to take that to Kate. There were a couple of those in that batch of boat building tools I bought at that auction in Brooklin last fall. It's a heavy-duty needle for sail-making. I'm sure Kate has lots of them, but I don't need it. You should take it with the jib."

"And where's the jib?"

"Oh, that's on the high shelf over there." David pointed, then watched as his daughter walked over to the dark corner and reached up to grab the white bag neatly stowed on the wooden shelf. She looked so much like Melissa, but the way she moved was more graceful and self-contained. Allie was taller by a couple of inches, too, and not as curvy as Melissa had been at that age. How strange, he thought, at about the same age her mother had been when she left, Allie came back.

Allie hefted the bulky sail bag onto her shoulder, and stopped by the workbench to pick up the needle.

"Wait, let me wrap it in some cotton to protect the point," said her father.

"And protect me, I hope!" added Allie. She took the cotton-wrapped needle from her father and walked out of the barn. "I'll see you for dinner," she called over her shoulder.

———ℓℓ———

Allie had been wanting to check in with Kate, to see how she was doing. She also had an idea that maybe Kate would be willing to take in Thomas during the SummerFest. Kate could use the money, and it might encourage her to move on from her grief. Or at least open up to the rest of life. Allie walked up to the Zellers' door, picking up the newspaper lying forgotten on the front step. Kate's probably working even though it's Saturday afternoon, she thought. This is the busy season for sailmakers; everyone gets excited about the start of the sailing season in early spring.

In her mind, she contrasted the two visions of Kate, before and after the accident with Toby. Shiny dark hair that framed her face in waves. Quick smile with crinkles around her eyes. Kate had always been ready to listen to Allie's questions. She had dispensed little advice but instead asked follow-up questions that led Allie to find her own answers. Kate used to be a warmly physical person, hugging Allie when she saw her, patting her shoulder in commiseration, or grabbing her hand in enthusiasm. She reveled in Allie's and her sons' successes and tried to lift their spirits when they felt dejected.

And now, Allie tried to do the same for Kate, but it didn't seem to have any effect. Kate's despondency was so deep, her sorrow so endless, that she seemed like a completely different person. Instead of someone who gathered friends around her and infected them with her sense of fun, Kate had turned into a loner who spent her days lost in misery. Would she be willing to even consider housing Thomas?

Thinking of Toby's death, Allie felt the tears rise in her eyes. Death was so horrible, so final. She could only imagine how awful it was for parents to lose a child. One minute he's laughing and running and behaving mischievously; the next minute, silence, nothing. Nothing! And never again. Never. It seemed unfathomable to Allie, the idea of never.

Toby's death had caused the end of many things, including Allie and Luke's relationship.

As she anticipated, when Allie dropped off the sail, Kate was friendly enough, but the dark circles under her eyes and the slump to her shoulders betrayed her continuing grief. She accepted the sail and said she'd be able to fix it by the beginning of June, and she told Allie to thank David for the sail-making needle. She didn't offer Allie a drink or a cookie, as she would have before the accident. Her body language conveyed the words she didn't have to say: "Leave me alone."

On her way out, Allie mentioned that Harris's horn teacher, Karin Anders, would be coming to town soon to play for the benefit gala. Kate thought the tickets would be too expensive for them to attend.

"I'm sure Harris could get in for free," Allie said. "And I think the volunteer committee is still looking for more help. Maybe it would feel good for you to get out and see people you know and do something fun."

"Thanks, Allie, you're sweet," responded Kate. "But I don't think so."

With Kate in such a negative mood, Allie decided it might be best to introduce the idea of providing housing for Thomas without coming right out and asking Kate. "There's an assistant conductor coming this summer. I've talked to him on the phone; he seems really nice, Thomas Ramirez. I think he's about 28 or 29. I'm having a terrible time finding a place for him to stay. The festival can offer payment for room and board, but there just don't seem to be any open spots anywhere in town. Do you have any ideas?"

"Hmmm," Kate said. "You're really having a hard time?"

"Yes, and we're offering $3,000, too. Even though he'll probably eat most of his meals, lunches anyway, at the barn."

"Would he have his own transportation?"

"Definitely."

"I might be interested."

"Really? That would be great!"

Allie left Kate's house feeling like a cloud had been lifted. Kate's darkness affected Allie, too.

Twenty-Six

"Good music... You have to sweat over it and bug it
to death. "   —*Keith Richards*

Allie rolled open the big doors of the SummerFest Concert Barn, letting the warm April sun pour into the performance space. The birds added their urgent songs to the fresh breeze that blew in through the open doors, dispelling the chilly air. It smelled rather musty, Allie thought. Luckily, the forecast for the next few days promised fair weather. By the time of the benefit concert, the barn would be aired out, warmed up, and welcoming as ever.

Allie set up the five chairs and music stands. The Summermusic Woodwind Quintet was performing at the benefit concert Sunday afternoon, and all five were arriving today to rehearse. Made up of the principal woodwind players—flute, oboe, bassoon, clarinet, and that honorary woodwind, horn—from the Kennimac SummerFest orchestra, the quintet didn't usually perform in other seasons or venues. They would need some serious rehearsal time to get their act together after months of being apart. Allie organized the chairs up in the usual U shape, the horn player at the back, flute and clarinet to the horn's left; bassoon and oboe to the right. Karin Anders was the horn; she'd be arriving soon. Allie wondered what fireworks would ensue.

So, far, the board and the musicians seemed to be at an impasse, each waiting for the other side to make a move. Allie had been making housing arrangements for all the musicians as if all were going as usual. But she also had fielded many calls from alarmed and irate players who thought she'd have the inside scoop.

She and Luke had talked to Karin and let her know about the terrific amount of community support the musicians were getting, but they were all still worried about Dr. Abbott's ulterior motive—to get rid of the orchestra in its current form. Karin was clearly angrier than ever but was being strategic about her temper. She hadn't even uttered the word "strike" to the board, as far as Allie knew.

How would Karin do when confronted with Dr. Abbott in person, Allie wondered. She had told Luke she'd do the set-up for the rehearsal so she could catch Karin before Karin could get into trouble.

She heard a car door slam outside the barn and two loud voices arguing. "Why should we take this kind of treatment?" shouted Kristen Kanafax, the oboe player. "It's insulting! I've never been treated like this before!"

"Krissy, trust me. I know what I'm doing," replied Karin, as she lugged her horn and equipment bag into the barn. She turned to Allie. "Get her off my back, will you," she said, half joking. "She's been on my case ever since we met up at La Guardia."

"Well, I'm upset!" continued Kristen. "I love coming here every summer. My kids love it. My husband loves it. I don't want it to change!" She set her bags down by the oboe's chair. "I just don't see how we're going to keep going as if nothing's wrong."

"I'm going to meet in person with Abbott on Sunday evening after the benefit. Let's see what comes from that," said Karin. "Right now, I want to get my horn out, warm up, and get ready to play the Neilsen Quintet." Karin opened her horn case and pulled out the horn and its bell. The horn was the dull gold of burnished unlacquered brass. Karin sat down, screwed the bell to the body of the horn, inserted the silver mouthpiece and brought it to her lips. As she warmed up, the liquid round tones of her horn's scales and arpeggios reverberated off the barn rafters and bounced around the cavernous space.

Kristen realized there was no point in continuing the conversation. She began putting her oboe together, first sticking the reed in her mouth to soften it up. When her oboe was assembled, she set it on a small stand and then arrayed her oboist's tools on the table beside her chair: razor-sharp knife; electronic tuner; mandrel; plastic pill bottle filled with water; extra reeds. She dunked the other reeds in the water to soften them up and began her warm-up routine. Soon the melancholy soulful wail of her oboe joined the sound of Karin's horn.

Allie got glasses of water for each of the players and set them by their chairs. After a few minutes, another car drove up to the front of the barn. Three doors slammed, and Steve Kennison, bassoonist, Carol McCreary, clarinetist, and Linda Scilly, flutist, came into the barn. They nodded wordlessly to the two already warming up and began to unpack their instruments as well. Soon the air in the barn was filled with the sound of all five instruments running up and down scales, tonguing and slurring arpeggios, playing over the knotty parts of the pieces they were about to rehearse.

It could almost be a contemporary composition, thought Allie. The sounds blended, yet were independent. Definitely sounded like something Charles Ives might have come up with. She lingered by the door, unwilling to return her desk in the bleak office.

"Shall we tune?" asked Karin, after a few minutes. Kristen hit an A on the oboe and, when she nodded that the pitch was centered, the other instruments softly joined in. Then, without a word, all five pulled out a page of music and began playing a Bach chorale together, working back into their sense of unity, breathing together and matching tone quality. It was clearly a routine they used before every rehearsal.

Allie envied them their close musical relationship. She'd played in chamber groups but not for an extended time. Her groups had never gelled to the point where communication came through another channel other than a verbal one. She let herself out the barn door, and almost collided with Sylvia Abbott, who was coming through with a determined look on her face.

Allie took a quick breath. "You aren't supposed to be here." she whispered. "I mean, we're not rehearsing until Saturday, when Thomas gets here."

"I'm well aware of that, Allegra," answered Dr. Abbott in a louder voice. "I wanted to make sure the woodwind quintet had all arrived. This benefit concert on Sunday afternoon is crucial. Allegra, would you tell Karin I'm confirming our meeting after the concert. And make sure the conference room is decent." As usual, it was an order, not a request.

"Sure," whispered Allie, closing the door soundlessly. She didn't want the quintet's rehearsal to be interrupted. If Kristen noticed Dr. Abbott was there, she might launch into an attack.

Twenty-Seven

"I can't understand why people are frightened
of new ideas. I'm frightened of the old ones."
—*John Cage*

A llie and Dr. Abbott wordlessly walked up the hill through the
apple orchard toward the main office of the SummerFest.
The phoebes and chickadees sang, flitting from tree to tree, and a
pair of hummingbirds competed for a chance at the hummingbird
feeder hanging on a branch. Forsythia and daffodils lined the driveway, and the sun warmed the newly greened grass and unfurled
leaves. In the distance, the bay sparkled, with reflected clouds
skimming the surface. If Dr. Abbott hadn't been walking beside
her, Allie might have opened her arms wide and broken out into
song like Maria in "The Sound of Music." Instead, she kept her
arms at her sides and inhaled deeply, secretly delighting in the
mingled scents of grass, breeze, and earth.

Dr. Abbott huffed slightly as they walked up the hill. Allie was
a fast walker. "Allegra," she said, stopping for a moment. "You do
see the necessity for the action the board has agreed to, don't
you?" She began walking again. "As a student of nonprofit arts
management, you must understand the importance of fiscal responsibility."

"I know it's a complicated issue," said Allie. "But I'm not sure I
understand the need for such drastic action."

"I strive for excellence, Allegra. And I believe in employing explosives—literal or figurative—when needed. I did it in my work and I do now as the leader of the board."

"But why get rid of the musicians' union?" said Allie. "That seems extreme..."

"I can tell you things about unions." Dr. Abbott narrowed her eyes. "Unions have caused financial hardship, injury—and even death—in my experience."

"Really? How so?" Allie was skeptical.

"Allegra, unions bombed an oil refinery construction site because the contractor was an open shop and didn't allow the workers to unionize. Union thugs set the bombs to go off at night when no one was working. But one went off too early. It killed a guard, and badly injured several workers."

"That's horrible," admitted Allie. "But I don't see what it has to do with the musicians."

"And union bosses—don't get me started. They've stolen money from their members, they've been involved in the mob..." Dr. Abbott was becoming more and more agitated.

Allie placed her hand on Sylvia Abbott's arm. "But Dr. Abbott," she said, "That is different from our local musicians' union. They're just trying to get a fair chance at decent wages and working conditions. After all, unions have done good things, too."

"I'm disappointed in you, Allegra. I guess you are too young and innocent to understand."

"I think you may be making a generalization that doesn't hold up." Allie was determined to speak up. "Unions have given lots of working people the chance to pool their individual power into a much stronger collective power. And because of that, they've been able to enjoy a higher standard of living. Imagine what factories were like before unions. They were horrible and dangerous."

Dr. Abbott shook her head. "Dangerous! It's unions that are dangerous. They must be stopped!"

Her vehemence was scorching. Allie didn't dare respond.

They walked in silence for a few minutes, then Dr. Abbott turned to Allie with a smile. "Change of subject—how is your Vivaldi coming along? We could get together and go over it, if you like."

"I think I'd rather wait until Thomas is here and we can put the whole thing together."

"I've decided to use an electronic piano for the harpsichord instead of bringing my harpsichord to the barn. It'll never stay in tune in the April weather. That's not a problem with the Roland piano. And since my part is not all that crucial, I don't think anyone will notice. Do you?"

"That probably makes sense."

"So, here's a question, Allegra."

Allegra stiffened, wondering what was coming next.

"Are you racing in the Wednesday series on the bay this year, I hope?"

The change in topic surprised Allie. "I don't think so. Our boat needs a lot of work and I don't think it'll be ready. Plus, I'll be busy here."

Sylvia Abbott had barely missed a race ever since she and her former husband had renovated their house on the bay. "I thought your father was working on Calliope already. What does he need to do?"

"Re-caulk the seams. It takes time, and I'm too busy to give him any help." Allie didn't mention that her father hadn't touched the boat until just a week ago. For months Calliope had lain upside down on two sawhorses in the barn, the tools and materials untouched since being set out on the workbench.

"Why not pay Seth at the boatyard to do it?"

Allie smiled ruefully. "Between my college loans and the new furnace we had to install last fall, it's just not in the budget." She was glad they'd reached the office door and could end the conversation. Dr. Abbott clearly had no idea what the Brewsters' annual contribution to the SummerFest cost them.

Luke was waiting for Allie in the office. He was taken aback to see Dr. Abbott follow Allie through the door, but quickly regained his composure.

"Hello, Lucas," said Dr. Abbott. "How are things coming for the summer?"

"On schedule," Luke said, trying not to clench his teeth. "Al, can you come check something out in the wood shop?" he asked. "I have a question about the conductor's podium I'm building."

Allie nodded, and the two of them headed out of the office and across the driveway for the wood shop.

"Jesus!" said Luke after they were halfway across. "What is she doing hanging around here? And haven't Karin and the rest of the woodwind quintet arrived? Is she trying to upset them or something?"

Dire Straits's "Brothers in Arms"[19] was cranked up in the wood shop. The blast of sound greeted Allie and Luke as they entered. "Ooh, good choice," said Allie.

"I'm tired of being in love and so alone." Luke lip-synched the words. "You're so far away from me, you're so far away from me, I just can't see," he mouthed, looking pointedly at Allie.

Allie shook her head at him and raised her eyebrows in skepticism. "Drop it, Lucas O'Donnell," she said over the music. "So, what's your question? About the podium, I mean."

Luke gave her an exaggerated look of disappointment, then walked over to the worktable. It was strewn with tools, pieces of wood, nails, and the other detritus of woodworking.

"God, Luke, how can you find anything in this mess?" Allie picked up a wooden-handled tool with a 5-inch spike at its end. "What on earth do you use this lethal thing for?"

"That's a spindle gouge," Luke answered. "Actually, that's for wood carving. Not the stuff I'm working on now." He picked up a drawing on the worktable. "This is basically what Anthony Bainbridge said he would like. And I can build that, no problem. The question is, what kind of wood should I use? I can get a good deal on some Ipe—it's usually quite expensive but we don't need much—and it lasts forever, but the color might not be right. And it doesn't take paint very well, so we'd have to stick with the natural color. Here's a photo of the wood."

Allie studied the photograph. "This isn't a question for me," she said. "I think it looks fine but it's up to Tony and George. I know Tony wanted to make sure whatever you built wouldn't squeak when he jumped around on it."

"Yeah, he's not a big man but he sure jumps around when he's conducting," said Luke. "Hey, is he coming to the benefit concert on Sunday? I could talk with him then."

"I don't think so. I haven't heard that he is, anyway." Allie turned to leave. "I'll mention the podium question to George. I'll tell him to check in with you."

"So, Al, have you seen Karin yet? She's here, right?"

"I have, but not to talk to about the board stuff. What more is there to say, anyway, until after she and Abbott meet?"

"How about Thomas What's-His-Name? Has he shown up yet?" Luke scowled.

"No, he doesn't get here until Saturday morning."

"Sounds like a *prima dona* to me. Showing up at the last minute."

"Luke, only a female opera singer can be a *prima dona*. And he's got a conducting gig that ends Friday."

"Well, I say he's whatever the Italian word for 'jerk' is."

Allie turned to leave. "There's only one person I know who is being a jerk..." she said over her shoulder.

Twenty-Eight

"Music is the divine way to tell beautiful, poetic
things to the heart." —*Pablo Casals*

A t twenty to ten on Saturday morning, Allie unlocked the
side door to the barn, preparing to rehearse with Sylvia and
Thomas, who was on his way from Boston. She had her iPad with
her cello part on it and her cello in its cherry red case. Setting
three chairs on the stage—one for Sylvia and one each for her
and Thomas—she opened her case and lifted out her cello. As she
tuned the strings, the door opened and Sylvia arrived, carrying a
padded leather piano stool.

"Oh, Allegra, I don't need a chair. I'll use this," she said.

Behind her, wearing a chagrined expression, came Luke, haul-
ing a large rectangular case almost six feet long. "My Roland—today's 'harpsichord,'" Sylvia said, motioning toward the case in
Luke's arms. "It weighs a ton. Thanks, Lucas, you can place it here."
She pointed to a spot on the stage.

For a few minutes, Allie went back to tuning her strings and
tightening her bow hairs, while Sylvia unwound a cord and
stretched it to the back of the stage to plug in the electronic piano.
She asked Luke to help her get the keyboard up on its stand,
turned it to harpsichord mode, and began warming up her fingers.

The concert barn was all wood inside, mostly oak—beams,
ceiling, floor, walls—and sound seemed to grow and become rich-

er as it bounced from surface to surface. The audience's chairs were made of maple in a graceful contemporary design. Cerulean woven-wool seat cushions, which could be itchy on the backs of bare legs on a hot summer night, softened the chairs' spare angularity. The barn's atmosphere held a complex scent: old and young wood, furniture oil, a faint odor of April's fresh greenery outside, the spicy scent of wool, and perhaps even the memory of ladies' perfumes and performers' perspiration lingering from past concerts. Sharp percussive harpsichord sounds (electronically reproduced) filled the barn, while gentle tones from Allie's cello laid down a velvety background.

In the midst of this, a loud car could be heard scattering gravel as it drove up to the barn entrance. A car door slammed, and soon Thomas hurried into the barn, carrying his cello case and a bulging messenger bag.

"I made it!" he said.

"Barely," said Luke, mostly to himself.

Sylvia rose from the piano bench and walked toward the front of the stage. "Welcome, Thomas. I'm Dr. Sylvia Abbott, the board chair and your harpsichordist." She held out her hand. "You made it just by the skin of your teeth. We're all ready to rehearse."

Allie waved her bow. "I'm Allie, obviously. Glad to meet you, Thomas. Oh, and this is Lucas O'Donnell." She motioned toward Luke, who was making his way out of the barn. "Luke is on the stage management staff of the SummerFest." Luke wore a sour expression as he exited.

"Glad to meet you all," said Thomas. Turning toward Sylvia, he added, "I'd like a moment to stop in the men's room before we begin, if you don't mind. I've been in the car for three hours, and I've had too many cups of coffee."

Sylvia nodded reluctantly.

They began rehearsing shortly, once Thomas had gotten himself settled in his chair and tuned his cello. The piece was only about three minutes long and the three of them soon hit a groove after a short discussion about the speed in which to play it. Sylvia thought the tempo should be faster than either Thomas or Allie wanted. Thomas pointed out that the movement was labeled "Adagio" (slow) in some scores, and "Largo" (even slower) in others, and finally Sylvia agreed to their wishes. Thomas rolled his eyes at Allie, unseen by Sylvia, and Allie smiled back.

The two cellos blended well together. Playing the first part as requested by Thomas, Allie could hear him matching her phrasing as he echoed her. They seemed instinctively to concur on where to slow down or play softer or louder. It was almost as if they had already rehearsed it together. The short piece was easy enough that the two of them didn't have to keep their eyes glued to the music. They traded smiles as they played through the notes. Allie couldn't help noticing how Thomas immersed himself in the music. He almost danced as he drew his bow across the strings. His expressions matched the emotion of the music, almost as if he were acting it out. Allie felt more free to add her own expression, trying for drama without overdoing it. As they played, it appeared she and Thomas were communicating on a level deeper than verbal communication. She felt the music's emotion, but on top of that was a giddiness, a pulse-quickening that she only occasionally experienced while playing.

Their connection brought the music to life. And behind the cellos' singing, Sylvia's steady rhythmic pulse kept it moving along. She seemed to sense when Allie and Thomas wanted to add a ritard, a slowing down of the tempo.

"This is going well," she said. "You both sound terrific. I know the audience will love it." Allie was surprised by how genuine Sylvia's smile looked.

After about ninety minutes, the three of them decided they had worked the piece into shape. "Any more," said Sylvia, "And it will sound over-rehearsed and boring."

As Thomas and Allie put away their cellos, Sylvia moved the electronic keyboard to the back of the stage, along with the piano stool. Then she came and stood by Thomas.

"I think I've met you before," she said. "You're not from Houston, are you?"

"Ye-es," he responded slowly. "We lived in Houston until I started middle school. Why?"

Allie watched the exchange with interest.

"Did you play the cello as a young boy? Maybe age eight or nine?"

"I did."

"At the Spence Program for Gifted Students?"

"I did," Thomas said, a memory slowing dawning. "Are you the woman who, who..."

"Who was the chair of the foundation that paid for that program, yes?"

"And then you cut the funding, right? It was terrible. My teacher had to leave Houston. My mother was..."

"Oh, Thomas," Sylvia interrupted. "It was the usual story. Mismanagement of funds."

"What? What do you mean? My mother was the bookkeeper. It devastated her. She couldn't find another job for months." Thomas's face was pink. "We had to move to Los Angeles to live with my grandparents. It was very hard."

"I'm sorry to hear that. But the mismanagement was really quite criminal. Your mother was lucky that the foundation decided not to press charges." Sylvia smoothed her blouse with a dismissive gesture. "Well, I hope that little history doesn't impede our performance tomorrow."

"I knew you looked familiar," said Thomas with a bitter expression.

"I'll see you both tomorrow," Sylvia said as she walked toward the door.

The two watched her go. Allie looked confused. Thomas was obviously furious.

"My mother was never the same after that," he said to Allie. "She died when I was in high school."

"I don't get it," said Allie. "How does someone like her leave a trail of anger and fear wherever she goes?"

ele

Allie and Kate had decided that the Saturday night before the benefit concert would be a good time to preview how it might be to have Thomas stay at the Zellers' during the six weeks of SummerFest. Thomas followed Allie in his car to Kate's house. Kate met them at the door, and Allie was glad to see that she had done some straightening up around the house in honor of Thomas's arrival.

"Welcome, Thomas," Kate said, extending her hand. "Chris! Harris! Come meet Thomas!" she shouted up the stairs.

The two boys ran down the stairs, Chris at a virtual tumble and Harris at a fifteen-year-old's lanky step-skipping ramble. Kate introduced them to Thomas.

"Is he the conductor who's living with us this summer?" Chris asked his mother.

"If he likes us," she answered, smiling.

"And if you like me," added Thomas.

"Well, I've got to go," said Allie. "Dad's expecting me for lunch, and Archie needs a walk. Are you coming to the concert tomorrow, Kate?"

"Oh, yes. They roped me into helping with the refreshments, after all. Plus, since you're playing your cello, I couldn't miss it." She winked at Allie.

"Oh, right. Thomas is playing his cello, too." Allie felt her face turn pink.

Thomas smiled. "I'm basically accompanying Allie. She's a fine cellist. Far better than I."

Allie cleared her throat. "Glad you're coming, Kate. You can make sure that Thomas finds his way back to the barn tomorrow, then."

Kate turned to Thomas as Allie closed the door behind her. "So, what do you think so far? Of the SummerFest, I mean."

"Seems like a good opportunity," said Thomas. "I'm excited to be working with a live orchestra for six weeks, and I know I have lots to learn from Tony Bainbridge."

"Yes, it's a pretty special place," said Kate. "Though I guess there has been some sort of trouble lately with the board."

"What trouble?"

"Well, from what I hear, the board is trying to cut the musicians' pay. Evidently Sylvia Abbott has convinced the rest of the board that the SummerFest is in financial trouble."

"Sylvia Abbott." Thomas grimaced. "I have some history with her. Not pleasant, either. It seems to be a pattern. Death and destruction in her wake..."

Kate narrowed her eyes. "You don't know the half of it." She shook her head. "Hey, let me show you around."

Twenty-Nine

"Everything is scary if you look at it. So you just got
to live it."   —*Mary J. Blige*

Sunday dawned a perfect spring day. By afternoon, the temperature was in the upper 60s, helping to warm the concert barn to a comfortable level. The crowd lingered outdoors until the last minute. Allie thought they were milling around because they were reluctant to leave the sunshine, but when she walked outside she was surprised to find several local people handing out flyers about the board's decision to cut the musicians' pay.

"Oh, yes, I've been hearing about this," a tall man in a madras jacket said, reaching for a flyer.

"That's why we wanted to come to this concert," said a woman near him, sporting a hot pink sticker with I Love SummerFest Musicians emblazoned on it. "We wanted to show our support for the musicians. We drove up from Boston."

"Well, I don't understand it," said a woman in a fluffy lime green sweater. "Why can't they all just get along?"

Allie smiled to herself. It looked like Luke and Karin had been busy.

~elle~

As the crowd of well-dressed Summerfest supporters finally swarmed to their seats, Allie could hear the faint tones of the members of the quintet warming up in the green room. She was happy so many people had bought tickets to this event. The tickets were expensive, and she'd worried that the outreach hadn't snared enough attendees. But it turned out that almost all the tickets were sold, and a few people even showed up to buy tickets at the door. At $150 a ticket, and $500 for tickets that included the reception with the musicians afterward, this event would bring in enough money to pay for the graphic design and printing of the summer's programs and posters. That meant the money brought in by ads in the program could go straight to the Summerfest coffers.

Allie checked in with the volunteers who were going to help with the refreshments at intermission and at the "exclusive" party after the concert. She was glad to see Kate Zeller was there, along with Harris. Her dad was, as well. Luke had also volunteered to help and had donned a jacket and a slightly ironic bowtie.

Allie came upon Thomas, sitting in the hall just outside the green room. He was staring intently at his phone, with an angry expression on his face. It changed to a welcoming smile when he saw her. "We go on at the end of the concert, right?" he asked.

"Yup. So you can sit in the audience if you like during most of the performance."

"I think I'll stay back here. I can hear it all fine from here. And can do my calming routine. Pre-performance nerves, you know."

"You?" Allie was surprised. "I know what you mean, nerves, but I would think..." She changed course. "What's your routine?"

"I listen to a piece I'm studying, and I conduct it to myself." Thomas paused, slightly embarrassed, then continued. "I conduct with this tiny conductor's baton my mother gave me. It's a stickpin, really." He held up a small version of a baton about three inches long and made of silver.

_ℓℓ_

The audience was excited to be there; chatter and laughter filled the barn. Many people in the crowd sported the fuchsia colored dots. A few minutes before starting time, Allie rang a small bell to signal the concert was about to begin. Then she headed back to the green room to let the quintet members know they should prepare to go on.

Precisely at 3:00 PM, Sylvia Abbott walked to the front of the stage. "Welcome, friends," she said. "I'm Dr. Sylvia Abbott, the chair of the board of directors of the Kennimac SummerFest Symphony. On behalf of the rest of the board, I'd like to thank you for supporting this important cultural institution. We're especially pleased so many of you chose to buy the premium tickets, and we look forward to talking with you after the concert about our exciting plans for the coming summer..."

Allie stuck her head in the green room and asked, "Everybody ready?" She received nods in return. "She's still talking," Allie explained. "But I think she's almost done."

From offstage, she could hear Dr. Abbott say, "Please give a warm round of applause to the Summermusic Woodwind Quintet."

"You're on," Allie said to Linda, who walked out with her flute, followed by the other members of the quintet. Acknowledging the audience's enthusiastic applause, the musicians bowed in unison and took their seats. The oboe, horn, and bassoon immediately launched into the opening bars of Milhaud's *La Cheminée du Roi René*[20].

The first half of the concert seemed to go quickly. Allie could see Dr. Abbott in the front row, looking around as the audience applauded. After the quintet left the stage for intermission, Allie was busy managing the refreshments and passing around trays of miniature crab cakes and glasses of Prosecco. Dr. Abbott stopped her at one point and asked where the wine bottles were, and Allie assumed she was going to help pour more glasses. A few minutes later, Allie noticed the glasses still stood empty and Dr. Abbott was not to be seen.

She quickly pressed Luke, George Park, her father, and Kate into service pouring wine, and the crush was contained. Kate looked better; she'd made an effort to dress for the gala. She'd put on lipstick and pulled her hair back with a favorite silver comb that came from the Indian Market in Santa Fe. Allie hoped Kate and Harris were sitting up close to the stage, so Harris could get a good look at Karin as she performed.

As she passed around the mini crab cakes, Allie noticed a clump of people over by the entrance. To her surprise, the voice of Tony Bainbridge rang out. "Marvelous, simply brilliant!" he was saying to one of the major donors. When did he arrive, Allie wondered, we didn't know he was coming. She hoped she hadn't missed some important communication, but a quick glance shared with George across the room confirmed he was as surprised as she.

After the requisite twenty minutes of intermission, Allie rang the warning bell and the audience reluctantly returned to their chairs. The quintet filed out with their instruments and took their seats, except for Karin, who stepped to the front of the stage with her horn.

"We are so glad to share this lovely spring afternoon with you," she began. "In fact, we're honored you were willing to come to a concert instead of going for a walk by the bay or digging in your garden." The audience laughed. "I want to thank Dr. Sylvia Abbott for her help in pulling off this benefit concert. In fact, she's going to have a surprise for you at the end of the concert that doesn't appear in your program." Karin shot a significant look at Allie, who was standing in the back by the entrance, then looked around for Dr. Abbott. "Let's give Dr. Abbott a hand," she added. The audience complied, but Sylvia Abbott refused to stand. In fact, she was nowhere to be seen. Allie couldn't believe it. Where could she have gone? Maybe she was warming up somewhere for the Vivaldi?

Satisfied that she'd completed her task, Karin spoke a few words about the next piece, "The Roaring Fork Woodwind Quintet" by Eric Ewazen[21], and returned to her chair. The quintet launched into the first movement.

The $500 per ticket reception was to be held in the Damon Pavilion, the special event space completed the year before. A flat-roofed glass box attached to the side of the Concert Barn, during the day the pavilion had a spectacular view of the fields rolling down to the bay. And on summer nights, a row of glass doors could be folded back, and the pavilion became a huge screened porch. Allie remembered a magical night last July when fireflies danced across the meadow, perhaps attracted by the twinkling lights. Practical, too, the pavilion was next to the kitchen, so drinks and canapés could easily be served from there. Allie loved the simple elegance of it.

As the quintet began the frenetic final movement of the Nielsen *Wind Quintet*[22], Allie headed toward the green room, expecting to see Thomas and Sylvia there, preparing for their special performance. Surprised that neither was there, Allie took her cello out of its case and checked the tuning of the strings. Were Sylvia and Thomas in the Damon Pavillion? It was getting late—they'd need to be ready to go on stage in a couple of minutes.

Allie left the green room and walked down the hall, glancing in the kitchen on her way to the Damon Pavilion. Though the kitchen was empty of workers, someone had already begun preparing the bowl that would hold the oysters on the half shell. A large shallow glass oval, the bowl would be filled with chipped ice into which the oyster shells would be nestled. Someone had set the bowl, an ice pick, and the special tool for opening oyster shells on the counter by the refrigerator, ready for someone to continue working as soon as the music ended. But Sylvia and Thomas were nowhere to be seen.

She pushed the door to the pavilion open. Vases bursting with lilies on the linen-covered tables perfumed the air. The top of Dr. Abbott's blond head was visible over the back of one of the wingback chairs that were scattered around the edge of the room, facing the fields and the bay. In relief, Allie sped towards her.

"Dr. Abbott, we have to hurry—it's almost time to go on," she whispered loudly as she crossed the large room. "Where's Thomas?"

How weird, thought Allie. Sylvia didn't move or answer.

"Dr. Abbott," she repeated. "It's time for us to go on." The woman didn't stir from her chair or respond.

"Dr. Abbott!" she said more forcefully. As she got closer, she heard the faint sounds of the audience's applause. I hope they clap loud and long enough to encourage the quintet to play an encore, thought Allie. We need the extra time.

Thomas suddenly appeared at the door. "We're on," he said.

"I know. But Dr. Abbott..."

She lightly shook the tweed shoulder of Sylvia's jacket as she came round the chair and recoiled in horror as the woman's head lolled to one side, eyes staring sightlessly into space.

A scarlet river of blood streamed down the front of Dr. Abbott's blouse from a hole in her neck. Allie's piercing screams traveled throughout the barn, immediately silencing the audience's applause.

Thirty

"Time is a great teacher, but unfortunately it kills all its pupils. "
—*Hector Berlioz*

C hief Knowles looked at his watch. Eight o'clock and he still
had a group of people to go through. Murder was not a common crime in his jurisdiction, and when it happened, it was usually
a crime of passion—husband shooting a wife, drug dealer shooting
a business rival, that sort of thing—and fairly straightforward to
solve.

This looked a lot more complicated. A prominent woman was
killed in a public place with several hundred people present, yet
no one had seen the crime or appeared to have committed it.
While there were several doctors in the building who all pro-
nounced the victim dead, it took the chief medical examiner,
Dr. Sheila Green, more than an hour to arrive from Augusta.
She agreed the victim was dead, and said, based on the extent
of rigor mortis, the victim had died between two and six hours
ago—which, of course, Chief Knowles already knew. The other
information from the chief medical examiner was equally useless:
some sort of sharp instrument that left a small round hole had
killed Dr. Abbott. Well, thought Knowles, I could have told you
that.

He'd had Officer Thomas seal off the crime scene in the pavilion and the two crime scene experts were still combing the room for clues. After Dr. Green had finished her examination, the body was bagged and carted away. Chief Knowles briefly questioned Allegra Brewster, the young woman who'd discovered the body, but she was too upset to be coherent. He'd come back to her after dealing with the hundreds of audience members.

One thing Allegra had told him was welcome news: they had a list of every person who had purchased a ticket. She brought the printout from the ticket window to him, and he'd distributed most of the list, people who were merely audience members, to the other junior member of his force, Officer Cheri Ouellette, so she could call people by name to question them. The list with "Heavyweights" written at the top he kept for himself.

It seemed to him the vast majority of the attendees were completely shocked to hear that a murder had occurred during the concert. Though he tried to keep the victim's identity secret in case he might flush out a suspect, it was obvious, after a half hour or so, a rumor had circulated naming Sylvia Abbott.

Many of the audience members could vouch for one another. If a person had been with his or her partner the entire time since arriving for the concert, then Officer Ouellette excused them quickly and let them go on their way. But if the person had attended alone, or had gone to the men's or ladies' rooms during intermission, then he or she might be allowed to leave, but a mark went down by their name. They would face further questioning tomorrow or the next day.

Once the word spread that the victim was Dr. Abbott, the responses were varied. Some people in her circle of friends expressed outrage that "such a thing could have happened." Many others in the crowd didn't know her personally and had no particular reaction except for a sense of horror at unwittingly having been present near a violent crime. Only a few people spoke negatively about the woman, saying such things as, "She was one hell of a bitch," or "She never gave me the time of day."

Chief Knowles could have spoken negatively about Sylvia Abbott himself. They'd had several run-ins since she'd moved to Kennimac. When her house renovation was first completed, she'd installed a security system, and the police had to deal with several false alarms. Knowles met with her to explain this was creating a lot of extra work for his limited force. "It's your job; don't complain to me," she had said. Another time, she had called an officer to her house on the pretext that someone had broken in. It turned out it annoyed her that kayakers were landing on her beach and she wanted the police to scare them off. The third incident had been more legitimate: someone actually had broken a window in the back of her house during the winter while she was away. It looked like an attempted burglary; according to Dr. Abbott, nothing was stolen. There were no real clues and, though the police had some ideas of who the hooligan might have been, there was no way to follow up.

After the last incident, Sylvia Abbott had arrived at the station—which was housed in the town office building that also contained the fire station—and berated Chief Knowles in a voice loud enough to carry down several halls and into many offices. His colleagues had ribbed him for days with quotes about being "an un-ambitious, small-town, closed-minded lay-about with no sense of priorities or responsibility."

As Officer Ouellette wrapped up the list of concert go-ers, the chief looked grimly at the list of attendees set on the music stand in front of him, the "Heavyweights." About twenty names remained, including the members of the performing group. He might as well start with those five. "Carol McCreary," he called out, standing at the front of the stage.

A tall woman dressed in an elegant black tunic and flowing black pants approached the stage and walked up to meet him.

"Carol McCreary?" he asked. She nodded. "Have a seat."

"Will this take long, officer?" Carol asked, sitting on the chair he had indicated. "I'm playing a solo next Sunday in Minnesota and I need to practice this evening."

"Shouldn't take too long, as long as you answer all my questions fully and truthfully." Knowles shuffled the papers around. "As I understand, you and the rest of your group were in that room down the hall from the kitchen during intermission. Is that correct?"

"Yes, we went back to the green room and had some water and relaxed for the 20 minutes."

"Did anyone leave?"

"I don't think so. Not for long, anyway. Well, wait... I think two of us went to the ladies' room."

"Do you mean you went to the ladies' room?" Chief Knowles couldn't stand witnesses who beat around the bush.

"No..." Carol was hesitant. "I think it was Karin and Krissy. They went out together, and they were only gone for a short time. I was busy texting with my daughter in Chicago, so I didn't pay attention." She grimaced and looked at him earnestly. "I might even be wrong about that."

"What was your relationship with Dr. Sylvia Abbott?"

"Relationship?" Carol looked nonplussed. "I didn't have one. I mean, I met her last summer, but I hardly could have picked her out of a crowd."

"Ok," murmured the chief, scribbling something down on his notepad. "Will you be somewhere nearby where we can reach you if we have further questions?"

"I have this concerto performance next Sunday in Minnesota with the Saint Paul Civic Symphony. Mozart's *Clarinet Concerto*. The second one, K. 622[23], not K. 581. I'm supposed to rehearse with them tomorrow night. My flight leaves at noon from Portland."

"Well, I'll make a note of that. We'll see what we can do to get you out of here."

"Thank you, Officer." Carol stuck out her hand.

"It's Chief. Chief Knowles," he said, rereading his notes and ignoring the proffered hand. "Where can we find you until you leave?"

"We're all staying at the Kennimac Inn."

"Ok, then."

"Do you mind if I practice in the green room until my ride is free to take me to the B&B?"

"No, I guess not." The chief waved her off and stood up, groaning as he stretched. "Kristen Kanafax?" he said loudly to the remaining attendees.

"Here," said Kristen, standing. She hurried toward the stage, a short slight woman with a worried frown. If she smiled, thought the chief, she'd look like an elf, with that fringed cap of gray-tinged hair and that turned-up nose.

"Ah," she said as she sat down, closing her eyes. "So sad. So regretful, almost, don't you think?"

Chief Knowles looked at her, confused. Kristen nodded toward the soft music coming from offstage. "The "Adagio" from the *Clarinet Concerto*. Carol wrings every smidgeon of emotion from that simple tune. Rather fitting, don't you think? Considering..."

"Let me ask the questions, Ms... Ah..." He had lost his place in the list.

"Kanafax. Kristen Kanafax." She leaned toward him. "It's a shame, too, because we were hoping Karin could talk some sense into the woman. They were supposed to meet after the reception. To talk about the board's decision."

"The board's decision?"

"Yeah, to ask the orchestra to take a big cut in pay."

"Oh. Well, first, let's establish where you were during the intermission."

"I was in the green room with everyone else, resting, checking my email. Getting refreshed, as it were."

"Did you or anyone else leave the room during that time?"

"I went to the kitchen to get more water. I don't know if anyone else left."

"To the kitchen? Was anyone else in the kitchen? Did you happen to look in the pavilion?"

"The kitchen was crawling with people helping serve the wine and the food. I didn't know any of them, I don't think. I didn't look in the pavilion." She squeezed her eyes shut in an attempt to remember. "I believe the door was closed."

"Do you know what time this was?"

"Well, the intermission had been going on for a while, but I still had time to get back and read a couple of emails on my phone and take a look at the music coming up in the second half of the concert. I'd say it was maybe five or six minutes into the break, but I'm not sure." She extended a delicate wrist. "No watch, see?"

Chief Knowles stared at the wrist for a moment, then shook his head. "Did anyone else leave?"

"The kitchen?"

"No, no, the room where your group was waiting during the intermission."

"I didn't see anyone else from the quintet outside the green room. I think a young man in a tux was sitting there. Or had been earlier, at least. Of course, I was gone for a while and I also wasn't paying much attention... Chief, how much longer do you think you're going to need to keep people here?"

"We're getting to the end. It won't be too much longer."

"Good," said Kristen. "I think the natives are getting restless."

As she got up to leave, a man who rivaled Chief Knowles in girth strode up on stage. His face was red and his expression livid.

"Knowles," he shouted. "This is an outrage! When are you going to let us go? My wife and I have been waiting for hours." He gestured to the now almost empty hall. "You let everyone else go. Why are you holding us?"

"Calm down, Howard." Chief Knowles made a placating motion with his hands. "I can talk to you and Lynnie next if you like."

As an elected member of Kennimac's Select Board and chair of the budget committee, Howard Kelly wielded considerable power over the police department's funding. Almost single-handedly, he could cut or increase the chief's paltry staff. He was used to getting his way. Chief Knowles doubted either Howard or Lynnie had any connection with the murder, so he prepared to give them a cursory interview.

"You know," Lynnie said in her high voice, before Knowles could begin. "I sure hope you don't suspect Howie and me, just because we've had that little argument with that woman. She was suing us, that's true, and for no good reason, but..." Howard put his arm around his wife and pulled her close to his side. She looked up at him from under his armpit.

"What Lynnie means, Chet," he began, "Is that we harbored no ill will toward Mrs. Abbott. It was all a legal misunderstanding, that's all."

"What was?" asked Knowles. "What legal misunderstanding?"

"Didn't you read about it in the Kennimac Weekly News?" asked the squeaky voice, muffled by Howard's suit jacket.

Howard glared at his wife and squeezed her harder. He cleared his throat. "Well, she thought we cut some trees that were on her property but were blocking our view. It was just a little mistake."

"But she was going to..." Lynnie added.

"She was asking for restitution," Howard interjected, "Which we of course were willing to pay. That's all."

"You cut down some of her trees?" Knowles thought he'd heard it all.

"She couldn't even see them from her yard. And they were going to grow tall enough eventually to block our view of the water." Howard paused to get control of himself. "But we would never have harmed her. Never."

"Hmmm," said Knowles, getting it all down on his notepad. "Well, tell me about intermission. Where were your seats? Did you leave the hall during the break?"

"We were in the second row, with the other major donors," said Howard. "We didn't go anywhere during intermission. I was talking with Joe and Don about playing golf next weekend and Lynnie was by my side. Weren't you, Lynnie." The last was a statement, not a question.

"Well... Actually, I went into the kitchen to help prepare for the reception in the Damon Pavilion. I was one of the volunteers."

The chief perked up. "Did you look or go into the pavilion?"

"Oh, no. We spent most of the time searching for the ice pick so we could break up the ice chunks for the oyster bowl. Finally found it in the weirdest place."

"And where was that?" Chief Knowles leaned forward.

"In the sink, mixed in with the dirty serving knives and spoons." She caught her breath. "You don't think...?"

"I don't think anything at this point, Lynnie," said the chief. "Are you two planning to stay in town over the next few weeks? We probably will want to ask you some more questions."

"Oh, we're both staying put, Chief," answered Lynnie. "Our house is on the Garden Tour this July, so I've got lots of work to do in the garden." Howard led her away. "Thank the Lord," she continued, her voice continuing as they walked down the stairs, "that the weather has improved, finally."

Thirty-One

"The musician is perhaps the most mod-
est of animals, but he is also the proudest."
—*Erik Satie*

C hief Knowles stood up and stretched, slapping his thighs
and backside as if to wake them up. Damn it, he thought,
there are still a bunch of people here. He noticed a fair-haired, no
nonsense type of woman making her way to the stage.

"Officer Knowles?" said Karin Anders.

"Chief," he replied.

"Ok, Chief Knowles," she amended. "Would it be possible to
take me next? I'd like to get the rest of our woodwind quintet
finished up. We're all feeling pretty exhausted and it would be
good to get back to the inn as soon as we can."

"You are...?"

"Karin Anders. I'm the horn player and, I guess you'd say, the de
facto manager of the quintet."

Her name ringing a bell, Chief Knowles looked through his
notes. "Ah, the Karin Anders who had an appointment with Sylvia
Abbott."

"Yes," she said, disconcerted. "But obviously it didn't happen."

"The same Karin Anders who left the green room during intermission. Am I right?"

"Yes. I went to the ladies' room."

"Did you talk to anyone while you were there, or on your way?"

"No. When I'm in the middle of a performance, I tend to keep to myself during intermission. For concentration, you know."

"Did you see anyone? You had to walk past the kitchen and the entry of the pavilion."

"Yes, there were a lot of people. Most of whom I didn't know. Let's see, Allie was in the kitchen, I think Luke O'Donnell was. Some board members, maybe. But I wasn't paying attention. I didn't know it was important, of course." She looked up at the barn's rafters and paused. "You know, I think Sylvia Abbott was in the kitchen, too. I think I can picture the back of her blond head and the multicolored tweed jacket she was wearing."

Chief Knowles tried not to betray his increased interest but couldn't keep his breath from quickening.

"You're sure about this?" he asked.

Karin winced. "Pretty sure. Not totally sure."

"What time did you pass by the kitchen?"

"It was just after we'd gotten to the green room. I set my horn down in its case and headed right out. I wanted to get back with time to relax. I also wanted to beat the line in the women's room."

"What was your relationship with the deceased?"

"Sylvia Abbott?" Karin looked straight at the chief. "She was a menace. She was going to ruin the SummerFest. I wanted to stop her."

"She's certainly been stopped now, Ms. Anders."

"And that's a problem. Because I'm afraid the board will just continue along with the plan she laid out. I wish I could have spoken to her..." Karin looked down, idly fiddling with her watch.

"You're wearing a watch. Did you wear that during the concert?"

"Yes, why?"

"Did you look at it when you went to the bathroom?"

"Not that I remember. No, I don't think so."

"Too bad," said the chief.

"Think we can go now?" asked Karin. "The quintet. Are you through with us?"

Knowles consulted his list. "There are two more of you I need to interview. But you and Kristen Kanafax and Carol McCreary are free to go, and I'll do the other two next." As she got up, he halted her. "We may want to talk with you in the morning. In fact, I'm sure we will."

"Thank you. We'll be here at least until noon."

Or maybe later, thought Chief Knowles, if all my questions haven't been answered. He watched Karin Anders leave the stage. A tall, wiry man with a shock of platinum hair walked up to her and said something. They talked animatedly for a moment, then she gestured for him to head to the stage. That must be Steve Kennison, thought Knowles. He wondered why the man looked so familiar.

"Chief Knowles," said the man, sticking his hand out to shake. Knowles was surprised by his British accent. "Anthony Bainbridge, here."

Knowles consulted his list. There was no Anthony Bainbridge on it.

Seeing the chief's questioning look, Bainbridge quickly explained. "I'm the SummerFest Music Director. I hadn't planned on attending this concert, but I had a couple of free days and thought I'd see how things were going up here. There's been a bit of a row, you might have heard."

"A row?" Knowles repeated the British pronunciation.

"Well, yes, a disagreement about the proper way to deal with a financial shortfall, shall we say. Anyway, I've got to hightail it back to Boston tonight—early morning flight—so I'm hoping you can fit me in now, so I can be on my way."

"I guess so. Can you tell me about your movements during the intermission? Who did you talk to? What did you see?"

"Let me think... I was in the hall the entire time. I talked to numerous people. Didn't notice anything out of the ordinary. I did tear myself away to run to the loo just before the beginning of the second half."

"You went to the bathroom?"

"The loo, yes."

"That's in the hallway outside the kitchen, right? Did you notice who was in the kitchen when you went by?"

"Oh, a crowd. Allegra Brewster, her father David, Lucas O'Donnell, George Park, and a group of female volunteers whose names I don't know."

"And they were doing what?"

"Let's see. Pouring champagne or whatever that plonk was, filling serving trays with canapés, washing up, that sort of thing. Oh, and one group was poking at a big chunk of ice with an ice pick."

"Oh? Do you remember who?"

Anthony closed his eyes. "David and some ladies, I believe. David had the pick. That's all I saw. I paid little mind to the whole scene—it was the usual pandemonium that occurs at events like this."

"And that was toward the end of the intermission?"

"Yes, I believe it was. Oh, and my assistant conductor, Thomas Ramirez, was sitting on a chair in the hall." Bainbridge chuckled to himself. "He was listening to something and conducting it with a tiny toy stick."

"Stick?"

"Toy conductor's baton."

"Oh. Tell me about your relationship with Sylvia Abbott," said the chief, changing tack.

"Ah," replied Anthony. "Here one must tread lightly. Mustn't speak ill of the dead and all that." He paused. "What you need to understand is that there is always some tension between the music director and the board of directors of an orchestra. At least in America—the structure's somewhat different where I come from. In my experience, in my American experience, boards often misunderstand their role. They get in there and muck things up."

"And? What about Sylvia Abbott? Did she 'muck things up'?"

"The board chair is the leader, in most of these cases. Sylvia Abbott was a bright woman. We did have our differences. I thought she was immensely capable."

"Capable of what?"

"No, I mean she had a highly developed intellect and business ability. She had that scientist's training; she could cut right to the heart of any matter." He smiled to himself. "Of course, that wasn't always comfortable for the people around her."

"Or for you?"

"Or for me," he agreed. "But I certainly wouldn't ever hurt her in any way. We could disagree, but it wasn't a violent disagreement. I admire her, to be honest." He lowered his voice. "But please don't pass that on to the musicians around here. They'd have my head."

"They didn't share your admiration for the deceased?"

"Oh, most definitely not."

Chet Knowles wondered if the music director was trying to deflect attention away from himself. Anthony Bainbridge appeared to be candid and charming. Perhaps too charming?

"You need to leave tonight?" asked the chief.

"Yes, bloody early flight from Logan tomorrow."

"Well, you may go. But we might have questions for you in the future. When do you expect to return?"

"I'm not scheduled to be back in Maine until the middle of June. Let me give my assistant's contact information to you—he always knows where to find me."

"You can pass that along to Officer Ouellette." Chief Knowles pointed to the young officer pouring over her notes in the dim hall.

The chief consulted his list once again and made a decision. He had two more musicians to interview this evening. The rest of the names on the list were at least familiar to him. As residents, they were likely to be available in the morning. He wearily stood up and faced the small group scattered among the front rows of the hall. Reading off the names of those he was releasing for the night, Knowles explained he wanted them to be available for an interview tomorrow, but he was letting them go for the night. Simultaneous sighs of relief filled the air as the reprieved group rose, stiff from sitting.

"Linda Scilly and Steve Kennison, I do need to interview you this evening," the chief said to the man and woman who remained seated, separated by a couple of chairs. He could sense their disappointment from the stage. "I'll try to make it quick so you can get over to the inn," he added.

The woman stood and said something to her colleague, who nodded in return as she made her way to the chief's interviewing setup. She carried a pink plastic bottle of water, which she set on the floor next to the chair. About 35, the chief reckoned. Maybe attractive when she smiled, but now looking somber and drawn.

"I'm interested in what you did and saw during the intermission," he said.

Linda flipped her long light brown hair over her shoulder. "I didn't leave the green room. I just sat there and checked my email, or chatted with the others. I didn't notice anything out of the ordinary."

"Did you see anyone come or go from the room?"

"I don't think so. Somebody may have left to go to the bathroom. Perhaps. But I really don't remember."

"You're quite sure you don't remember?" asked Knowles.

"No. Sorry. I don't." Linda shrugged her shoulders and yawned. "I'm sorry. I'm tired, that's all."

"Can you tell me about your relationship with Sylvia Abbott?" Knowles didn't hold out any hope her answer would be enlightening.

"Not much to say," she answered, confirming his supposition. "I met her last summer when she was introduced as the board chair, but other than that..."

"Alright, thank you. I can let you go. Would you ask your colleague to join me?"

Steve had seen Linda stand up as if her interview was finished, and he was already on his way. He hurried up to the stage, a bit out of breath. Steve Kennison was definitely the elder of the quintet—in his late fifties or early sixties, Chief Knowles guessed.

"Have a seat, Mr. Kennison," he said. "I'm interested to hear about your activity and observations during the intermission."

"Of course," said Steve. "I was having trouble with my reed. I'm the quintet's fagott..."

"What did you say? You're what?"

"Fagott. Bundle of sticks. That's German for bassoon." Steve cleared his throat. "Just trying to inject a bit of levity..."

"So, you are the bassoon player. Go on." The chief wasn't smiling.

"Ok, well, the reed I'd chosen for the concert was acting up. So I had my head down, sitting at the table and scraping away at that reed and another just in case, so I'd have better luck in the second half of the concert. I hadn't realized the weather would be so dry. We double reed players have these problems all the time."

Chief Knowles thought back to the layout of the room. "So you couldn't see the door, correct?"

"Correct. But I was listening and taking part in the conversation. I've had enough practice that I can scrape a reed and talk at the same time." His eyes twinkled.

"And?"

"Well, of course there was a lot of talk about the board's decision to cut musicians' salaries. Some unkind words about the deceased, that sort of thing. Kind of sorry about that now, in light of subsequent events." He smiled ruefully, then added, "No talk of harming her in any serious way. I mean, we all agreed we'd like to throttle her but had no intention of... I mean, that's just a figure of speech." He recoiled. "She wasn't strangled, was she?"

The chief shook his head. "I'm not currently at liberty to say. Tell me, did anyone enter or leave the room that you know of?"

"Well, I remember Kristen went to get water because Linda had emptied the green room's pitcher into her water bottle. At some point, George Park stuck his head in the door and said we were playing wonderfully and the audience loved us. Someone else may have gone out—Karin, perhaps?" He knocked his head with his fist, as if to dislodge a memory. "Yes, it was Karin. She ran out to the little girls' room."

"Okay," said the chief. "You've said a little about the group's feeling about Dr. Abbott. Now, tell me about your own relationship with her."

Steve looked uncomfortable. "Well, I knew her a bit. The others aren't aware of this, but," he paused and cleared his throat again, "We went on a couple of dinner dates two summers ago. We met at a wine-tasting and discovered a mutual love of French wine. Had several dinners, but we didn't click for some reason."

"The relationship ended then? Or did it continue?"

"Ah, well, it ended. I got the feeling it disappointed her we didn't continue, but we remained cordial. I only saw her at SummerFest functions last summer."

Chief Knowles considered whether to delve deeper into this line of inquiry or to accept Steve's statements at face value. Fact was, Knowles was tired. He scrubbed his now stubbly face with his roughened hand, trying to disguise a yawn. "Thanks for your time," he said. "You've been helpful. We may have further questions; you're staying at the B&B?"

"Yes, I'm leaving tomorrow afternoon. Heading to Vermont to visit an old friend."

"Alright then. Have a good evening."

The two men stood. Steve strode off toward the green room to pick up his bassoon, while Chief Chester Knowles gathered up his papers. He looked at his notes in consternation. He hoped he'd gotten it all down. Damn it, his handwriting was getting worse. He hoped he'd be able to decipher it all in the morning. Fagott, he thought, who'd want to play an instrument called that?

"Luke," he shouted to Lucas O'Donnell, who was waiting to turn off the lights and close up the building. "We're done for the night in here. If the crime scene crew is finished, you can head home. Officer Thomas here will spend the night."

His young colleague, Officer Ouellette, was waiting by the door. She looked as worn out as he felt. It was draining and not a little daunting, this idea that a murder had been committed in Kenni-mac. And the three of them bore the responsibility for catching the perpetrator. This case would be harder than any case in his thirty years of experience. That goddamn Abbott woman—she was trouble from start to finish, he thought to himself as he walked out into the chilly spring night and got in his car.

Thirty-Two

"Imagination creates reality."
—*Richard Wagner*

A llie sat, forlorn, at the kitchen table. The rest of the house was dark, and for once no music spilled from any of the various devices scattered throughout its rooms. Her father, looking pale and suddenly old, had gone to bed almost as soon as he'd arrived home. He had asked her how she was doing, but his question seemed hollow. Allie worried he had just taken a deep dive on his downward spiral.

She couldn't get the image of that round hole with the red line dripping down the crisp white silk blouse out of her mind. Allie rubbed her own throat, wondering at the thin layer of skin, all that lay between life and death. Those glassy eyes. Dr. Abbott dead was completely different from Dr. Abbott alive. Cold in a different way. Flaccid. Vulnerable, maybe. Now Allie would forever associate the scent of those stargazer lilies in the pavilion—that spicy/sweet smell—with the awful scene. Nausea rose in Allie's throat once again and she swallowed, fighting the urge to throw up.

The clock on the microwave said 11:48. Too late to call anyone. Luke might still be awake, but he'd get the wrong idea if she called him now. Allie knew she couldn't go to bed yet. She'd lie there, those images imprinted on the inside of her eyelids. She looked around for a magazine or newspaper—something to take her mind off the scene replaying in her mind. Outside, the moon had risen, shining through the maple trees in front of the house. The trees' shadows drew an intricate web on the lawn in the silvery light. Allie had always loved nights like these. Even in the midst of misery, she was mesmerized. As a young child, she and her mother had sat in the dark, watching the silhouettes of the tree branches and the nighttime animals—skunks and raccoons—silently padding about, digging for grubs or heading to the garbage can. Once, on a snowy moonlit night, they'd seen an ermine, reflecting silver off his white coat, slither between the rocks in the stonewall by the driveway.

Her mother. For a moment, a familiar flash of anger lit up Allie's mind. Stop it, she told herself. Stop making yourself more miserable than you are. Just stop.

Was Dr. Abbott a mother? Allie didn't think so, but she didn't know for sure. There was an ex-husband, Allie knew. He'd been around when Dr. Abbott and he had restored that fancy house and set the town talking. But then he disappeared; Maine wasn't for him. Or maybe Dr. Abbott drove him away—Allie didn't know what happened.

She went to the kitchen door and opened it. For a night following such a warm April afternoon, it was remarkably chilly. Allie wrapped her sweater around her shoulders and stood on the threshold, leaving the door open behind her. The light from the kitchen spilled out onto the steps and Allie observed her own shadow, long and thin, stretching through the bright rectangle. She heard rustling in the yard—perhaps a small rodent scurrying away from the threatening brightness. From down the driveway by the main road came the loud singing of the spring peepers. The pond was not visible from the house, but the sound of the spring peepers carried well enough to keep her up at night.

Allie concentrated on their sound for a moment. Something unusual caught her ear. There it was again, a human voice singing with the tiny frogs. Almost an operatic keening, maybe a tenor or alto range. Male or female, she couldn't tell. It was melodic, minor, improvisational—no tune she'd ever heard before. The eerie sound transmuted the cheerful natural chorus into something sinister. Who was doing the singing? Allie went down the kitchen steps and out into the yard. The peepers immediately stopped and the human singing ceased as well. In a panic, Allie ran back up the steps and locked the door behind her.

Thirty-Three

"Money doesn't talk, it swears."
—*Bob Dylan*

That proper noun, "Kennimac," was a misnomer. Originally called Oyster Dumps in the 1700s and most of the 1800s, the name was changed in the 1870s in an attempt to sound more exotic and attract a "better sort" of resident, especially in the summer. It was changed by the same people who were getting rich mining those eponymous oyster shell heaps. Located along the banks of the tidal Kennimac River, which fed into the bay from the ocean, the heaps were actually garbage piles left from millennia of annual oyster feasts held by native peoples. Through the centuries, the oysters decomposed, and the heaps became giant repositories of calcium. The mined material was sold for fertilizer and made some of the townspeople quite wealthy.

Winding five miles from Lake Winnicasset to the sea, the tidal Kennimac River widened into the first bay after passing through a series of falls. It then narrowed again, flowing another short distance until it collected in the second bay, this one much deeper but still tidal. It was the east side of the first bay, known locally as Little Salt Bay, on which the former dairy farm—now the site of the SummerFest—was located. The Kennimac Inn was directly across the shallow bay on the west. Lined with old farmlands, old summerhouses, and a few new homes tucked discretely into clumps of trees, Little Salt Bay was the calmer, more bucolic of the two bays. While seals occasionally made their way into Little Salt Bay, the most notable non-human residents of the bay were horseshoe crabs, oysters, and sea birds—gulls, herons, osprey, and cormorants. In the spring, alewives ran up the river into Little Salt Bay, attempting to climb the falls to reach the lake above. During that time, osprey and bald eagles fished the alewives relentlessly. But when the alewives left, the big raptors left with them.

If it was bald eagles you were seeking, the first bay, known as Big Salt Bay, was rife with them. Deeper and more treacherous, with shoals and lone rocks lurking just below high tide, Big Salt Bay was the home of the sailing club, and many of the newer, grander summer homes perched on its shores. The main part of the town of Kennimac straddled both sides of the bridge that crossed the river between the bays. The town consisted of several streets of commercial buildings made almost entirely of bricks baked from the clay of the Kennimac's riverbanks. Banks, several restaurants, a bookstore, clothing and housewares boutiques, and an imposing library lined the main street, with other shops and restaurants, along with residences—some simple, some not—clogging the alleys and narrow streets that radiated from the main street. Quite picturesque, there were still a few poorly remodeled storefronts, a few buildings with peeling window frames to leaven the quaintness. And swooping above the main street, from one hairy black tilting utility pole to another, electric and phone wires scribed a tangled path above the cars, bicycles, and pedestrians.

As in any Maine town with a large population of summer people (sometimes called the "summer complaint" by year-round residents), there was an uneasy relationship between the two groups. Each depended on the other, but their motives were often misunderstood by their counterparts. To add to the confusion, many of the now year-round residents had begun as summer people. Perhaps they'd spent childhood summers at a family compound and chose to raise their own young families in the place they remembered as idyllic. Or they'd visited as adults and decided to retire there, marveling at the bargains one could purchase with the proceeds from a Connecticut or Boston-area real estate sale.

Sylvia Abbot straddled both those categories. She had spent summers as a child at her family's summerhouse next to the sailing club. Her career with an oil company had kept her in Houston, with only infrequent forays to Maine, while her cousins and aging aunts and uncles inhabited the summer house. Childless and wealthy, she and her husband, Charles, chose instead to travel to Europe during summer vacations. But when retirement beckoned, she convinced Charles to consider Kennimac. It turned out her relatives had dwindled, with their interest and bank accounts dwindling as well, and Sylvia and her husband bought the property for what they considered a steal.

Alas, retirement suited each of them, but in different ways. Charles Abbott was happy with the frenetic energy needed during the renovation phase of their time together in Maine, but once they renovated the house to their liking, they realized spending time together was not. He needed to be in the midst of the action; Kennimac was too quiet and insignificant. They parted, reasonably amicably, and Charles moved to a co-op apartment just off Fifth Avenue. Sylvia had never been there. By the time of her murder seven years later, the two of them had essentially moved on.

In the meantime, Sylvia Abbott had worked to become a part of the Kennimac community. Before Charles had left, they'd joined the sailing club, known as the Big Salt Bay Sailing Club. She'd bought the Osprey and found people to crew with her at the Wednesday races each summer. A fierce competitor always, she burned through crew, at least two per summer; no one could find much fun in listening to her withering comments when the boat fell behind the lead. To her chagrin, she never won the annual cup, perhaps because she and her ever-changing crew never were together long enough to develop a working rhythm.

Dr. Abbott sprinkled her money around to various local worthy causes: the library, the hospital, and of course, the SummerFest. She donated several sailing dinghies for the sailing lessons at the club. This strategic generosity enabled her to snag invitations to fundraising events and hobnob with people whose investment accounts could match hers. But she knew most of those friendships were superficial. She longed to make friends who were interesting and vibrant and fun to be with, not just well-to-do.

She did put her own labor into volunteering at the sailing club, helping with the various race series, even the ones for kids. Sometimes she wondered if her life would have been more exciting if she'd had children. Then she thought of the emotional baggage that seemed to come with having children. Not that she'd raise them the way most parents did today: lenient, easily bamboozled, inattentive, trying to be friends. No, her children would have been different and superior, she was sure.

Sylvia had a sense that something was missing in her life. Not Charles. They had never been all that close—more like business partners. But several times, Sylvia had reached out to people in Kennimac to foster a more meaningful type of friendship. But it hadn't worked out, not with any of them, and that made her angry.

Thirty-Four

"When I was a little boy, I told my dad, 'When I grow
up, I want to be a musician.' My dad said,
'You can't do both, son.'" —*Chet Atkins*

The Kennimac Inn was a mishmash collection of turrets,
gables, porches, and bay windows. The Victorian-era house
hadn't been updated much, except for comfortable beds, fresh
paint, and modern appliances in the kitchen. One significant
change was a row of French doors installed in the dining room
that opened onto a brick patio facing Little Salt Bay.

Monday morning, the five members of the Summermusic Quintet sat around the table in the Kennimac Inn's dining room, blink-
ing in the bright sunlight reflecting off the bay outside the windows. The five looked pensive; conversation was sparse as they
chose from the pastry-laden breakfast served family-style on the
large oval table.

"I have to say, it seems like a bad dream," said Kristen, brushing
croissant flakes from her fingers. "I wonder when the police will
show up here."

"I know. I couldn't sleep at all last night." Karin looked at her
phone. "It's eight o'clock. I bet they'll be here soon."

"There's nothing more to tell them," said Carol. "I told them
everything I knew—which was essentially nothing. And I need to

practice." She set down her cup of coffee and headed back to her room.

"Boy, is she ever paranoid about her gig this weekend," whispered Linda. "She's not usually so uptight. Anyway," she continued in a normal voice, "I wonder what the effect of Abbott's death will be on the SummerFest. I don't imagine that it will grind to a halt. I mean, George runs things, not the board."

"Yeah, but there's the question of how to handle the board's decision about the orchestra." Kristen spoke up. "Even without Abbott, the board's decision still stands. I wonder who becomes the chair now..."

"Wouldn't that be David Brewster?" asked Steve. "He's the vice chair."

"Now, that would be interesting," said Linda, with a giggle. "He voted against the rest of the board, didn't he? He could probably find a way to overturn the stupid decision. Hey, maybe he killed her to stop it from happening? Seriously though, what do you think, Karin—can he change the board decision?"

Karin brushed her hair out of her face. Of all the quintet members, she looked the most sleep-worn. "It's hard to say. I know she had some allies. And David Brewster is not someone who looks for conflict." Karin rolled a sausage around her plate with her fork.

"What did you guys think of the police chief, what's-his-name?" Linda looked at each of her colleagues.

"He needs a stronger brand of deodorant," said Kristen.

"I know!" said Linda. "Did you notice the sweat marks under his arms? I wonder if he was nervous or something."

"Well," said Karin, "I don't think he deals with a fucking murder every week here in Brigadoon-slash-Kennimac. He seemed like a decent guy, trying to do a good job. I bet he's under tremendous pressure. I mean, someone was killed, for Christssake, and the murderer is still out there. The town must be going nuts."

"Sucks to be him," said Linda.

"Pretty much," agreed Kristen.

"The one I'm worrying about is poor Allie. I wonder how she's doing?" added Karin. "She was white as a sheet when I saw her after the fact. I think she'd been barfing her brains out."

Steve, who'd been scrolling through his email on his phone, looked up. "Have any of you ever seen a dead person?" The others shook their heads. "Well, I have," he continued.

After a moment's pause in which he didn't follow up, Kristen interrupted. "And...?"

"Oh, well, they don't look right. Not like themselves. Like it's against nature, somehow. Like an insult to life or something." He shrugged. "I can't seem to explain it, but the sight is something you never forget."

"Who was it you saw, Steve?" asked Kristen gently. "I thought we knew all your stories."

"This one you don't," he answered. "It was my older brother. The one who died in a car crash, remember? I don't think I've ever mentioned I was in the car. I don't like to talk about it much." Steve looked pensive. The others studied their plates.

"More coffee?" The inn's owner, RuthEllen Cox, bustled into the dining room. "I just heard from Chet Knowles. He'll be here in about a half hour. Can I fix anyone any more food before he arrives?"

They all shook their heads. The center of the table still sported a wide assortment of muffins, breads, ham, sausages, and fruit.

"I'll have more coffee," volunteered Karin, and the other three followed suit.

"Where's your clarinetist?" asked RuthEllen.

"Can't you hear her?" asked Steve. They all became silent and listened. A faint reedy sound leaked from one of the upstairs rooms.

Thirty-Five

"There are only two things worth aiming
for, good music and a clear conscience."
—*Paul Hindemith*

A llie stretched and pushed off the covers. She had finally
fallen asleep and slept deeply. The memory of Dr. Abbott's
sightless eyes rushed into her mind. Allie felt nauseous again.
Who could have done such a thing? It was so horrible. And how
shockingly little effort it took to end someone's life.

She had seen a dead body before, but somehow that was different. When they brought Toby Zeller to the dock after his sailing
accident, he didn't have a mark on him. When the seawater gushed
out of his mouth, it seemed as if he would start coughing and
come back to life. He looked like a sleeping angel, lying there on
the wood with his curly gold hair haloed around his head. But
yesterday, Dr. Abbott had seemed most definitely dead. That evil
little hole in her neck, that trail of blood down her front.

Allie shivered. Get busy, she told herself. Think about something else.

Archie had already departed, surprisingly; he wasn't an early
riser. Allie sniffed the air in the house. No scent of bacon, toast, or
coffee coming up the stairs. Bright sun streamed in her windows,
the wind ruffling the unfurling leaves on the hawthorn tree. She

checked her phone. 8:30! Allie scrambled out of her bed and slipped a baggy corduroy shirt over her t-shirt and boxers.

The kitchen showed no sign of breakfast, but her father's car was still in the driveway. No sign of Archie either. Allie ran back upstairs and checked her father's room. The bed was unmade; his pajamas lay atop the rumpled quilt.

"Dad?" she called. "Dad, are you here?"

There was no answer. A flash of white in the field outside caught Allie's eye. Archie, running toward the house. That was odd. She went down to the kitchen door to let him in. "Oh, good boy," she said, scratching his back as he wriggled between her legs, his tail wagging frantically and his body trembling with excitement. "Happy to see me, are you, my good boy?" She looked up the field, past where Archie had shot from, expecting to see her father following after, but no one came clumping toward the house in tall green field boots. In fact, she noticed, his boots were right here, next to the door.

Hmmm, thought Allie. Where could he be? She'd assumed he'd been taking Archie for a walk, but clearly that wasn't so.

"But then," she asked the little dog, "How did you get out?" Archie looked at her and cocked his head, as if he didn't quite understand the question. "You'd tell me if you could, I know," she said.

After grabbing a piece of toast, Allie headed upstairs to get dressed. As she brushed her teeth, her phone rang. An unfamiliar number flashed on the screen, so she let it go to voicemail.

As she finished rinsing, her phone ran again. It was the same number. This time, Allie answered. She was surprised to hear her father's voice.

"Hi, Allie, how did you sleep?" he asked.

"Once I feel asleep, fine," she said. "Where are you?"

"That's why I'm calling. I'm at the police station. Chief Knowles picked me up this morning. He had some questions he wanted help with. We're all done, so I was wondering if you could come and get me."

"Sure, Dad." Allie paused. "Is everything okay? I mean, I know it isn't—there's been a murder, but is everything okay with you?"

"Me? Yes, things are fine. I'd just like to get some breakfast and start the day at home. I'll be waiting on the sidewalk for you to pick me up. Leaving soon?"

"Right now. See you in a few minutes." Allie hung up the phone, puzzled. Why had the chief brought her father to the station? Did the chief think her dad knew something? Was he a suspect, even? Allie shook her head. Not her dad. He would never do something so violent and cruel. No matter how angry he was.

Thirty-Six

"The ocean scares me."
—*Brian Wilson*

A llie noticed her father was wearing the same clothes he'd worn to the concert the day before, minus the tweed jacket. His white oxford shirt was rumpled, with a faint coffee stain on the front. His hair, too, stood on end as if he'd repeatedly run his hands through it. His eyes drooped—not just the bags under his eyes but his eyelids as well. The color of his skin, his expression, his kneed-out pants, everything signaled exhaustion and defeat. She turned down the radio broadcast, NPR's "Morning Edition," as he got into the car.

"Hello, Archie," he said, feigning cheerfulness. "Hello, love." He rubbed Archie's ears and kissed Allie on the cheek. "What a morning already," he sighed.

"What time did you go to the station? Did Chief Knowles call first? I never heard the phone ring."

David Brewster smiled wryly. "You were still snoring when I left. I know you didn't hear a thing. Thank goodness. I think we all deserve a long rest after yesterday."

"But why did you have to go into the station? What was that all about?"

"Chester knows I'm a good source of background information. He had a lot of questions about Sylvia and the goings on at the festival. I was happy to help. We have to get this crime solved as soon as possible, for the sake of the festival, Allie. I've already seen some emails from board members about postponing this season. If we do that—close for a season—that'll be the end of the festival forever. It's almost impossible to revive once you've stopped."

Allie thought her heart was going to stop. Suspend the Summer-Fest! She hadn't thought of that outcome. That would be the end of the festival and the end of her first professional job. "Dad, they would never do that, would they? I mean, wouldn't you have a lot to say about it?"

David sighed. "I don't have as much power as you might think. Sylvia brought a new group of people to the board, people who are not as historically connected to the enterprise as you and I are. I don't run the board, and I don't have the financial resources to throw my weight around. I just don't know..."

"But you will fight to make sure that doesn't happen, right?"

"Yes, I will. But I think the best thing any of us can do is figure out who did this. I'm especially anxious to find the murderer because of what that experience must have done to you, Allie."

The vision of Sylvia Abbott flashed before Allie's eyes once again.

"Dad, I was thinking," Allie said, turning into their driveway. "I never knew Dr. Abbott. I mean, she was more of a caricature than a real person to me. I guess I saw another side of her when we rehearsed the Vivaldi. But you knew her a lot better. What was she like?"

"She was a complicated person. Let's talk over scrambled eggs and bacon."

The comforting scents of coffee, toast, and bacon soon filled the Brewster kitchen, along with the familiar lighthearted strains of Respighi's *Ancient Airs and Dances, Suite I*[24] on the classical radio station. Allie gave George a call to say she'd be late getting to the SummerFest office; he told her not to hurry. "Who knows what we'll be doing today or from now on," he said dourly.

"So, what sort of things did the police want to know?" Allie turned the radio down and looked expectantly at her father, who seemed to delay the conversation by first deliberating over his music choice and then setting the table and elaborately buttering his toast.

"Chet wanted me to tell him everything I know about Sylvia and the board."

"Such as...?"

"Well, your mother knew Sylvia as a child, you know, although Sylvia was older. According to Melissa, Sylvia was quite a tomboy. I think her childhood summers in Maine were important to her, growing up. From what I heard, her parents were pretty uptight and demanding—she was their only child and they put pressure on her to be perfect. All she wanted to do at that age was to race her dinghy, climb trees, and run with the pack of boys. She was a warrior, according to Melissa. Never afraid, always pushing the rest to do something a little daring, a little dangerous even. I think your mother was afraid of her, if you can imagine such a thing."

"What sort of dangerous things did Sylvia do?"

"Let me think what your mother told me. Okay, here's an example: she challenged a couple of kids to swim out to Cook's Island and back with her. But she was a much stronger swimmer; most of the kids around here hadn't had formal swimming lessons. But they couldn't stand being upstaged by a girl, so two guys—Buddy Templeton and Ted Prouty—took her up on it. She teased the rest of them mercilessly. But Buddy and Ted practically drowned. As I recall, one of the grownups near the docks jumped in a rowboat and ended up fishing them out of the bay, while Sylvia swam back to shore with no problem. That certainly raised everyone's opinion of her physical abilities, but it didn't make her any friends."

"Humiliation doesn't usually."

"It sure doesn't. And Sylvia never understood that. To this day. Or at least yesterday, I guess."

"Was that the way her parents treated her?" asked Allie.

"It may be. I guess they didn't think much of the neighborhood summer kids—that was the impression they gave Melissa. And they stopped coming to Maine when she was about fifteen. Melissa never saw Sylvia again, since your mother was gone by the time Sylvia and Charles came back here to retire seven or so years ago."

"By which time Sylvia had become a full-blown bully?"

"Oh, no, I wouldn't say that. Sylvia had many good points."

"Are you just trying not to speak ill of the dead?" Her father's defense of the person with whom he'd been at loggerheads on so many issues surprised Allie.

"No," he said, stretching out the word. "She was smart, and she was honest. You knew where you stood with her; she didn't hide her feelings."

"But she sure seemed to lack imagination," argued Allie. "And compassion. Like, didn't she see how much pain her idea of breaking the musicians' union would cause the SummerFest? What was up with that, anyway? And Thomas, the new assistant conductor, had a previous history with her in Houston when he was a boy."

"She told me something last week that I think sheds some light," David Brewster said. "Did you know she invited me over for drinks?" Allie shook her head. "Well, I think she felt bad I was still not onboard with her plan. And I was willing to listen, although I knew she wouldn't change my mind." He folded the cloth napkin that had been in his lap and laid it on the table. "Anyway, she told me about her family's troubles with the unions back when she was a child. Her father had invested in some utilities, power plants of some sort. The builders were an open shop construction company. And the unions hated that. They actually bombed several of the construction sites. It killed a worker, I think. Anyway, that completely colored her feelings about unions."

"I know; she told me something similar. But why did she think that had anything to do with the SummerFest and the local musicians' union? She was always so totally convinced she was right."

"That's for sure. Nothing could shake her sense of being right about something. We all know that," her father agreed. "Well, you probably should get up to the office and see what's happening. Archie and I are going to work on Calliope, aren't we, Archie?" David Brewster reached down and scratched the little white dog's ears. Allie was pleased to see her father didn't look so tired and depressed; he seemed to have gathered energy as he spoke.

Thirty-Seven

"Nothing primes inspiration more than necessity."
—*Giacchino Puccini*

George Park and Chief Knowles were deep in conversation as Allie entered the SummerFest office. "Good to see some color back in those cheeks of yours," Chief Knowles said to her as she settled at her desk and turned on her laptop. "I hope you'll have a chance to talk with me later this morning?" He aimed a questioning look at Allie. "Right now I'm supposed to be at the Kennimac Inn, talking with those musicians before they head south."

"I should be here all day." Allie looked at George, who nodded. "So, anytime is fine with me."

"Good. I'll come by after lunch then." Knowles heaved himself out of his chair. "Thanks for your help, George. We'll figure this out."

After he had left, Allie asked, "What's he thinking, George? Did he give you any hints?"

"It didn't sound like they've zeroed in on any suspects. He was asking me about what I saw at the intermission—if anything new had come to mind last night. I was so busy trying to help with the refreshments while ingratiating myself with various donors that I didn't notice anyone else. What do you remember, Allie?"

"There were lots of people milling around. The kitchen was chaos. Dr. Abbott stopped in early on—I'm guessing she went into the pavilion from there." Allie took a deep breath, thinking about what happened in the pavilion.

"Luke and Dad were pouring the Prosecco," she continued. "I was loading up trays with crab cakes. Several people were trying to get the oyster tray ready for the pavilion reception. There was so much coming and going, it was pretty crazy. Thomas was sitting in the hall by the green room with headphones on. And I think Kristen Kanafax came in to get some water."

"Who were the other people getting the reception stuff ready?"

"Hmmm. I think it was Mrs. Kelley and Mrs. Swift... and Professor Schimler. They were trying to get this huge mound of ice chunks to break up so they could spread the ice out on the oyster platter for the oysters to sit on. I think my dad and Kate Zeller also pitched in. They were all taking turns going at it with an ice pick." Allie paused, realizing what she had just said. Ice pick. Round hole oozing blood. Could the pick have been the murder weapon? She felt woozy.

George raised his eyebrows. "Ice pick? Wonder if Chief Knowles heard about that."

"I can tell him when he comes back this afternoon," said Allie. Hoping to change the subject, Allie asked if it was okay if she listened to some music. George said it was fine. In fact, he needed to get back to the financials he'd been working on earlier in the morning. Allie inserted the earphones and soon the restrained notes of the opening of Scarlatti's *Sonata in d minor* (L. 108) filled her head. She began the work of updating the donor list. A thought occurred to her. She put the music on hold and pulled out the earphones.

"George, we need to send out a message about Dr. Abbott," she said. "I think we should do a press statement and an email to our list."

George rubbed his forehead. "Christ, you're right. We need to get those out immediately. I've already gotten about five media calls, and I have a ton of media email queries. Would you mind drafting the email, Allegra? I'll work on the press statement."

"You might want to record your statement so TV and radio newscasts can use it in their broadcasts. That should keep them off our backs for a while. I can help with that."

"Great idea. Just let me draft it." George's forehead was turning red from being rubbed so much.

Allie put the earphones back in and started thinking. Email. Short and simple. It's all that was needed. She started on the message.

The Kennimac SummerFest Symphony regrets...—too perfunctory. She started again. The Kennimac SummerFest Symphony was saddened...—no, too emotional. (And possibly untrue.) The Kennimac SummerFest Symphony was shocked...—that was maybe too true and probably inappropriate. Jeez, this was hard. Finally, she settled on:

Dear <first name> <last name>,

As a friend of the Kennimac SummerFest Symphony, you know what a close knit community we are—musicians, audience, directors, and staff. We each have an important role to play in the artistic and financial success of the organization. Yesterday we lost a member of that community, Board Chair Sylvia Abbott, who died while attending a benefit concert in the SummerFest Barn. Dr. Abbott was a strong leader of the board; her presence will be missed. As we sort out the repercussions of her death, we will continue to keep you informed.

Yours truly,

George approved it and suggested Allie also insert the professional headshot of Sylvia Abbott she had had taken when she assumed the chairmanship. Soon the email was winging its electronic way to the thousands of SummerFest email subscribers. Within minutes, the office line began ringing with calls from concerned friends of the symphony who hadn't heard the news.

"Allie," said George. "We'll never get anything done if we have to answer the phone all day and repeat the same story to people over and over. Would you mind putting a new message on the phone? I think you can basically say the same thing as in the email, except include that we have no news to add at this time, or something to that effect."

Allie thought for a moment, then started writing.

"George, do you mind if I include the "info@" email address, in case people have more questions?" She knew a dead end message wouldn't satisfy them. Some of them, at least, would like a conversation. Finally, she was ready to record.

"Thank you for your interest in the Kennimac SummerFest Symphony. As you may have heard, our community has recently lost a valued member, our board chair Dr. Sylvia Abbott. At this time, we have no further information about her cause of death or the board of directors' interim leadership. If you have further questions or wish to communicate with SummerFest staff, please send us an email at info @summerfestsymphony.org."

The calls continued throughout the morning, but voicemail picked up after the first ring. Allie knew she'd eventually have to go through the emails—hey, wouldn't that be a good job for a volunteer or a board member?—but she wasn't going to worry about that. Right now, she would worry about her upcoming interview with Police Chief Knowles. And most of all, she would worry about who the murderer was.

Thirty-Eight

"To send light into the darkness of men's
hearts—such is the duty of the artist."
—*Robert Schumann*

A s the door to the office began to open, Allie expected to see
Chief Knowles enter. Instead, Luke's head poked around the
door.

"Lunch?" he asked the room's inhabitants. "Any plans?"

Allie thought he was inappropriately jolly. She didn't feel light-
hearted, although Scarlatti's tickling melodies had lifted her mood
somewhat. "Nope," she responded.

"Brought a sandwich," grunted George.

"Warm sunny day. Staff in need of relief. How about a picnic
under the apple trees?" Luke tried his most winning smile.

Allie didn't have the energy to resist. "Fine. If you get me a
sandwich—turkey and avocado. And chips. And a root beer. And
be quick about it." She took a ten-dollar bill from her wallet and
handed it to Luke.

"Your wish, your highness, is my command." With a knightly
flourish, Luke backed out the door and headed off to Favreau's
Country Store to fill the lunch order.

George lifted his eyes from his spreadsheet and looked at Allie.
"I thought you were trying to stay away from him," he said.

"True," she replied, "But I'm starving."

"Ah, the young queen has her price, just like everyone else in the kingdom," mocked George.

"Today, yes," Allie agreed with a rueful smile.

ele

Not only did Luke's ingratiating grin seem inappropriate, but the sunshine pouring over the budding apple trees gave no hint of the tragedy of the day before. Allie and Luke sat in silence for a minute or two, the crunch of chips and the fizz of opened soda bottles joining the buzzing of the industrious bees plying the clover blossoms in the grass.

"Penny for your thoughts," said Luke.

Allie finished chewing before replying. "What else? We have to find out who did this."

"Isn't that more a job for the police?"

A small bird, emboldened by hope for crumbs, hopped nearby. "The birds and the bees," exclaimed Luke, breaking into song, "Let me tell ya 'bout the birds and the bees and the flowers and the trees and the moon up above and a thing called love..."

"Enough!" protested Allie. "Luke, I'm not in the mood for your stupid musical jokes."

Luke laughed. "If only I had my ukulele, you would have loved it."

"Yeah, right."

"So, why are you in such a bad mood? I mean, ding dong the witch is dead, right?"

"Luke! That's horrible! And anyway, can't you see the danger this puts the SummerFest in?" Allie thought about the word danger. "And there's a murderer out there. Who knows if he will strike again?" She shivered.

Luke gently brushed off a petal that had fallen onto Allie's hair. "You don't need to worry, Allie. No one will want to harm you."

Allie pushed his hand away. "Don't be so sure. I was the first person to see the... to see Dr. Abbott. I don't know anything, but the murderer might not realize that. And I have no clue who this evil person is. Right in our midst. It could be you, for all I know."

"Hold on, Allie. It's not me. Jesus! That's not funny." Luke scowled. "I can't believe you said that!"

Allie shrugged as she wrapped up the second half of her sandwich. "Look, I'd better get back to the office. Chief Knowles is coming by to interview me. Not to mention, I do have work to do. Hopefully, the musicians will arrive here in a couple of months. We have a lot to do to get ready."

"Yeah, yeah, yeah. I have work to do, too." Luke got up and gave Allie a hand. "I'm sorry you're so upset about this, Allie. I know it's gotten to you. I wish I could do something..."

Allie relented slightly. "Well, thanks for getting lunch. And let me know if you see or hear anything that might help figure this out."

Thirty-Nine

"Say what you want to say, let the words fall
out. Honestly. I want to see you be brave. "
—*Sara Bareilles, "Brave"*

"So, let's go over what happened, moment-by-moment," said
Chief Knowles. "Close your eyes for a minute, Allegra, and
try to recreate in your mind what you saw during intermission.
Not just what you saw in the pavilion but leading up to that time.
Officer Ouellette will take notes." He paused for a second as a
thought struck him. "You know what? I think it might help you if
you did an actual walk-through of those twenty minutes, timed
with a watch. Can we get into the Concert Barn?" He turned to his
colleague. "Is there still someone on duty down there?"

Cheri Ouellette called the trooper guarding the crime scene on
her walkie-talkie to let him know that they were on their way.

Allie was nervous about going there but she thought it might
help her remember. She, the chief, and Cheri walked down to the
barn, and the officer let them in.

The hall was still in disarray. It had been shut up all day and
was much cooler than outdoors. Audience chairs were scattered
around the floor, and the musicians' chairs and stands were still
on the stage. The smell of unrefrigerated crab cakes and the tang
of sour wine mingled with the woody smell of the barn.

"So, just take us through your actions during the intermission, Allegra."

"Ok." Allie took a big breath. "When the quintet started the last piece before intermission, I went into the kitchen and began to get the trays ready." Allie walked to the kitchen, followed by the chief and the two police officers. The kitchen was a mess, full of dirty dishes and trays of leftover food. Bottles of flat Prosecco lined the counter.

"I opened the refrigerator and got the crab cakes out and arranged them on the platters. Wait, first I passed Thomas Ramirez, sitting in a chair in the hall. He had his eyes closed and had earphones in, listening to music."

"Thomas Ramirez?" asked the chief. "I don't remember seeing that name anywhere on the lists."

"Oh, he's the assistant conductor this summer, and he and I and Dr. Abbott were scheduled to perform a short piece at the end of the program."

"Did he know the deceased?"

"Oh, no. Well, he might have, a little. From a long time ago. She was on the board of a foundation that his mother worked for—something like that."

"Where might I find this person?"

Allie gave Thomas's contact information to Officer Ouellette. "He probably drove back to Boston last night. I know he had a conducting job he was finishing up there."

"So, alright. Continue with your recollection, Allegra."

"When the applause ended, I walked out and set a tray down on the side table. Luke, my dad, and a few volunteers from the board went into the kitchen to help, and I think Luke took out the rest of the trays. Dad and I were pouring the wine; I was getting worried because we needed to get it out to the crowd ASAP. That's when Dr. Abbott came into the kitchen. She asked me something about the wine, and I assumed she was planning to help pour, but then she disappeared..."

"What exactly did she say to you? Can you remember her exact words?" Knowles looked at her intently.

"I think she just said, 'Where's the wine?' I thought she meant the Prosecco, but I guess she meant the wine for the reception in the pavilion."

"So, people were coming and going in the kitchen. Can you tell me who you saw?"

Allie closed her eyes, trying to remember the scene in the kitchen. "Well, as I mentioned, my dad, Lucas, two volunteers from the board, Esther Swift, and Professor Schimler. Also, Carolyn Kelley. Kate Zeller came in partway through; she must have seen we needed help. Dr. Abbott. Kristen Kanafax came in and got water. George helped pass the trays around when he saw how busy we were."

"Did you notice anyone walk by in the hall?"

"I think I saw Karin Anders head to the ladies' room. I think Anthony Bainbridge walked by on his way to the mens'. Maybe Steve Kennison, too." She stood in the kitchen, trying to re-enact her motions from the afternoon before. "There may have been others. And I was paying more attention to what was happening in the concert hall than who was walking to the bathrooms. The refreshments were disappearing faster than we could refill the trays."

"Think now, Allegra. Is there anything you saw in the kitchen that you haven't mentioned? Anything unusual or unexpected?"

Allie turned around in the kitchen, looking intently at the left-over mess. She noticed the puddle of water in and around the platter that was to hold the oysters. "People were trying to break up a big frozen chunk of ice cubes."

"Who was?"

"I know one of them was Mrs. Kelley. She has that voice—hard to miss. She means well, though, I think," Allie added hastily. "Then other people helped at times. I think my dad, Kate, probably others I didn't notice."

"What else?" Chief Knowles looked over to make sure Cheri Ouellette was getting it all down.

"Well," Allie said slowly, "I remember they had a hard time finding the ice pick. Mrs. Kelley asked me if I'd seen it. Then someone—Dad or Kate?—found it in the sink already." The import of that hit Allie. "But that was too early, right? I mean, someone couldn't have already killed Dr. Abbott and returned the ice pick, could they?"

"We can't rule anything out at this point," said the chief.

Allie was silent. Can't rule anything—or anybody—out *at this point*, she thought. She shivered.

"Does everything look about the same as when you last were in here?" asked Chief Knowles.

Allie surveyed the chaotic room again. "Yes, I think so. I don't know why it is such a mess, though. I thought some volunteers were going to clean up after intermission. I guess they decided to wait until later so they could listen to the second half of the concert." And then I discovered a murder, she added to herself.

"Ok, then. Good work, Allegra. Let's move into the pavilion and see what you can remember there." Chief Knowles untied the yellow police tape that cordoned off the door to the pavilion.

Allie could feel a sense of panic rising in her chest. The heavy scent of lilies was overpowering. The wingback chair where Sylvia Abbott had been sitting was still there, facing out to the fields and shore. Outside, the sun shone a deceptively cheerful clear light, glittering on the water in the bay beyond.

She took a deep breath. Her voice began with a quaver. "I... I walked in here and looked at the wine on the back table, which hadn't been opened yet, and I knew because the red needed to breathe—that's what Dr. Abbott had said," Allie stopped to take a breath, "And so we should open it a few minutes before the event." She looked around the room. It was spotless, just as before. The twenty or so stackable chairs were still scattered around the perimeter, the unopened bottles of wine and the wine glasses were still standing in neat rows on the black tablecloth covering the table in the back of the room. Views of the fields and bay filled the windows, which extended on three sides of the large room.

"The door was unlocked, correct?" the chief asked.

"Yes, but it had been unlocked earlier, before the concert, when the caterers delivered the wine and wine glasses."

"Ok, Allegra, now take us through what happened after you entered the room and checked on the wine." Officer Ouellette spoke in a gentle voice.

"Umm, I saw Dr. Abbott. I could see her hair... the back of her head above the chair. I thought she was just sitting quietly. She... I said something, and she didn't answer. I thought she didn't hear me. She... So I said it louder, and she still didn't answer. So I... I stepped closer." Allie wiped her tear-filled eyes. "I came closer and touched her shoulder and... and... her head moved and I saw..." Allie put her hand over her mouth.

"Easy, now, Allegra."

"Her eyes were open, but they were just staring. It was so horrible! There was blood on her blouse and I could see this hole in her neck..." Allie couldn't continue.

"And so what did you do then?"

"I think I screamed. Well, I know I did. I screamed and ran into the kitchen. And then I ran into the bathroom and threw up."

"Did you notice what happened next? Who responded to your screaming?" Chief Knowles signaled silently to Officer Ouellette to make sure she was capturing it all.

"Kate Zeller followed me into the bathroom and held my hair back while I threw up. When we came out, my dad was calling 911 and Luke was locking the door to the pavilion."

"That was a smart move on his part," said Knowles.

"Kate and I went into the kitchen and I said something terrible had happened to Dr. Abbott and we had to call off the reception. I was so freaked out. I was shaking, and I had a hard time talking." Allie was embarrassed by how panicked she'd been. What a wimp I am, she thought disparagingly. The panicked feeling was returning; her legs felt wobbly. "Can I sit down, Chief Knowles?" she asked.

"Of course." The policeman waited while Allie settled herself in a nearby chair. "Speaking of sitting down, what about the arrangement of the chairs? Are they the same now?"

She looked around and tried to think back to yesterday. "I think they're pretty much the same," she said, closing her eyes to help her picture the scene. "Wait, I think there was another wingback chair next to Dr. Abbott's. Yes, I'm pretty sure there was. As if someone else had been sitting there." Allie looked doubtful for a moment. "You don't think my memory is playing tricks, do you?"

"No, this is important. Keep going; you're doing fine. Where would you place that other chair?"

Allie stood up and moved a chair from a group nearby, setting it at an angle to the chair Dr. Abbott had been sitting in. She moved it closer, then farther away, then once more, a little closer. "I think it was about here," she said. "But I'm not positive." She paused for a moment, lost in thought. "The odd thing is, I think it wasn't there when I came back in, when the police—I mean you and your team—had arrived, was it?"

"I don't believe it was."

"Why would someone have moved it? Could it have been a clue, do you think?" Allie's mind was racing through the list of people who could have moved it. At the top were her father and George. And Luke. And Thomas? Where had Thomas gone after she found Dr. Abbott?

Forty

"The duty of youth is to challenge corruption."
—*Kurt Cobain*

George was waiting for Allie in the office when Chief Knowles finished questioning her.

"How did it go?" he asked. "Could you shed any light?"

"I tried my best, but I'm not sure how helpful I was."

"Do the police seem to have any leads?" His expression was strained.

"I couldn't tell. Chief Knowles didn't give me any hints, that's for sure." Allie slumped into her desk chair. "I hope he figures this out soon. I'm never going to get a good night's sleep until he does."

"And we'll never get any work done. The phone rings continually; the emails pour in. And we have an upcoming season to prepare for."

"Speaking of emails, Chief Knowles said they've taken in Dr. Abbott's computer and are going through her emails. Maybe that will turn up something."

"She was a damn prodigious emailer," said George. "If she had any secrets, they'll find them in her email, I'll bet."

"I was wondering, have we heard from Dr. Abbott's ex?" asked Allie. "You'd think he would have at least a little interest in his former wife's murder."

"I don't know," said George. "Charles was not a very emotional man. He may be glad, for all we know." George half smiled. "Hey, maybe Knowles should investigate him. Wouldn't it be great if the murderer was someone from away, like Charles Abbott?"

"Yeah," concurred Allie. "Or someone we'd like to see locked away for a good long time. Any political figures you'd like to exile?"

"Plenty!" The two smiled at each other. It felt almost normal.

"Okay," broke in George, becoming serious again. "Well, there's work to be done here. Some of the board members want to call a meeting," he said. "I think it's a good idea. We can't let what happened jeopardize our upcoming SummerFest season. So, I guess you need to send out an email notice to the whole board."

"Do we have a date?"

"I think we're aiming for two weeks from today at five o'clock, here. As vice chair, your father should preside. I just talked to him and he seems happy to do it."

"Should I include an agenda in the email notice? I'm guessing it will be pretty short. Agenda Item I: Which one of us murdered the chair?" Allie stifled her smile when she saw George wasn't smiling along.

"David and I talked about that. He wants to think about it tonight and get back to us. It will be, basically, one, choose the interim chair and, two, discuss whether to proceed with the board's decision to ask the musicians for cuts. Of course, those two items could take a long time to resolve."

"No kidding." Allie nodded in agreement. "I'd better get this right out."

from: ABrewster@Kennimacsummerfest.org
to: Board of Directors
date: Monday April 20 at 3:45 PM
subject: Save the date, May 4th, 5:00 PM

Considering recent events, Vice Chair David Brewster has called for an emergency board meeting on Monday, May 4th, at 5:00 PM in the conference room of the Summerfest offices.

Please respond to this email to let us know whether you plan to attend.

Thank you,
Allegra

Responses came in quickly from most of the board members. The majority of them were eager to get together again and take some sort of action, even if they couldn't solve Dr. Abbott's murder. Allie wondered if one of them already knew who the murderer was. She decided she needed to listen to something light and upbeat and settled on *Cello Submarine*[25], the 12 cellists of the Berlin Philharmonic playing their renditions of Beatles tunes—an oldie but goodie.

As she began working on the musicians' housing contracts—oh, joy—Allie reflected on how much better she was feeling than just a few hours earlier. Maybe this feeling of dull despondency interspersed with short flashes of panic would eventually go away. Talking with people she cared about seemed to help. Maybe a get-together after dinner with Kate would raise both their spirits.

She texted:

Kate, how bout a beer ths evening? I can bring over a couple of brews around 8. pemaquid or seadog?

Allie was surprised she didn't get a text back immediately. Kate must be busy or away from her phone, she thought. Back to the contracts.

At five, as Allie was finishing up the contracts and printing them out for those who didn't want an electronic version, her phone chimed.

Sorry. Not tonight. Homework patrol with Chris and Harris.

Well, okay, thought Allie.

Forty-One

"I like beautiful melodies telling me terrible things."
—*Tom Waits*

A llie got home late. She could tell by the open peanut butter jar on the counter that her father had already eaten his usual dinner—a peanut butter and jelly sandwich—when nothing else was on offer. He sat at the kitchen table, Archie at his feet, papers from his SummerFest board file folder spread in a semi-circle in front of him. A notepad, dense with writing, occupied the center. As Allie entered the kitchen, her father put down his pen and looked up.

"Hi, Dad," Allie said, hanging up her jacket and setting her bag down. "Had any brilliant ideas?"

"It seems to me we can nip Sylvia's plan to get rid of the union in the bud. I've been looking over the list of board members, trying to figure out who might be convincible. I think there's a slim majority who'd go along with me."

"Well..." Allie thought for a minute. "Since there are now an even number of board members, you'll need..."

"I'll need eight members to join with me."

"Okay, so let's assume Henson, Campbell, Davis, Vogel, and Osbourne won't. That's five against for sure. I bet Esther Swift will be on your side, though, and she'll bring a lot of the others. The old guard."

"Right. And Arnold Schimler will probably agree with me—he tends to go along with the leader." David Brewster drummed the table with his fingers. "I think I can limit the nays to seven. I hope so, anyway."

"So are you feeling hopeful? It sounds like you have a good chance."

"Oh, I will prevail. There's no alternative." Allie's father sighed. "I'll tell you what, though, I'm not looking forward to it. One thing that worries me is how much time the other members will want to spend talking about what happened. I just hope I can get them to focus on what we need to accomplish at this meeting, and instead of speculating on Sylvia's murderer."

"It'll help that you're sending out the agenda ahead of time."

"Right. Why don't you grab something to eat and we can figure out the agenda right now."

Allie made herself a peanut butter and jelly sandwich and sat down at the table. "What if..." she started. "... Here's an idea: what if you delay the discussion about Dr. Abbott until after voting on how to proceed with the musicians?"

"Good thinking. That would provide an incentive to get through the decision-making part of the meeting. I wonder if I could even get Chet Knowles to come and speak about the investigation's progress."

"Wow, that would be helpful. And if you let people know that's happening, they'll show up for sure. Although I bet everyone will show up, anyway."

David Brewster called the chief and got a quick response that, yes, he'd be willing to come, as long as he didn't have to be somewhere else. Allie's father ended the call, laughing.

"What's so funny?" she asked, after he hung up.

"Chet said maybe the meeting will give him an opportunity to meet the murderer." He paused for a moment. "Guess that means they haven't figured out who it is yet. He did sound stressed out."

"I wish it were over. And I'm not the only one who hates not knowing," said Allie. "Okay, let's get this agenda figured out." Her eye lit on a handwritten note among the pieces of paper on the table.

> *David, another night of wine and roses tomorrow? Let's see if we can recreate the magic.*
> *XOXOX S·a*

"Dad, what's this?" Allie picked up the note and handed it to him.

Her father stared at it for a moment. "Oh, that's nothing. Sylvia and I shared some wine a few times."

"The magic? What's she talking about?"

He sighed. "Sylvia went a little overboard. I think she was lonely. Charles had left her several years earlier and, well, she was looking for companionship."

"It sounds like more than that. Was she looking for romance, too?"

"We had a few dates, Allegra. That's it. You were at grad school. And Sylvia and I are both adults. Were." He thought for a moment. "She wasn't all bad, you know. And she had a heck of a wine cellar. We actually spent much of the time playing chess. She could be fun if you were in the right mood."

"You mean, if *she* was in the right mood. Wow, I can't believe you dated." Allie shook her head.

"'Dated'—I'd hardly call it that. It didn't last long. Let it go, Allie. Hey, I thought you were going to type up the agenda."

"I'll do it tomorrow in the office. It won't take long."

Forty-Two

"Life is like a beautiful melody,
only the lyrics are messed up."
—*Hans Christian Andersen*

After a restless night, followed by a quick walk down to the frog pond and back with Archie the next morning, Allie headed to the office. She was concerned about what she'd learned about her father and Sylvia Abbott the night before but tried to put it out of her mind. Even so, she was finding it hard to concentrate on the agenda. Eventually she managed to finish it and send it out to the board. George had texted saying he had a meeting and wouldn't be in until 11:00 or so.

Around ten o'clock, the door to the office opened and a balding man in a stretched-out green polo shirt entered.

"Excuse me," he said. "I'm Kevin Springer. The police have hired me to check out the computers—to see if there's any connection to the murder of Sylvia Abbott."

"Oh," Allie responded, surprised. "Sure. I'm Allie Brewster. I'm the assistant director. You can take a look at mine first." She rose from her chair and motioned to him to sit there. "Let me contact our executive director, George Park, before you start getting into his desktop."

Springer wedged his considerable beer belly behind Allie's desk and began delving into her laptop's directory. She noticed with dismay that the nails on his pudgy fingers were edged in black. Even so, they moved deftly across the keyboard. He obviously knew what he was doing.

"Wowser! Heck of a music library you got here," he said to her. Allie cringed.

"George," Allie said into her cell phone. "There's a man here, a computer expert sent by the police named Kevin Springer. He's supposed to look at our computers for links to Dr. Abbott's murder. Is there anything on your desktop you want me to save before he starts in on yours? He's looking at my laptop right now."

George didn't seem too worried about the search. He asked Allie to save a few documents that were open, just in case. "It's pretty much all on my laptop, too," he said.

After a half hour on Allie's laptop, Springer swiveled Allie's desk chair around and said, "Nothing here. Have you worked here long?"

"Only since last November."

"Well, you keep an amazingly clean, well-organized computer. Everything's neatly filed. I don't often see that." Allie felt ridiculously proud at his comments. That's pathetic, she thought, looking for praise for the way you file your computer documents. Her audible sigh was matched by a grunt as Springer stood up.

"Is this your boss's computer?" he asked, pointing to George's aging desktop model. He made his way over to George's chair and plunked down. Allie tried not to notice how loud his breathing was from the exertion. She returned to her desk and readjusted her chair. Her laptop seemed the same as before, and she returned to the task she'd been working on when Mr. Springer arrived. Every once in a while, she looked over at him. Unlike when he was looking at her laptop, he was now rapidly typing away, frowning as he worked. Several times, he cleared his throat. His breathing remained labored.

Finally he said something. "I've copied some files, but I may need to impound this computer. I'm going to call Chet, uh, Chief

Knowles, to find out what he'd like me to do." Springer pulled at the collar of his shirt as if to gain some air.

"Really?" Allie frowned. "I'm sure it's nothing. I mean, George didn't have anything to do with the murder."

Springer cleared his throat but offered no more information. "I'll just step outside to make the call," he said. "Please don't contact your boss or touch the computer while I'm gone."

Allie looked at George's computer as Springer stepped out of the office. What on earth could he have found? And didn't George use his laptop most of the time, anyway?

"The chief says to bring the computer in." Springer moved toward George's desk.

"Wait a minute," said Allie. "Is that necessary? How are we going to get our work done preparing for the festival?" She had an idea. "Can I copy the contents of his computer on a thumb drive?"

"Ms. Brewster, I don't think that would be possible. How big a thumb drive do you have? Wait, let me check something." His grimy fingers moved quickly over the keyboard. "Yeah, as I thought. He backed most of this up in the cloud. So you should be able to access any documents you need for the festival planning."

"I guess that's ok." Allie didn't think she should argue with him further.

Springer unplugged the bulky CPU, gathered up the cords, and lugged it out to his car. He came back with a document that he asked Allie to sign. "It's a receipt that says you acknowledge I've taken the hard drive for further investigation." Allie signed the document and Springer left.

Allie immediately texted George:

computer guy took yr hard drive

George answered shortly:

You're kidding! I wonder why. Nothing of interest on it.

Allie responded:

i was worried that would make it harder to do our work

George reassured her:

Shouldn't. It's all on my laptop. And in the cloud. But it's weird that he took it.

Allie agreed.

maybe he's just not that competent LOL

Forty-Three

"There is no feeling, except the extremes of fear
and grief, that does not find relief in music. "
—*George Eliot*

W hen George returned to the office, he told Allie a group of
board members and others had decided to hold a memorial service for Sylvia Abbott. It seemed she had no close relatives
who were interested in organizing a funeral, but her local friends
thought some way of marking her life was needed, especially in
light of the way she'd died.

George hadn't taken off his coat yet. "Of course, they've asked
us to help. John Campbell called me on my way back here." George
was none too pleased. "Well, we probably have the easiest way of
getting the word out," admitted Allie. "What do they want us to
do?"

"They were hoping to hold the service on Saturday morning in
the Concert Barn. But I told them the police probably would still
have the barn cordoned off with crime scene tape. I don't know if
that's true, but it seems plausible. So John hung up and conferred
with the others. Then he called me back with their second choice."

"So where will it be?"

George told her the next option the group was considering was
Sylvia's church, St. Cecilia's Episcopal. "It's not very big," said
George, "but as Sylvia was a member, it seems fitting."

"What about the Sailing Club?" asked Allie.

"I suggested that, too," said George, "but John said they'd decided it was too informal."

"Too shabby, more like it. Oh, well, St. Cecilia's will be fine." Allie never attended church at St. Cecilia's—her grandparents had been members of the First Congregational Church—but she'd attended many activities there, from weddings to funerals to concerts. Even her Brownie troop had met there in the community room when she was little. "What exactly are they asking us to do?"

"Two things. Care to guess?"

Allie thought. "For sure, one is to send a notice out to our local list. What's the other? Pick out some music?"

"You're close. They want us to organize some live music. I suggested you might play something on the cello."

"Really?" Allie winced. "I don't thi..."

"Nonsense. You'd be great. After all, you and Thomas were prepared to play at the benefit concert. Do you suppose he'd come back?"

"He said he's conducting concerts both Saturday and Sunday, so no. And I don't have anything ready to go. I haven't been working with an accompanist, either." Allie looked down. "Except for Sylvia," she said in a small voice.

"Hey, I negotiated $300 for you." George was adamant. "If I were you, I'd take the gig. It's only for a few minutes of reflection during the service. I think they already have hired a bagpiper to do the processional and recessional music. And the organist will accompany the hymns."

"I don't know... I should talk to Anne and see what she suggests..."

"Well, do it quickly, Allie. They want to get this organized as soon as possible." As George turned to hang up his coat, he noticed the spot by his desk where the missing computer terminal had been located. "Guess that guy did take it, huh?"

"Yes. For whatever reason." Allie looked up the phone number of her teacher, Anne Kirschner.

⁓eℓℓ⁓

Anne answered after only one ring.

"What's up, Allegra? How are you? I heard about what happened Sunday. Karin posted the news on the musicians' private webpage, so it spread like wildfire. So awful! Everyone must be in a state of shock."

Allie swallowed, feeling a lump in her throat at the sound of her beloved teacher's voice. "Hi, Anne. Yeah, it was terrible. But that's not why I'm calling. Well, it's sort of why I'm calling. I mean, it's related."

Anne waited for Allie to get her thoughts together.

"You see," Allie continued, "There's a memorial service for Dr. Abbott on Saturday and they want me to play something, like an interlude, during the service. I don't know if I should do it. I don't have anything prepared..."

"Nonsense, Allie. This is an honor. And it's such an emotional event; cello is a perfect instrument to express the depth of feeling. How about playing one of the Bach cello suites? You know them well."

"And I love them, but I don't know... I think I would be too nervous up there by myself... Especially because I'm the one who..."

"Oh, right. You discovered the body, didn't you. Yeah, ok, let's think of another option. Do you have a pianist handy who could work something up with you?"

"Not really. And I won't have unlimited time to rehearse, either. The church organist will be there—do you know any pieces for cello and organ?"

"Hmmmm." Anne was thoughtful. "There are a few possibilities, but organ is so overpowering." Anne continued thinking. "Oh, I have the perfect idea, Allie. How about the Ravel *Sonata for Cello and Violin*[26] you and your father worked up a few years ago?"

"It's not easy. And neither of us has played it recently."

"Think about the slow movement, the "Lent." That's not difficult—you just need to keep it moving and play with a lot of expression. But would your dad be willing to do it with you? From what I've heard, he and the board chair had clashed rather acrimoniously lately."

"That movement is beautiful. And you're right, it's not too hard. It would be fitting." Allie was slowly getting used to the idea of performing at the memorial service. "I'll ask Dad if he'd be willing to do it. He and Dr. Abbott disagreed, but I know he's sorry about her death."

Allie and Anne talked for a few more minutes, until Anne's next student arrived. Allie promised to let her know what she and her father finally decided.

Forty-Four

"Music in the soul can be heard by the universe."
—*Lao Tzu*

A llie and her father got to work on the Ravel. Practicing together seemed to bring a sense of peace to both of them. David was wholly engaged in the music, showing an intensity in his playing that Allie hadn't noticed in a long while. He was lavish in compliments about her playing and musical interpretation.

While they practiced on Thursday afternoon, Allie's thoughts drifted to the rehearsal with Thomas and Sylvia. She was enjoying practicing with her father, but the rehearsal with Thomas felt different. What was so intoxicating about that experience? She pictured Thomas's lock of wavy hair tumbling over his forehead and the way her pulse jumped when his eyes met hers across his music stand.

As she was putting her cello away, her phone ran. It was Thomas, as if conjured by her thoughts of him.

"Hey, Thomas," answered Allie.

"Allie? Do you have a minute?"

"Sure. What's up?"

Thomas paused. "A Kennimac police officer came to question me this afternoon."

"What? Are you here in town?"

"No, no. I'm in Boston. I got a call this morning from Officer Ouellette, asking where she could find me this afternoon." He exhaled. "I had a hard time convincing her that I had a rehearsal this afternoon. She seemed to think 75 orchestra musicians could change their schedules so she could interview me at three o'clock." He paused again.

"Uh-huh?"

"She changed some things around and was able to get here by noon."

"How'd it go? She seems pretty reasonable, I think. At least compared to her boss."

"Reasonable?" His voice rose. "She gave me the impression that I am a murder suspect!"

"Seriously?"

"Someone must have mentioned to the police that I was sitting in the hall near the door to the room where... you know... Remember? I was sitting on a chair, listening to a recording with my eyes closed, practicing how I would conduct it. You remember, right?"

"I do. But why is that a problem? There were a lot of people around there..."

"But the policewoman told me that 'not everyone had a history with Dr. Abbott.' How did they know about that?" His voice rose. "As if I would have killed her. It's just ridiculous. It's insane. And then I had to go conduct the rehearsal, but I couldn't concentrate. It was terrible."

Allie thought for a moment. Had she been the one to mention Thomas's mother's issue with Dr. Abbott?

Allie cleared her throat. "I was the one who told the police you were there. They had me do a run-through of my actions just before I found... I might have mentioned that you had a slim connection with Dr. Abbott from a long time ago, but I didn't say it was a problem, or you held a grudge, or anything."

"You told the police that! No wonder they suspect me. I can't believe you did that, Allie. I thought you were a friend."

"I didn't say anything more than maybe you might have known Dr. Abbott many years ago. They asked me if you had any connection." Allie sought to calm him down. "Thomas, if they really thought you were a murderer, they would have brought you in and charged you. Don't you think? Maybe it's just their usual procedure. After all, they have many suspects. Maybe she was just trying to rattle you."

"Wait, I didn't tell you the worst part. She took my little baton stickpin—you know, the one my mother gave me."

Allie felt her throat constrict. That small round hole. That small *red* round hole.

"Allie, what if they really think I'm guilty?" Thomas sounded panicky. "What should I do? Should I find a lawyer?"

"Thomas." Allie tried to summon up the confidence she didn't feel. "Thomas, I don't think you should worry. They'll figure out that you're not guilty. Don't let it interfere with your gig."

Allie heard a muffled sob. Was he really that worried? That seemed overly dramatic.

"Thomas, I'm sure you have nothing to worry about."

"I hope you're right," he said in a shaky voice. "You'll tell them I'm innocent, won't you? If they ask, I mean. Don't mention me, if they don't. Dios mio, this is a disaster!"

"Thomas. Take a few deep breaths and try not to think about it. Focus on your work." Allie saw she was getting another call. "I've got to go, Thomas. Will you try to relax? The police are talking to everyone. Everyone who was there. We are all suspects for now. Until they find the person who..."

⁓ℓℓ⁓

The incoming call—from Luke—had gone to Allie's voicemail before she could answer it. A beep signaled he had left a message. Allie was inclined not to listen, but then reconsidered. Maybe Luke had some news.

Hey, Al, guess you're not available. I just wanted to check in and see how you are. I know how shocking it must have been to find Abbott. And damn dangerous, too—the murderer could have been lurking nearby. I know how hard you take things; you have such a soft heart and so strong a sense of justice. I heard that you and your dad are playing at the memorial service on Saturday. That's cool. I know you'll play beautifully, even if it feels super emotional for you. Anyway, I thought it might help you if we talked. Yeah. Um, well, I miss talking about important things with you. There's no one like you—you're really special to me, you know. I still feel... Yeah. Well, call me back if you want to talk. You know I'm always here for you.

Allie felt the tears well up in her eyes. Luke... it was tempting to call him back. But, no. Those days were past. She chose to practice the cello instead.

Forty-Five

"If you play music with passion and love and honesty, then it will nourish your soul, heal your wounds, and make your life worth living. Music is its own reward." —*Sting*

St. Cecilia's Episcopal Church sits on the banks of the Kennimac River as it makes its way between the two bays. The half-timbered church, visible from the center of town, is a distinctly English-style edifice built in the late 19th century by wealthy residents of Kennimac (the recently renamed Oyster Dumps). Its architect was brought from England, and his design was a pastiche of the 15th century English style known as English Gothic. Pseudo or not, the church nestles into the sloping river bank with stone-paved garden walks surrounding it, creating a picturesque view from across the river.

On Saturday morning at twenty minutes to ten o'clock, people started streaming into the small nave of the church. Decorated in olive green and maroon stenciled patterns similar to those of the English designer William Morris, the ceiling is punctuated with carved beams arching over the nave and sanctuary. Allie and her father sat in the boxed-in choir area off to the right of the altar, both dressed in their concert black attire—David in his tux and Allie in a simple sleeveless floor-length black silk dress topped off with a diaphanous white scarf-like collar. David had brushed his hair back, which gave him a distinguished black-and-silver-tinged mane. Allie had swept her caramel colored hair up and held in place by a large comb in a style Kate had taught her years before.

Allie noticed Officer Cheri Ouellette and Chief Knowles were both at the back of the church, their eyes roaming over the gathering. They stood among many other people who couldn't find seats in the crowded pews. The predominant colors worn by the congregation were navy and black, and expressions were somber. The air in the church was thick with whispers, and clashing perfumes overlaid the scent of the gardenias on the altar. Allie gave silent thanks that they did not use lilies in the bouquet.

As the minister spoke, Allie looked through the congregation. George nodded solemnly when she caught his eye. Most of the board members and their spouses were there, along with many of the people who'd attended the benefit concert just one week before. The Kelleys were there, Carolyn Kelley already dabbing at her red nose with a hanky. Allie spied Luke standing in the back, not too far away from the police chief. Luke had not attempted to tame his curls, but he had put on a wrinkled button-down white Oxford shirt and khakis. Very formal for him. His face wore a concerned expression, his brow furrowed. When he looked at her, Allie looked away quickly, deflecting eye contact.

A sudden flurry of movement at the entry caught Allie's attention. It was Thomas, moving through the standing crowd. He stopped short when he noticed the two police officers. Thomas looked at Allie, pushed back that lock of hair, and raised his eyebrows. Her breath quickened, and she shot him a questioning look. What was he doing back in Kennimac? Didn't he have a concert to conduct this evening in Boston? Allie glanced down at her folded hands, perplexed.

The minister's sermon was short and rather impersonal. He mentioned how generous Sylvia Abbott had been with donations for various church projects, but he exuded little warmth in describing her as a member of his congregation. When he concluded his sermon, he invited anyone who wanted to remember her to stand and give reminiscences of Dr. Abbott. At first no one stood up, and Allie felt sad there wasn't even that small bit of affection shown for the murdered woman.

Then a tall man with gray sideburns who was wearing an expensive-looking suit stood up about halfway up the pews. A slight buzz circulated around the room as people recognized Charles Abbott, Sylvia's ex-husband.

"I don't know too many of you," he began. "But we all have something in common, and that's the fact that Sylvia Abbott touched us in some way. I met Sylvia in graduate school. We were both studying for PhDs in geology in Texas. She was the only female in the class. She had spunk, let me tell you. One of our professors flat out told her he would not give a woman a passing grade in his class because he didn't believe females should be geologists. That didn't deter her. She invited the head of the department to review her work, which he did. She asked him what grade he would have given the work, and he said it was definitely deserving of an A. When she showed the department head that her prejudiced professor had failed her, the head overruled the professor.

"So, yes, Sylvia was ambitious, had high standards for herself and everyone else, and could even be a bit annoying at times, as many of you probably experienced one time or another." He waited for the titter to die down. "But you can't deny she loved Maine, and she loved this town. Once we moved back here and fixed up the house, I couldn't dislodge her to save my life. She didn't want to miss anything you all were doing, whether it was sailing, or making music, or opening a new store, or what have you. She loved this place more than her parents had, and I think she had hoped to spend her old age here. Now that's not going to happen." Charles Abbott looked down and paused for a moment.

"I just hope to God you find who did this to Sylvia. You've all lost a fine woman, someone who would have stood up for you when times were tough. I hope you'll all stand up for her."

"Thank you, Mr. Abbott." The minister scanned the congregation. "Is there anyone else... Ok, Ted, uh, Mr. Prouty, go ahead."

Ted Prouty was standing up toward the rear of the pews. "I knew Sylvie, that's what we used to call her, I knew Sylvie when she was a summer kid back when we were young. She wasn't afraid of anything. She sure as heck showed up Buddy and I on many occasions. But the thing was, she could challenge you and scare you half out of your wits, but at the end of it—whether it was sailing in a lightning storm..." He nodded as some in the crowd gasped. "Or diving off a thirty-foot-high rock into Sampsons' quarry—you felt like you accomplished something. She knew what she wanted and she know how to get it, but lots of times, in the end you realized it was what you wanted, too. I'm darn sorry we've lost Sylvie, and especially the way we did. I'm hoping Chet and his crew bring justice sooner rather than later." He turned around and looked pointedly at Chief Knowles, then sat down abruptly.

"Thank you, Ted." The minister looked for other speakers, but no one stood up, so he motioned to Allie and her father to play. They brought their chairs and music stands out to the center of the sanctuary, then carried out the cello and violin and sat down. Since it had been several hours since either instrument had been played, they tuned briefly. Then David set his violin down and Allie took a big breath in and drew her bow across the string to begin the cello's opening lament. For a second or two, Allie felt shaky and the fingers of her left hand, pressing on the strings, felt weak. Then the sorrow of the music filled her. She looked at her dad and his eyes were full of tears. She vibrated each note and closed her eyes. When her father's violin joined the music, she dropped back and let him lead. Together they wound their way through the music, laying into the dissonances where they occurred, letting the pain and anguish of the music reverberate.

During the seven-minute piece, there were moments of reflection but also of fury. Without thinking about it, Allie knew somehow the audience was experiencing the same emotions the music expressed. She and her father took turns leading, depending on who had the more important line. Spent and weary, the piece ended with a quietly sad diminuendo, the sound slowly slipping away in ancient-sounding modal harmonies.

Allie and her father had practiced the piece a total of about four hours over the course of the preceding days, working out every technical detail, matching tone and volume. But they had never just let go and played it without analytical thought, the way they did just then. When finished, they sat. David slowly lowered his violin and Allie her bow. They looked at the congregation and saw tissues and hands wiping wet cheeks. An almost shocked silence hovered over the pews.

Finally, the minister rose and said, "Let us pray." He ended his prayer with the familiar:

"Go forth into the world in peace;
be of good courage;
hold fast that which is good;
render to no one evil for evil;
strengthen the fainthearted;
support the weak;
help the afflicted;
honor everyone;
love and serve the Lord,
rejoicing in the power of the Holy Spirit;
and the blessing of God almighty,
the Father, the Son, and the Holy Spirit,
be among you and remain with you always."

The congregation quietly chimed in with, "Amen." Suddenly, the doors to the nave were flung open, and the piper began his raucous but also mood-lifting rendition of the traditional tune known as "Going Home," which also appears in Dvorak's *New*

World Symphony[27]. The congregation filed out, released and re-lieved, most heading home on a beautiful spring morning to return to the smaller joys and tragedies of daily life.

As Allie wiped down her cello and laid it to rest in its case, she felt a gentle touch on her shoulder. Esther Swift looked up at her, her eyes still watery. "Allegra, my dear, you and your father just demonstrated the power of music. Thank you for sharing that with us."

Behind Esther loomed the tall figure of Thomas. And behind Thomas, Allie glimpsed the back of a rumpled Oxford shirt as Luke turned on his heel and headed for the door..

Forty-Six

"If music be the food of love, play on."
—*William Shakespeare, Twelfth Night*

"**N**ice job on the Ravel, Allie." Thomas smiled. "Glad I made it in time to catch that. You and your dad blended well. And you kept the tempo moving."

"What are you doing here? Don't you have a concert to conduct tonight? In Boston?" Allie set her bow in the cello case without loosening its hairs, then remembered. She fumbled with the bow, trying to take it back out again, her hand shaking ever so slightly.

"I do, but that's not until eight o'clock, so I don't need to leave here until about four." He shifted the navy blazer slung over his shoulder. "I thought we might get a bite to eat somewhere."

Allie felt the heat rise in her face. Why did she always blush when Thomas was around? It was maddening. "Ok, sure." She turned to her father, who was snapping his violin case shut. "Dad, this is Thomas Ramirez, the assistant conductor for the Summer-Fest this summer."

David Brewster stuck his hand out. "Pleased to meet you, Thomas. Allie tells me you're a fine cellist, to boot."

"These days, I'm mostly an out-of-practice cellist. But I'm sorry I didn't get to perform the Vivaldi with Allie at the concert last week. She was really rocking that first part." He laughed. "I just had to follow along for the ride."

"She's grown into a damn fine cellist. No question."

"Dad, we're going to get a bite to eat. Want to join us?"

"Thanks, no. I'm going to get back to the house and work on Calliope. That's the name of our little sailing dinghy," he said in an aside to Thomas. "There's a chance I may get her in good enough shape to hit the water this summer. You two have a nice time." He picked up his violin case and headed for the door.

"Where shall we go?" asked Thomas. "I don't know this place very well yet. Where do you suggest?"

Allie thought of her depleted checking account and almost empty wallet. "There are good pre-made sandwiches at The Green Reaper. We can grab a couple and go sit at the beach or something." She looked at her concert outfit and Thomas's nice clothes. "But we're not really dressed for a picnic..."

"I have a blanket in my car. We can sit on that." Thomas put on his jacket and bent to pick up Allie's cello case, as if to carry it for her.

"Whoa, no one carries that but me." Allie took the case from Thomas, their hands touching briefly on the handle.

—ele—

Though it was a sunny Saturday, it was still April and chilly at the beach. Passing three splintery picnic tables, Thomas carried his blanket down to the sand and spread it out, while Allie brought the bag with their sandwiches and drinks. A few seagulls were gliding overhead, and a band of sandpipers skittered along the shallows, but otherwise Thomas and Allie had the beach to themselves.

At first, they chatted about Thomas's concert the night before, which had gone well. He seemed much calmer than he had been on the phone several days earlier. He explained that he'd received a notice about the memorial service, and Allie remembered that she'd added him to the email list of musicians when Dr. Abbott had given his appointment the thumbs up. Allie let Thomas know that, even though they hadn't had a chance to make a pitch at the benefit concert for donors to underwrite his stipend, funds had flowed in. There would be enough money to cover it.

They also discussed the idea of Thomas living at Kate's house for the six weeks of the SummerFest. Allie filled him in on Kate's story, explaining how her middle son, Toby, had died and the effect that had on Kate and the rest of her family. Thomas listened but soon shifted the conversation to the music that the SummerFest Orchestra was scheduled to perform, and he wondered which pieces Tony might allow him to conduct in concert. Allie assured him that Tony always had his assistant on the podium several times throughout the summer, and she related a few funny stories where things didn't go off as planned, such as when the off-stage "cannons" in a July Fourth performance of Tchaikovsky's *1812 Overture*[28] missed their cue and came in late, throwing the piece's ending into chaos.

Behind all the conversation, Allie wondered why Thomas had come. Was it to gain information about the SummerFest? To attend the memorial service? To see her? Something else? Finally, she had to ask. "Thomas, why are you here? I mean, really?"

"If I said I wanted to get to know Kennimac better, would you believe me? No?" Thomas shifted his long legs on the blanket. "You're so intense, Allie," he said. "I did want to talk with you. To see you. And I want to know, too, if you know any more about what happened. Like, who are the police looking at? Have they found the culprit? I'm still worried that they're thinking of me."

Allie shivered in the cool breeze.

Thomas continued, "I don't want you to think I had anything to do with it. But there's something maybe you should know." He stopped for a moment. "Hey, are you cold? Should we get back in the car?"

"I'm fine." Her gaze was unflinching. "What do you mean, there's something I should know?"

Thomas ran his hand through his hair. For a few seconds, he stared at the water, saying nothing. Then he took a breath in and shook his head. "I did some stupid things when I was a kid in L.A. For a year or so, when I was 12, 13, I got mixed up with some bad kids. We stole a car and got caught. I don't have a record, but I always worry that someone will discover what I did and the word will get out. And there goes my career."

Allie squinted into the sun. "Why would that be a problem now? You were a kid. It was a long time ago. It was just a joyride. Lots of teens do that."

"Not really—someone got shot. I didn't have a gun, but one of the other kids did. He shot the car's owner in the leg."

"Oh. A car-jacking."

"Yeah. A car-jacking. I've regretted it ever since."

The wind had picked up, and high overcast clouds had veiled the sun. The sandpipers had flitted away. Only the gulls remained, hopeful that the remnants of lunch were for them.

"You're getting cold, I can tell," said Thomas. "I should head back to Boston, anyway." He clasped Allie's arm. "Do you think less of me, Allie? I wouldn't want that. You believe me, right?"

"Of course. You were a kid. You made a mistake."

"Quite a few, actually." He turned and gave her a serious look. "You won't tell anyone, will you?"

Allie shook her head.

"I'd like to kiss you..." He leaned toward Allie and turned her chin towards him.

She closed her eyes. She was sinking, sinking, floating... Warmth flowed through her veins and she gave way to the sensation. His lips were soft, his tongue insistent. He gently pushed her back on the blanket and unbuttoned the top of her blouse. His kisses traveled down her neck and chest as his hands slid her bra up. The second his lips teased her right nipple, an electric charge shot through her. She moaned. The sound of a zipper being undone joined their labored breaths.

A faint sense that something seemed wrong fought with Allie's desire.

"Thomas," she whispered. "I... this is... I don't think we should..."

He lifted his head. "What? I should stop?" He rolled on his back. "I thought you wanted this, too." He sat up.

Allie squeezed her eyes shut. "I thought I did, too. But it's too soon. I..." She sat up, adjusted her bra, and buttoned her blouse. "It will complicate everything."

"Jesus! It doesn't have to. It's just a casual hook-up. It doesn't have to mean anything." Thomas pulled her to him. "Come on..."

She shook free and stood. "No, Thomas, we should get going. You don't want to be late for your concert."

Thomas joined her, picking up the bag with the sandwich wrappings and empty drink bottles. Allie grabbed the blanket by two corners, and shook it out with a loud snapping noise, which caused the gulls to fly off in a flurry of wings and squawks. She walked to the car in front of Thomas, wondering if her burning face was bright pink.

ell

Except for the rattle of its loud muffler, silence prevailed in Thomas's car for most of the way back to St. Cecilia's. As he drove into the church parking lot, he turned to Allie. "Tell me the truth. Are you afraid of me because of my history?"

Allie shook her head. History? No, she thought. What scared her was the way he made her heart rate jump. And then he said it was just a hook-up to him. Not good. She shook her head again.

"That's my old junker," she said, pointing to Pablo. "Thanks for the ride."

"See you in June, I guess, Allie," Thomas replied. "Unless something comes up..."

What did he mean by that, she wondered, as Pablo coughed into action.

Forty-Seven

"When I wished to sing of love, it turned
to sorrow. And when I wished to sing of sorrow, it was transformed for me into love."
—*Franz Schubert*

The next few days passed uneventfully, though the work-
load was heavy. Calls and emails from concerned Summer-
Fest supporters continued to pour in. The organization's official
response occupied much of Allie's time. She didn't hear from
Thomas again and assumed he had calmed down.

As she turned off her laptop and got ready to leave for the day
on Friday, Luke strode in.

"George isn't here. He's already gone home," she told him.

"I didn't come to talk to George," Luke responded. "I came to
talk with you. First of all, any news?"

"About?"

"Ha! Don't play dumb with me, Sherlock!" Luke picked up a
pencil and brandished it in a mock-threatening manner. "Murder
most foul. Whodunnit!" he said. "Haven't you solved it yet?"

Allie sighed. "Jesus, Luke. What's up with you? Do you think it's
a joke?"

"Just trying to lighten the atmosphere around here, Al." Luke
smiled. "And to that end, I have some music down in the wood

shop I want you to hear. And it looks like my timing is perfect; you're packing up to leave."

Allie tried to reset her frame of mind. "So, what is it?" she asked.

"Come and find out," he answered. "I think you'll like it—I know I do."

"Alright. Take me to your music."

The two walked down the hill to the wood shop. It was now late afternoon. Their shadows touched and merged on the gravel road in front of them. As they approached the shop door, Luke stopped Allie.

"You wait here 'til I tell you to come in," he said.

Allie knew this about Luke: he loved surprises. He was an inveterate gift giver and practical joker. You never knew which you would get—a thoughtful present or a silly joke—and it kept you a little off kilter. It was endearing and annoying all at the same time, Allie had to admit.

Luke stuck his head out the door and motioned Allie inside.

As she entered, he hit a button and the most danceable music she'd ever heard filled the shop. "I love how they use the reverb. It sounds like we're in a huge room," she shouted above the music. "What is it?"

"It's this Norwegian group from the '80s. I think they were called 'a-ha.' You can guess what this is called, right?"

"'Take On Me'[29]? What does that mean?"

"Whatever!" Luke started dancing around the table saw in the middle of the room, waving his arms in the air and doing as close to a disco dance as a man of his era could approximate. Allie couldn't help laughing. He danced up to her.

"Feel better?" Luke fingered the collar of Allie's sweater and quickly kissed her, but Allie pushed him away. "Not you, too," she muttered.

"What? Al," said Luke. Light from the low sun slanted through the dusty windows, burnishing his gold-tinged waves. "Why don't you trust the way I feel about you? It's the same as it always was. I can't just be your *friend*." He said the last word with distaste.

"Luke, you know why." Allie looked away from his imploring expression. "Two summers ago... Tiffany Mitchell... Does that ring a bell?"

"Let's talk about that, Allie. You told me we needed a break. You told me there were more important things." Luke looked down at his hands, which were fidgeting with the tools on his workbench. "You were so sad about Toby's death and you wouldn't let me console you. You pushed me away." He absentmindedly picked up a tool. "Tiff. She was nothing. Just someone to have fun with, a casual hook-up—no more—and it ended soon after it began. It was you I cared about, but you told me to get lost. I was... lost."

"You wouldn't give me any space. You couldn't seem to understand what I was going through. You seemed to take it all much too lightly, like it didn't really matter..." She took a breath. "And then I saw you with Tiffany. You two looked serious to me. Lip-locked. I..."

"Wrong, Allie," Luke interrupted. "You wouldn't let me in. I wanted to be there for you. I still do. I care about you. It's been driving me crazy. I'd do anything for you. Anything! Can't you see that?" He shrugged. "Anyway, Tiffany was kissing me; I wasn't kissing her back. She wanted it—I didn't care. She's nothing compared to you, Al."

"I don't know, Luke. I just don't know." Allie could feel her defenses withering. He was so earnest, his eyes so warm. But... she'd been so hurt before. Allie looked down at the tool in Luke's hand, a small wooden-handled metal spike. "What's that you're holding?"

Luke looked down and, as if it were hot, dropped the tool onto the workbench. "Oh, that. That's the spindle gouge," he said, trying to appear nonchalant. "You know, I showed it to you a few weeks ago."

"What's it for again? It looks dangerous."

Allie couldn't quite believe what she was thinking.

"It's for carving, like I said."

"But you don't do any carving here, do you?"

"Well, I was working on something..."

"What? Can I see it?"

"Uh, no, you can't."

"Why not?"

"Well, I can't tell you."

Luke looked into Allie's concerned eyes. "What?"

Allie backed away. "I have to go. Now. I have to get home."

She turned and left, not stopping when Luke called her name. Her face was hot and her heart pounded. Luke? It couldn't be Luke. No, it couldn't be. What was wrong with her? She suspected everyone, even people she loved, or used to love, she amended. This was hell, this constant feeling of suspicion. She stopped and wiped the tears from her cheeks. It would be good to focus on something mundane, like figuring out what to have for dinner with her dad.

Forty-Eight

"My music is best under-
stood by children and animals."
—*Igor Stravinsky*

Allie woke early the next morning after a disturbing dream. In it, Luke was holding the spindle gouge and waving it around. The driving beat from that song he had played was thumping in the background. But he was speaking to her in soft wooing tones and even though she knew there was some sort of danger radiating from him, she was flooded with desire. Then he morphed into Thomas. Thomas was holding her and... The sound of her own moaning woke her from the dream. Immediately, she clamped down on those inexplicable feelings and buried them somewhere unreachable.

Doubt still remained. What if Luke was the killer? Or Thomas?

Allie rubbed her eyes and looked at the clock. Six a.m.—way too early to start a Saturday. Although, she probably should plan to go in to the office to catch up on work—things had been so crazy over the past week. She groaned. Another day. Another day of pretending everything was normal while churning inside with doubt and fear. Why couldn't the police come up with an answer? What was taking so long? Allie lay in bed, weighted down by feelings of hopelessness and depression. Suddenly, a furry white bundle jumped up on her bed. Archie began licking her neck and rolling around in the covers, trying to get her to scratch his belly.

"Oh, Arch," she said, "I haven't forgotten you. Let's take a walk in the field before I go to work." Reinvigorated, Allie slipped into faded jeans and flannel shirt. Noticing her cello in its open case, she thought maybe an hour of practice would make her feel better, too. At least it would give her brain something else to think about.

Archie ran down to the door, excited at the prospect of a walk. As she stepped outside, Allie registered the manic birdsong and the earthy smell of growing plants. Late April—soon it would be May. Green fields. A warm breeze with a promise of summer. The scent of lilacs from the bushes framing the barn. Allie felt herself relax as she took long strides in the grass while Archie dashed around her in widening circles, full of joy in the fresh morning. Every third or fourth rotation he'd pass close by her as if to say, "Run with me! Be happy!" She couldn't help laughing at his antics. The grass was still bowed down with dew; Allie's sneakers and jeans were soon soaked. Swallows dipped and glided from the fields to the barn, and some sort of warblers were singing a complicated song. Allie tried to copy it but her whistling skills weren't quite up to par. She took a deep breath and smiled to herself. Some parts of her world were okay, anyway. She watched a bumblebee nose its way through a patch of crocuses. "Time to go in, Arch," she called, looking forward to putting in some time on her cello. Maybe she'd practice the cello parts from the second movement of Beethoven's 7th Symphony. No, too somber, she decided. Better: *Sicilienne* by Gabriel Fauré[30].

Forty-Nine

"It never seems to occur to people that a man
might just want to write a piece of music."
—*Ralph Vaughan Williams*

A summer music festival in a winter-ravaged place like Maine
is special because the warm days are so precious. Every day
of 75 degree sunshine is a gift; every trip to a swimming hole or
hike up a hill is a celebration. A general sense of giddiness infects
the members of a string quartet rehearsing under the shade of a
maple tree; they laugh as the breeze turns their pages of music or
a ladybug lands on the second violin's bow.

The fields around the SummerFest were especially suited for
outdoor playing. Over successive years, various ensembles had
created their own little refuges: a stage built of rough planking on
the shore, a mown path to a circle in a far corner shaded by large
maple trees. The cows in the neighboring field often drew close
to listen as a horn quartet played by the fence. And the musicians
left the campus to perform as well—the wide sidewalk in front of
the Sea Coast Book Shop was a perfect venue for a brass quintet,
and the float at the end of the town dock often hosted a flute duo,
playing from memory while their toes dangled in the water.

The summer and year-round residents of Kennimac looked
upon these musical inhabitants with indulgence. Yes, the Saturday night concerts snarled traffic on Main Street, but the locals

knew the benefits outweighed any hassles. Many of them earned a few extra dollars by housing a musician or two in their home, sometime the same musicians year after year, lodgers and locals becoming close friends. Others owned businesses that gained customers from the summer influx. And best of all, for six weeks, glorious sound filled the air. As Mina Treat, Kennimac's postmistress put it, "You just can't help but wear a smile when you hear snatches of the Haydn *Trumpet Concerto*[31] as you walk to the town office to pay your property taxes."

⎯⎯ℓℓ⎯⎯

Monday morning, Allie carefully worked the pile of envelopes out of the SummerFest's post office box and into the canvas bag she had brought. She was pleased to see how many orders for season tickets there were. She wouldn't know until she entered and tallied them, but it looked as though the count might already be ahead of last year's season ticket orders. I'd better check, she thought; we need to save some seats for critics and musicians' freebies—stuff like that.

As she walked past the post office customer window, she caught Mina Treat's eye. Mina waved. "You're getting a veritable avalanche of mail these days, Allegra," she said. "Good thing. Glad to know the festival's friends are coming through."

"No kidding," said Allie. "Pretty soon I'll need to bring a wheelbarrow or something." The only downside, she added to herself, is that I have to handle all these orders. Enter them in the database, mail out the tickets, answer questions. I wish everyone would order their tickets online and pick them up at the will-call window or load them onto their smartphone. "Not complaining, though," she said out loud. She lugged the bag of mail to her car and headed back to the office.

Allie thought George would be happy to see the huge pile of mail she carried in, but he hardly seemed to notice. "George, look!" she prodded.

"Oh, good." He glanced up briefly. Then it seemed to register, and he got up and came over to look. "They're mostly orders," he said. "That's a relief."

"George, everything ok?" asked Allie. "I'd have thought you'd be more excited. I mean, it looks like the season is going to be a success, even with..."

"Yes, yes, it does," said George. "I guess it does. His phone dinged, and he read the text. "I've got to go... I've got to run out for a few minutes," he said.

Allie began her work on the pile of mail. It would be great to report to the board tonight that ticket orders were flowing in. The plans for the meeting were all set. She decided she'd pick up some cheese and crackers and bunches of grapes; food would help keep the board members in a positive mood.

I think I'll send Tony Bainbridge an email to let him know we're getting an enthusiastic response to the ticket mailing, she thought. Although, maybe I should wait until I talk with George. And he'll want to let Tony know about the result of the meeting. It's his job to contact Tony.

ell

The day wore on. George was gone for several hours, so Allie listened to music without her earphones. Loudly. She tallied the ticket orders: already up to 83 percent of last year's season ticket orders with two months of sales to go. Wait until the board heard that! She sent a text to George to let him know and called her dad to tell him the news, but neither answered. I'll try Dad later, she thought. George rarely responded to texts if there wasn't a question to answer. Allie ran out to the store and picked up the snacks for the meeting. In the parking lot, she tried her dad again.

Still no answer. He must be in the barn working on Calliope, she thought.

As she set out a water glass, napkin, copy of the agenda, and notepad and pen at each place, Allie danced around the conference table, "air-conducting" and playing "air-harpsichord" to Bach's *Concerto #5 in F minor for Harpsichord and Strings*[32]. The increase in season ticket sales, combined with three large anonymous donations that came in the previous week, meant the board meeting had a chance of going well.

But when the second, more somber, movement of the concerto began, her mood changed with it. Why hadn't her father returned her calls? Should she worry? What was up?

The meeting was scheduled to begin in an hour. Where was he? What was he doing? Allie called the house phone once again; once again, there was no answer. She decided to go home and make sure everything was alright. She needed to change out of her jeans for the meeting, anyway.

Fifty

"Music begins where the possibilities of language end."
—*Jean Sibelius*

Allie took the steps to the kitchen door two at a time. "Dad?
Dad?"

The kitchen was empty but Allie heard music coming from the
living room. It was Krishna Das[33], her father's go-to music when
he was suffering from anxiety. Oh crap, Allie thought. He's in bad
shape.

As she approached the living room, the scent of marijuana
wafted toward her. Great, she said to herself, he's anxious and he's
stoned. That will go over really well at the meeting.

"Dad?" Allie turned down *My Foolish Heart*. David Brewster
opened his eyes, surprised to see her. He was wearing a frayed,
coffee-stained denim work shirt and faded baggy jeans—his usual
barn outfit.

"Dad, the board meeting? You are supposed to run it in less than
an hour." Allie stood with her hands on her hips. She couldn't help
herself from adding, "And you've been smoking..."

"Ah, yes, so I have." Lifting his eyebrows, David Brewster looked
at the ashtray by his side. "Allegra," he began, "Yes, I'm going to the
meeting. And I'm going to run it. And the board is going to do the

right thing by this organization I love, the musicians whom I love. But it won't be easy."

Allie's face softened. "I know that, Dad."

"So, help me get spiffed up. Should I wear a power tie?" He smiled ruefully.

"Do you even have a power tie?" Allie laughed. "I think you should wear whatever you feel good in."

"Damn right. I need to be comfortable if I'm going to tell all those self-righteous, self-centered rich jerks on the board to go to hell."

"Really? That might not be the best way to approach it. How about diplomacy?"

"Well, you're probably right, as usual. Here, find me some fighting music to psych me up." He handed his music remote to Allie, who scrolled through. Wagner? Too atavistic. Beethoven? No, Tchaik. 4^{34}. Those resolute opening chords of the brass choir would do it. And then the softer but urgent violins... perfect! Allie started the recording, then followed her father to his closet, where he picked out a worn but clean L.L Bean blue and white tattersall shirt and a red tie. She brushed off his tweed jacket and helped him into it, and pushed a springy batch of his hair into place.

"You look the part now, Dad," she said. "They'll pay attention to you."

"I know this is important to you and lots of other people, Allegra." Her father looked serious. "But it's important to me, too. I have to succeed, for the sake of this organization. I have to win once in a while, you know." He broke his solemnity by smiling at his daughter. "Now, we need to hurry if I'm going to be there in time to start the meeting."

Fifty-One

"Music is the social act of communication
among people, a gesture of friendship,
the strongest there is." —*Malcolm Arnold*

A llie and her father arrived at the office with ten minutes
to spare, Allie still in her jeans. Oh, well, she thought, this
meeting's not about me. She was surprised to see George's car
wasn't in the parking lot, but he rushed through the door soon
after they arrived.

"Looks good," George said, surveying the conference room.
"You've done a good job of getting ready. Sorry I wasn't here to
help."

"And what about the season ticket sales?" prompted Allie. "Did
you get my message? Isn't that amazing?"

"It is," said George. "When we get to that part of the agenda, I'll
call on you to give the numbers."

Board members began arriving for the meeting. Allie was re-
lieved to see her father, more confident now, meet them at the
door, shaking each person's hand and saying a few words of welcome. Back on his game, she thought.

The conference room was full of chatter as David Brewster took
his chair at the head of the table. George sat to his right, and Allie
sat in a chair against the wall.

"Thank you all for coming on such short notice," he began. "We have a lot to settle tonight if we hope to keep the festival moving forward. And, not to drop a spoiler, but I think you're going to hear some numbers later that will assure you our audience wants us to keep going." He looked down at the agenda, then swept his eyes around the table. "The first thing I want to say—and I'm sure you all agree—is how sorry I am Sylvia isn't here. Her death is a tragedy, and it's a huge loss for the Kennimac SummerFest. I would like to suggest that a committee of board members and friends of the SummerFest work on coming up with a way of commemorating her service to the organization."

Allie leaned forward. She hadn't heard her father mention this before.

David Brewster continued. "Ken Henson, John Campbell, Helen Davis, Alice Vogel, and Ron Osbourne, I'd like you to participate in this memorial committee; I know you were close to her. I think you would have the best idea of what would be meaningful and appropriate."

The five board members looked at Brewster warily. They had come to the meeting expecting a fight. But now it appeared the vice chair was extending an olive branch.

John Campbell broke the silence. "That's a fine idea, David. I'm sure we could come up with a suitable idea. I know we all miss Sylvia and deeply regret what happened." The others nodded in assent.

"Lovely, David, lovely," said Esther Swift. "I move that such a committee, a committee in memoria be formed, with the members listed by the acting chair."

"And I second," quickly added Arnold Schimler.

"Discussion?" asked David, looking around the table. "Seeing none, all those in favor say 'aye.'" Everyone voiced their agreement. "Nay? It's unanimous then. John, would you be willing to chair this ad hoc committee?"

"I would, happily."

"And I recommend you consider inviting a few community members to join the committee. Perhaps even a musician or two?" he added.

"We'll see," said Campbell.

"David, dear," said Esther, "May I be recognized to speak?"

"You may."

"I would like to propose we appoint you the permanent chair of the board, rather than simply the acting chair." Everyone at the table leaned in a bit and watched David Brewster for his reaction.

"Thank you, Esther. That's a terrific vote of confidence and I appreciate it. I really do." He smiled. "But I don't think that would be appropriate at this time. I'm happy to continue in a temporary position, of course, leaning heavily on our fine staff," he said, gesturing toward George and Allie, "But there is too much up in the air. And I'm not prepared to take on that responsibility long-term."

A simultaneous exhalation of air from several members was barely audible.

Whew, Allie thought, that's now two things her dad handled well.

"Next on the agenda is the musicians' contract. But before we get to that, I want to insert a bit of context. I'd like to let George and Allie fill us in on how the season seems to be progressing, especially considering what happened."

George nodded to Allie.

"As you all know," she began, "we've sent out two of the three season ticket mailers. One went out at the end of March and one went out, coincidently, the Monday after... we had already scheduled it at the printer's... after the benefit concert." Allie stopped for a moment, tangled in memories. Then she continued, "And, as of today, we're already at 83 percent of last year's total season ticket holders."

"How does that compare to last year's sales at this point?" asked Professor Schimler.

"We're way ahead," answered Allie, looking at her laptop. "Last year at this time we had only received 60 percent of our total season ticket orders."

"I don't need to tell you that this is excellent news," added George. "It's a demonstration of the faith and affection of our audience."

"Yes," picked up David Brewster. "It's significant, and it's something we should keep in mind as we discuss how to handle the musicians' contract. So, shall we?"

David passed around a sheet that described the current state of the negotiations and another sheet that showed the current finances.

"Let's start with the financial picture," he said, picking up the second sheet. "As you can see, the deficit left from last year has been met. Three large anonymous contributions arrived last week to make up the difference. For which we should all be extremely grateful," he added.

Many of the members of the board darted looks at each other, trying to figure out who among them might be the mysterious donors. Esther looked up, her eyes magnified by her glasses' thick lenses. "It wasn't I, if that's what you're thinking."

But I'm sure it was thanks to you, thought Allie. The three donors were all good friends of Esther's, and faithful festival attendees.

"As you can see," said David, "we now no longer have a deficit. And the prospects for the coming season look strong. Therefore, we may want to revisit the proposal we put before the musicians last month. George, would you please refresh everyone's memory as to what that was?"

George cleared his throat. "Yes. The proposal asked for a 35 percent reduction in pay, several unpaid performances, and required an essay from each musician detailing his or her dedication to the festival."

"And we know how that was received by the musicians," said David, "as well as many members of the public."

"It seems to me," said Professor Schimler, "that the board should reconsider this proposal, in light of the change in financials, etc."

"But the musicians' union..." began Helen Davis.

"Has always worked in harmony, forgive the pun, with the SummerFest management," interrupted David. "I've been a part of this organization from the beginning, on both sides of the table. The musicians and management have always enjoyed a positive relationship. It would be a shame to lose that now."

"May I make a motion?" asked Esther.

"You may, of course, Esther," answered David.

"I move we rescind that proposal and revert to our former agreement with the musicians."

"I second," said Peter Drumlin.

Allie typed the notes, but she found it all hard to believe. Had Dr. Abbott simply bullied the rest of the board into following her orders? Were they all actually concerned about the welfare of the festival? Allie was skeptical. Well, whatever was motivating them, it was all good.

"This definitely merits discussion," said David. "George, please go over the items in the previous agreement with the musicians. I want us to be totally informed about what we're voting on."

George rustled through some papers in the file folder he had brought to the meeting. "Here it is," he said. "Basically, this is a standard work agreement. I won't read all the particulars—you can stop by my desk at a later time and read it through if you're interested—but the agreement says the musicians are hired for a six-week season, with a maximum of eight two-hour services per week, at a base rate of $1500 per week. Because this is not a year-round position, we don't offer health insurance, but we do contribute to a retirement plan. The $1500 figure would be the same as the previous three-year contract."

"Whoa. Wait a minute." Ron Osbourne raised his hand. "That's effectively paying them almost $100/hour. That's the equivalent of about $200,000 a year. And they only have to work 16 hours a week. That's a hell of a deal; I'd like to take it myself!"

"Excuse me, Ron," said George. "But don't focus on the hourly rate. Those 16 hours are for formal rehearsals and concerts during the week. But there are also informal rehearsals of chamber groups, not to mention hours each day spent on individual practicing. And $1500 per week only adds up to $78,000 a year, not $200,000."

"It's been at that rate for three years?" asked Alice Vogel. "Might we consider a slight increase, along the lines of a cost-of-living increase? I mean, well, we don't want to lose them to some other summer festival..."

"I'll make a motion to that effect," said Professor Schimler. "George, could we absorb a three percent increase?"

"Well, we made more at the benefit concert than we had expected. And ticket sales are going well. Plus, some sizable donations have been flowing in." He nodded. "I think we could handle it."

"And it would send a positive message to the musicians," said Helen Davis.

"Are we ready to vote on the amendment, then?" asked David. He looked unfazed by the change in attitude by the board members, but Allie guessed he was as surprised as she was. George was easy to read; he wore a startled look on his face. David asked for a vote. "All those in favor of amending the motion to adopt the previous agreement with the musicians by increasing the base pay by three percent, say aye."

It was unanimous. And the vote to approve the entire amended motion was almost unanimous; only John Campbell and Ken Henson voted nay. Allie had to fight the temptation to tweet the news or send a text to Karin Anders.

"Thank you all for that," said David. "It is a positive way to begin our rebuilding. And now, as promised, I believe Chief Knowles is here to give us an update on the investigation. Allie, would you please invite him in?"

Fifty-Two

"I don't know anything about music. In my line, you don't have to. "
—*Elvis Presley*

C hief Chester Knowles was waiting in the outer office, having arrived ten minutes earlier and let himself in. He'd been able to hear the conversation in the conference room, thanks to the register's opening in the wall. He rose stiffly as Allie opened the door to the conference room.

"Chief Knowles, they're ready," she said, beckoning him.

"Thank you, Allegra," the chief said. He entered the conference room and set a notebook on the table. David Brewster moved his chair to the side so the chief could take the head of the table. Allie began to bring another chair, but Knowles shook his head. "I'll stand," he said.

"Thank you for agreeing to meet with us, Chief," said David. "As you can imagine, we are all most interested in hearing how the case is progressing."

Chief Knowles placed his palms on the table and leaned forward. "I appreciate your interest. Thank you for inviting me," he said. "I wish I could tell you we have the culprit in hand, but we're not quite there yet." He looked around the table. "Almost, but not quite."

Allie noticed George wasn't looking at the chief. Instead, he was staring at his hands, which were clenched tightly on the table in front of him.

"Well, what then can you tell us?" asked Helen Davis.

"We know quite a few details now, Ma'am. We know the perpetrator was known to Mrs. Abbott."

"Dr. Abbott," murmured someone.

"We know the victim, *Doctor* Abbot, was familiar with her attacker," he began again, "because there was no sign of a struggle, and there was an indication that the culprit was sitting near her just prior to the attack. The victim died almost instantly."

"What about the murder weapon?" asked Ron Osbourne.

"A small pointed tool of some sort," the chief replied.

"So, you know the killer knew Dr. Abbott," said John Campbell. "What else do you know? Male, I assume."

"Could be either," said Knowles. "The killer didn't have to be very strong. Just needed an element of surprise."

"Was this premeditated, do you suppose?" asked Helen Davis.

"Hard to say, Ma'am. It was certainly planned, but maybe only a few minutes before. It could be a crime of opportunity. But it certainly was someone who had a beef with the lady."

"No leads?" asked Professor Schimler.

"Oh, we think we have a pretty good idea. We're just not quite ready yet to say who that is."

The board members shifted uneasily in their chairs.

"Is there anything we can do to help?" asked David Brewster.

The chief paused and regarded him for a moment. "No. Just don't any of you take any trips out of town," he finally said.

John Campbell laughed. "Are you serious?" he asked.

"Dead serious," was the response. Someone's cellphone vibrated in the silence that followed.

David Brewster cleared his throat. "Well, then, Chet, we thank you for your time and wish you the best of luck in clearing this up soon."

Other board members added their thanks in subdued tones.

David stuck out his hand, but the chief had turned away from the table and made straight for the door. Allie accompanied him out through the office as he grabbed his coat. "Thanks for coming," she said, opening the outer door.

"Welcome," he replied over his shoulder.

Shortly thereafter, the members of the Board of Directors of the Kennimac SummerFest solemnly left the building.

Allie and her father rode home together. "Dad, you handled that meeting brilliantly," she said.

"Did I?"

"I can't believe what you accomplished—and without a fight. Wait until Karin and Tony hear about this. They'll be ecstatic."

"Suppose so."

Allie looked at her father's silhouetted profile. He seemed distant. Anxiety's returning, she thought. She marveled at his ability to rally and then sink low again.

Fifty-Three

"There's nothing remarkable about it. All one has
to do is hit the right keys at the right time and the
instrument plays itself."   —*Johann Sebastian Bach*

An hour after Allie and her father arrived home, Chief
Knowles was at the door, with Officer Cabot standing a few
steps down.

"Is your father home, Allegra?" he asked as she opened the door.

Oh crap, she thought. Yes, he's lying on the couch in a pot-in-duced stupor. Not the best way to greet an officer of the law.

"He's a little indisposed right now, Chief Knowles. Is there
something I can help you with?"

"No, it's your father I need to see. Right now." The chief seemed
stern.

David Brewster shuffled to the door, his eyes blood-shot and
sleepy. "Chet? What's up?"

"David, I'm bringing you in for questioning regarding the murder
of Sylvia Abbott. I think you know more than you've told us so
far. I think you're hiding something—something that incriminates
you. You can either come willingly or I can arrest you."

Allie's father looked at the police officer blankly. "You what?
Chet?"

"Dad!" Allie grabbed her father's arm. "Dad, the chief wants to
question you about Dr. Abbott." She turned to Chief Knowles.

"Why not do it here? You can ask him what you want to know here."

"This is serious, young lady. I want your father to understand just how serious. That's why I want to bring him to the station."

"But, I..." David Brewster still looked bewildered.

"It's not necessary, Chief Knowles," Allie broke in. "No one is taking this lightly."

"There's no arguing, either of you." Knowles pulled a pair of handcuffs out of his pocket.

David Brewster waved his hand. "Hold on. Of course I'll come willingly. I have nothing to hide. I've told you everything, Chet, and it's all true."

Shocked, Allie watched as Chief Knowles took her father's arm and escorted him to the squad car.

Fifty-Four

"Hell is full of musical amateurs."
—George Bernard Shaw

C hester Knowles was not a complicated man. The son of an alcoholic lobsterman and a bright but frustrated housewife, Chet had tried to live up to the higher standards his mother set him. He knew the force of her thwarted ambitions; he'd heard her verbal abuse of his father year after year. Yet, even though he excelled in school, he wasn't able to meet her expectations either. Though he could handle the course work, it only took one semester at the University of Maine to show that he was not cut out for academic life. He wasn't comfortable with the open-ended class discussions, the variety of viewpoints held by his professors and classmates. It seemed like there were far too many gray areas—Chet preferred things to be uncomplicated and black and white. His mother was furious when he received his second semester grades, along with a letter encouraging him to withdraw from school. She berated him for not trying, for deliberately sabotaging her dreams for him.

The saddest thing for Chet was that he actually had tried, but university was not the right place for him. All that reading and talking about abstract ideas made him feel itchy.

The one good thing that came of his time on the Orono campus was meeting Saralynn Cutler. By the end of the semester, they were seriously going steady, and she didn't seem to mind that he flunked out. Saralynn was a devout Catholic, and during her second semester at the University of Maine she decided to transfer to Saint Joseph's College in Standish. Not only did it give her the opportunity to major in theology, but she would be closer to Chet, too. She convinced him to attend mass with her at the conservative church she had discovered.

During the years Saralynn was at St. Joseph's, Chet lobstered with his father. Carl Knowles was a small wiry man with a bitter expression. He wasn't particularly happy to have Chet as his stern-man and made that clear by making nasty remarks to the other lobstermen at the dock about his son, "the pansy, who thought he was too good for fishing," who "was such a fairy, he couldn't hack college, either." So Chet focused on saving money and thinking about Saralynn. When she graduated, they got married and moved to Portland, where Saralynn found a job at a church-sponsored pregnancy center, counseling young women with unwanted preg-nancies to either keep their babies or give them up for adoption.

Saralynn encouraged Chet to explore various career oppor-tunities. A temporary stint as a security guard convinced him he'd like a job in law enforcement, and he enrolled in the Maine Criminal Justice Academy in Vassalboro. The hourlong commute from Portland was challenging, but Chet was enthusiastic about the classes and graduated with honors.

As the years went by, Saralynn's conservative beliefs became ingrained in Chet as well. He thought his work fit in perfectly with his religion. He did reasonably well (though not according to his mother), moving up through the ranks from police officer in Portland to finally becoming the chief of the small police force in Kennimac.

Saralynn was an outspoken activist against Maine's same sex marriage law and was crushed when the law passed. Chet, al-though maintaining a lower profile, equally abhorred homosexu-ality and was sure it was a mortal sin. He was glad there didn't seem to be many homosexuals in Kennimac and therefore, he didn't have to have much to do with them. He was damned glad he didn't have to defend any of their so-called rights. In fact, he'd gotten into trouble last summer when arresting for drunk driving someone he knew to be gay. Luckily, Officer Cheri Ouellette had heard him berating the accused and stepped in to defuse the situation.

When he realized his long-time acquaintance, David Brewster, was actually "one of them," he could hardly contain his disgust.

Fifty-Five

"Some days there won't be a song in your heart.
Sing anyway." —*Emory Austin*

Her father? A suspect? Allie was dumbfounded. There was absolutely no way her father could murder anyone. No way. I'm going to have to find out who the actual murderer is, she thought. But she couldn't think straight—she could only picture the confused expression on her father's face as they led him out the door, and the bullying tone to the chief's voice.

Her phone rang. *Thomas* flashed the caller ID. Without thinking, she answered numbly, "Hello?"

"Allie." Thomas's voice sounded strong. "What are you up to this evening?"

"Oh, God, Thomas, they just took my dad in for questioning." Allie drew a shuddering breath. "I don't know what to do."

"Wow. I guess that's good news for me, but it sucks to be him. Why do they think your father did it?"

It surprised Allie that Thomas seemed so unconcerned about her father's situation, especially after he'd been so upset when he was questioned.

"Thomas," she said. "I have to go. I need to figure out some way to help my father."

"Yes, sure. Good luck. Hope it all works out," Thomas said. "See you." And he hung up.

Allie thought about Thomas. He actually had a motive, slim though it was. The pressure from the police must have waned, and he decided he wasn't in danger of being charged. But what if he...? She tried to remember where Thomas was after she had discovered Dr. Abbott's body. She didn't remember seeing him anywhere. Of course, she was not exactly herself at that point—puking in the ladies' room, practically passing out, her head awhirl. But Thomas had been so upset about Officer Ouellette taking his keepsake, the baton stick pin. His reaction was way too dramatic, she thought. And then so low key tonight.

And what about Luke and the carving tool he had?

And George had been acting weird. He was not at all his usual efficient self.

Oh, my God, Allie thought, shaking her head. I can almost make it seem as if *anybody* is guilty. But I don't have any proof about anyone. Much as she hated to admit, there was only one person she could think to call.

Fifty-Six

"Some people have lives;
some people have music."
—*John Green*

"**A**llegra? What's the emergency?" Her mother's voice was scratchy with sleep. "Do you know what time it is here?"

"Mom." Allie was afraid she would start crying and not be able to talk. "I'm sorry, Mom—I forgot to check the time. But Dad's in trouble."

Melissa's impatient sigh was audible. "What do you mean? How am I supposed to help from Zurich?"

"It's kind of a long story." Allie inhaled. "So I was meaning to call you. Sylvia Abbott died. I found her."

"You found her body? How did she die?"

"It was awful. Someone killed her, Mom."

"What?" Melissa's voice rose, the sleepiness erased. "Oh, honey, how horrible for you!"

Allie wiped the tears from her cheeks and nodded, wordlessly.

"Do they know who did it? What does your father have to do with this?"

Her voice cracking, Allie explained that Chief Knowles had taken David in for questioning. There was silence while Melissa digested the news.

"That god-damned Sylvie," she finally said. "She has always been so difficult. But why would someone go to the trouble of killing her? Certainly David wouldn't. Of course he wouldn't." Almost to herself, she added, "He wouldn't have the gumption."

"Mother!"

"Anyway, I thought he and Sylvie were friends. Dating, even. I'd heard that from Charles Abbott, Sylvie's ex. I ran into him at an economic conference in London two years ago." She paused. "I did think at the time that they made an unlikely couple. And when I heard nothing about it from you or David, I assumed it was a false rumor."

"I guess they went on some dates. That's what Dad said. But it wasn't a big romance or anything."

"I'm sure it wasn't. I can't imagine they would get along. They are complete opposites."

"What should I do? I mean, Dad's at the police station. We have to do something."

"Have you called a lawyer?"

"No. Who should I call?"

"I think the best choice would be Nat Roy. He's very good. And he likes David."

"I should have thought of that," said Allie. Then another thought halted her. "But the cost..."

"Don't worry about that, Allegra. I'll transfer some funds. Let's just get your father some decent legal representation."

They talked for a few more minutes. Melissa asked Allie if she was seeing anyone these days. "Not Luke?" she queried. "Definitely not," answered Allie. Allie apologized for waking her up, and her mother replied that it was ok—in another hour it would be time to get her day started.

"Call me anytime, honey. Let me know what happens. And I'm glad I could help."

Fifty-Seven

"The only love affair I have
ever had was with music."
—*Maurice Ravel*

S itting across the metal table, David Brewster looked at the printed emails in Chief Knowles hands. "Yes," he said with a sigh. "She kept writing me. She didn't want me to stop seeing her. She wouldn't accept the fact that our affair was over. But it was over. I tried to tell her that. And I've already told you all that, too."

"I think there was more to it," said Chief Knowles. "She threatened to expose you. And you were afraid people would find out you are gay. So you killed her."

"What? Me, gay? That makes no sense! I'm not gay. You know that, Chet."

"Sylvia Abbott certainly thought you were homosexual." He started reading out loud, "'My darling David, why should I write darling now? You have betrayed me. How could you have toyed with me, letting me think you loved me, when it seems you can't ever commit to a relationship with a woman!' Knowles emphasized the last words, repeating them—'you can't ever commit to *a relationship with a woman.* You drove Melissa away and now you're pushing me away. I feel used and confused. I can't let this charade go on. I will let people know about the real you before you hurt another unsuspecting woman...'"

Chief Knowles looked up from the printout. "And here's how you responded: 'I'm ending this, Sylvia. You obviously wanted more from our relationship than I did. Please stop the drama before you drive me to do something more drastic than ignoring your phone calls.' The chief shook the printout at David. "You were afraid she'd spill your secret, weren't you?"

"No, it was nothing like that." David searched for words. "I didn't care. I knew she was angry and hurt. I didn't pay much attention to her threats."

"But you were worried about your reputation..."

"What? In this day and age? Even if I were gay, being gay isn't a problem. And, for your information, I am not gay. You are confused."

Chief Knowles cleared his throat. "You lied about your relationship with the victim. You said it was, quote, 'a light-hearted, momentary affair.' Yet even as recently as a few days before you murdered her, the two of you had cocktails."

"I was trying to get her to see reason about the SummerFest board. I didn't kill her," insisted David. "I'm... I mean, there's no way I would do such a thing."

"We have other incriminating evidence," said Knowles.

"Like what?" David was incredulous.

His incredulity was met with the chief's smug smile. "I think you'd better call your lawyer before you say anything else."

"I have nothing to hide."

"Your lawyer would be a better judge of that. But if you want to waive that right..."

A deep voice outside the door stopped the chief.

"Yes, I'm his lawyer," said the voice. "And he needs representation."

Chief Knowles got up and opened the door.

"Hello, Nat," he said wearily. "How the hell did you get here so fast? Brewster hasn't even made a phone call yet."

"But his daughter did. I got here as fast as I could." Attorney Nat Roy wore a Burberry raincoat over a plaid flannel shirt and faded jeans. His cropped, gray-tinged curls topped an athletic six-foot-four-inch frame. His slightly hooded eyes and expressive mouth varied from sardonic to questioning as he turned from Chief Knowles to David Brewster. "Hello, David. Don't say another word."

David Brewster looked up, his face lined and weary. "Allie called you?"

"She did. And, lucky for you, I hadn't started talking to Jack Daniels yet this evening." Nat gave a belly laugh, then cut it off as he looked back at Chief Knowles. "What the fuck do you have going on here, Chet? You know there's no way David Brewster could be responsible for the murder of Sylvia Abbott."

"That's where you're wrong. The evidence is strong. I believe he's guilty."

"God knows what you believe or what your so-called evidence is. But before you cause anymore havoc, I'd like to speak with my client."

Chief Knowles slammed the door as he left the questioning room.

The lawyer pulled out the folding chair across the table from David Brewster and sat down. "So, what is going on?" he asked.

David was hunched over, his arms tightly folded across his chest. He didn't answer for a moment, then finally raised his head and lifted his eyebrows. "He thinks I killed her."

"But why? What would give him such a crazy idea?"

David shrugged his shoulders. "He found some old emails..."

"About?"

David took a breath and straightened up. "Sylvia and I dated for awhile. Briefly. Years ago. No big deal. But she wanted more to come of it than I did."

"Sounds like Sylvia," Nat interjected.

"Yes, well, she couldn't leave it alone. She was angry. And she got it into her head that I was a misogynist, that I couldn't commit to a relationship or something."

"And?"

"That's it. Evidently the police have her emails, and Chet has gotten the wrong idea about Sylvia's accusations."

"What do you mean?"

"Well, she was claiming she would let other people know that I'd let her down somehow."

"And that's supposed to be grounds for murder?" Nat wrinkled his brow.

"No, well...," David rubbed his eyes. "It's almost too incredible to believe, but Chet seems to think she was saying I was a homosexual and she was going to expose that. For which he thinks I killed her."

"Oh, for Christ's sake. Seriously? That can't be all he's got."

"That's all I know about." David gestured with open palms.

"Ok, let's start at the beginning. Do you have an alibi for the time of the murder? It was during the concert, right?"

"I think it happened during or just after the intermission. I was working in the kitchen during intermission, getting corks out of wine bottles and helping prepare the ice for the raw oysters. There was a small crowd of us; I'm sure they'd all vouch for me."

"How about when intermission was over? Did you stick with them? Go sit down in the audience?"

"Unfortunately, no. I was so pleased the turnout for the concert was so high. I went out into the parking lot to count the cars. I could still hear the music; the barn doors were open. But it was so beautiful outdoors..."

"Did anyone see you out there?"

"I doubt it. I didn't see anyone else. I ran back in the barn when I heard Allie screaming."

"Hmmm." Nat scrutinized David, his mouth pursed. "Have you told me everything about your relationship with Sylvia Abbott? No secrets, David, if I'm going to defend you successfully. Did you sleep with her?"

"Twice. Well, sort of. It was awkward. I wasn't interested in her in that way but I felt it would hurt her feelings—she was rather insistent. But the second time I couldn't fake it. I just couldn't. And I guess it did hurt her feelings. As shown by her emails. Which I decided to ignore. I figured she'd get over it and she did."

"But a woman scorned..."

"I know, I know. 'Hell have no fury like...' But she really did move on. I think she was seeing someone in the orchestra soon after we called it quits. And I tried to remain friends but she didn't want that."

"Oh, you probably reminded her of her failure to be attractive to you." Nat rubbed his stubbly jaw. "So how would you characterize your relationship afterwards?"

"Civil, I guess. Business-like. We pretty much avoided each other."

"Knowing Sylvia—and I do, from the Wednesday sailboat races—civil was generally a stretch for her. That woman was one tough cookie." Nat looked at his Rolex. "Hell, it's late, Dave. Let's get you out of here." The lawyer stood up and opened the door. "Chet!," he shouted.

The police chief sauntered down the hall to the questioning room, his bald spot glistening in the glare of the florescent lights. "Can we finally get back to business?"

"Your business is a bunch of baloney, Chet. I don't know what you think you're doing, but unless you're ready to charge my client with a crime, I think we're done here." Nat motioned for David to stand up and follow him.

"Whoa, now. You can't just walk out of here. We're not done." Chief Knowles blocked the doorway.

"Are you ready to make a charge?" Nat moved closer to the door. He was several inches taller than the chief and in better shape. He looked down at the chief. "Well, are you?" he challenged.

Chief Knowles narrowed his eyes. You bastard, he muttered under his breath. He inhaled loudly. "This case needs solving, Nat. But, no, I'm not ready to charge anyone." He gave David Brewster a sour look. "You're free to go."

David stood up, rubbing his neck. "I need to call Allie and tell her I'm fine and everything's going to be ok," he said to Nat.

"She's quite a girl, your daughter," he responded.

David held out his hand for Nat to shake. "I'm glad you came," he said. "I actually do believe everything will be fine."

"Stay positive, man," answered Nat.

___elle___

David Brewster went straight to bed once he'd reassured Allie he hadn't been charged with anything. Allie offered Nat a cup of decaf, with a questioning look.

Nat took the coffee, refusing her offer of cream or sugar. He settled into a kitchen chair and took a sip. "Chet's got it all wrong, Allie. He thinks your father killed Sylvia Abbott because she was going to expose him as a homosexual."

"What? That's crazy!" said Allie. "That's the most insane thing I've ever heard. He's not gay and even if he were..."

"I know. He would never murder someone to keep it a secret. Don't worry. They don't have a case," Nat said. "But what would help is if someone would confirm his alibi. He says he went out into the parking lot to count the cars. Did you see him?"

"No, but there must be someone who did. There's a window in the kitchen that looks right out on the parking lot, and the door is a glass door, too."

"So, if you want to help, Allegra..."

"Of course I do!"

"Then talk to the people who were in the kitchen during intermission and find out where they went afterwards."

"We've got to clear Dad, Nat. You know he isn't guilty of anything."

"You bet. We'll clear him. Stay cool."

———❦———

Back at home, Nat poured himself a double of Jack Daniels and
took a gulp. Chet Knowles was an idiot, he thought, shaking his
head. Nat had grown up in the next town to Kennimac, adopted as
an infant. His adopted family was well known in that part of Maine
during his youth: one tall black high school basketball star, one
tiny Chinese gymnast, and a Colombian social butterfly. Nat had
left for college vowing never to return, tired of feeling as though
every move he made was exposed, that everything he did would
be judged. But after law school and working as a public defender,
he decided he missed the Maine seashore and woods. And his
parents. He realized he'd never wholly fit in anywhere—that was
just a fact of his life. He wasn't going to let that sour him. Instead,
he would learn to use it to his advantage. And he had, rising to be
a respected member of the community and a successful defense
attorney, with cases across northern New England.

Fifty-Eight

"A creative artist works on his next composition because he was not satisfied with his previous one."
—*Dimitri Shostakovich*

It was too late for Allie to call anyone, though she wanted to. But she realized that she'd probably get a better response if she waited until morning. And besides, calling Luke late a night, well, he'd probably come running to her, and she didn't want that. But she wanted to find out who might be able to lend her father an alibi.

She sat in the dark, much as her father often did. Activating the music system, she selected Borodin's *String Quartet No. 2*[35], the third movement, "Notturno," to start. It was melancholy but also had a sense of hope. That it was written in a major key helped. The section that was a conversation between the four instruments, with the cello and viola posing questions, seemed to mirror her feelings. As the ending of the movement died away, she clicked off the remote and sat in the silence, thinking.

Clearly, since they had focused on her father, the police had no idea who the real killer was. Allie thought back to the day of the murder. Her dad had been working on Calliope that morning. When he arrived at the concert barn, he'd shown her a wood screw he'd brought in his pocket and asked her to remind him to stop at the hardware store on the way home to find more screws to match. The police couldn't think the screw was the murder weapon, could they? After all, it was much thicker and would have made a jagged hole. Allie closed her eyes, sickened once again at the thought of the hole she saw in Dr. Abbott's neck.

So, if it wasn't her father, who was it? Who would have wanted to kill Dr. Abbott—not just figuratively; that was a lot of people. Allie smiled in spite of herself. They had to figure this out. She had to, that is. She couldn't ask anyone to help her. Luke, Thomas, George, Tony, Kate, Mrs. Kelley, Karin, the rest of the quintet—they were all suspects. No one had observed a stranger walking past the kitchen. Occam's razor, Allie thought. The simplest hypothesis is probably the most likely. KISS: keep it simple, stupid. No, the culprit was bound to be someone who knew Dr. Abbott and knew the building.

Who had been acting strangely? Luke had certainly been explosively angry about the treatment of the musicians. Allie knew he had a temper, but he was also quick to calm down, too. Maybe something had set off that temper, though. Did she remember Sylvia Abbott saying anything to Luke? She just didn't know.

And Thomas had seemed inordinately worried about the questioning by the police. Had they found out about his trouble as a juvenile? What was the story with his baton stickpin? Why did the police officer take it—and what had they discovered about it?

Kate. Well, Kate wasn't herself, but that had been true for months. Kate commiserated with Allie about the direction Dr. Abbott was taking the board, but she didn't have any reason for personal animosity toward the board chair. Plus, Kate seemed so mired in her own passive hell it wasn't logical to think she had the force of will to do something so violent.

Carolyn Kelley was a suspect because of her proximity, but really, thought Allie, she hardly had the brains or the nerves to pull off something like Dr. Abbott's murder. She could barely handle helping with the refreshments; she'd been so nervous and spilled so much wine that Luke had had to take over from her. Plus, she wasn't an evil person. And, by definition, mused Allie, the murderer had to be evil.

Karin Anders and the other musicians of the quintet hardly seemed to be possible suspects. They would have had to kill Dr. Abbott and then get right out on stage and start playing almost a split second later. Allie wondered if anyone would have the nerves to play the second half of a demanding chamber music concert after just having committed murder. Her thoughts strayed to the tools used by some of the woodwind players. Now, those definitely were possible murder weapons. Even so, it all seemed too far-fetched to focus on them.

It had been a surprise that Tony had showed up at the concert. But she hadn't seen him near the kitchen or the hallway to the Damon pavilion. And unless there was some other connection between Tony and Sylvia Abbott that she didn't know about, Allie couldn't see why he'd kill her over the musicians' contract.

George definitely had been acting odd. But he was under a lot of stress, the same as Allie was. Probably she had been acting strange, too. Both of their jobs were under attack. But killing Dr. Abbott wouldn't solve George's problem even if she was the one causing the stress, because her death threw the organization into even greater shambles. Allie respected George, but she reflected she didn't know him well. He was always professional, but his anger at Dr. Abbott had been discernible, if held in check. But it was no more than anyone else's anger, was it?

Allie switched on the lamp beside her chair. Archie, stretched out on the floor by her feet, sleepily opened his eyes. "Time to go to bed, buddy," she said. The little dog staggered to his feet and wobbled to the stairs. "You and me, both," Allie said to him. "You and me, both."

Fifty-Nine

"The old idea of a composer suddenly having a
terrific idea and sitting up all night to write it
is nonsense.
Nighttime is for sleeping."
—*Benjamin Britten*

Allie woke up the next morning ready to go to battle for her father. After a short walk through the fields, with Archie alternately prancing around her tall green waterproof boots or dashing off to chase a squirrel, she quickly grabbed a peanut butter and jelly sandwich and sat at the kitchen table with her phone.

Her first call was to George.

"Allie!" he answered the phone with uncharacteristic energy. "Early, aren't you? Listen, that was quite a job your dad did last night! I'm still in a state of shock and awe."

"George." Allie's somber tone stopped George from continuing. "George, I need you to help me. And I probably won't be in to work today."

"What's come up?" George asked.

"They... the police... Chief Knowles, anyway..." Allie stopped to calm herself.

"Something about the murder?"

"Chief Knowles brought my father in for questioning last night."

"Your father? David? Why?"

"Yes. He suspects Dad of killing Dr. Abbott." Her voice broke. "Look, can I call you back? I need to get a drink of water or something."

"Call me right back," George quickly replied.

Allie stood for a moment and inhaled deeply. If she was going to be of any help, she was going to need to get control of herself. "Shit," she said as she turned on the tap and filled a glass. "Shit, shit, shit, SHIT!"

At the sound of her yelling, Archie scrambled out from under the table and ran into the living room. Allie laughed bleakly. "Sorry, buddy," she said.

Sitting back down at the table, she redialed George's number.

"Ok," she said, "I think I've got a better handle on myself."

"So let me get this straight, Allie. After the meeting last night, Chet Knowles came to your house and arrested David? I don't get it. That doesn't make any sense..."

"You're right; it's crazy. Chief Knowles has this insane idea that Dr. Abbott found out Dad is gay, which he isn't..."

"No, he's not gay."

"And Knowles thinks Abbott was going to expose him, so he killed her to stop her from doing that."

"He thinks your father killed Sylvia to avoid being exposed as a gay man, which we all know he wasn't. Is that what you're telling me?"

"Yes."

"That's just plain nuts. What evidence does he have for this accusation?"

"According to Nat Roy...," started Allie.

"Oh, good, I'm glad Nat is already involved. He was my first thought."

"My mother suggested I call him—I phoned her in desperation after the police left with Dad."

"Smart thinking. Anyway, what is Knowles basing this on?"

"Nat said they found some emails between Dad and Dr. Abbott. You'll find this hard to believe, it's unbelievable to me, but they went on a few dates."

"Your father and Sylvia?"

"Yes, about two years ago. And she wanted it to turn into something more but he didn't, so she got mad and wrote some nasty emails."

"Typical. But why would that make anyone think she was going to throw him out of the closet?"

"I don't know. I think Chief Knowles is so anxious to catch the killer that he's hallucinating or something. Anyway, Nat Roy says the best thing I can do is help establish an alibi for Dad at the time of the killing. So I need to check in with as many people as I can to find someone who saw him leave the kitchen after intermission to stand in the parking lot."

"He was in the parking lot?"

"That's what he says. He was counting the cars. And I believe him."

"Of course. I don't doubt it, either. So, let me see. I was sitting in the back row of the audience for the second half of the concert. I didn't see anyone leave but I wasn't looking in that direction."

"You sure about that?"

"I am, but who else might have seen him? How about the people working in the kitchen? I know Lucas was there. Howard Kelley's wife, what's her name? Oh, Carolyn. Start with those two. I'll bet one of them saw your dad go outside."

"Oh, God, I hope so," said Allie.

"And Allie, be careful. It wasn't your father who killed Sylvia, but it was someone close. Don't go accusing anyone else; just stick to getting a strong alibi for David. And don't worry about coming in today. The important thing is for you to find that alibi."

"Thanks, George. I totally appreciate it."

"Keep me in the loop."

"I will. Bye."

Allie ended the call and looked at her phone. There was something niggling in the corner of her memory. Something not quite right. Oh, George hadn't mentioned Kate Zeller. But she must have been there, too; he just forgot. I'll call Kate first, she thought. Of the three of them—Kate, Lucas, and Lynnie Kelley—Kate is probably the most observant. She took a bite of the peanut butter sandwich, forcing herself to swallow past the lump in her throat. God, this sucks, she thought. I've got to figure this out.

After a sip of water, she dialed Kate.

"Allie, what is it? Not a good time." Kate put her hand over the phone but Allie could still hear her yell at Harris that he was going to be late for school again if he didn't hurry it up.

"Kate, can I call you back? It's extremely important. The police..."

"What about the police?"

"They brought Dad in for questioning last night. Knowles thinks that Dad... that he is the one... Dr. Abbott's...."

"What! You're kidding! Yes, call me back. In about half an hour or so." Kate hung up.

Allie still remembered Luke's number, so she quickly punched it in.

⁓ℓℓ⁓

"Allie?" he answered her call with a yawn. "What are you calling so early for?"

Hearing his sleepy unconcerned voice reminded Allie how everything had changed. Her voice broke as she said, "Luke, the police arrested Dad last night."

"What! Did they catch him selling weed or something?"

"No, no." Allie managed a ghost of a smile. "No, Chief Knowles thinks he killed Dr. Abbott."

"What the fuck? That makes no sense whatsoever. Your father is the kindest, gentlest person I've ever met. He couldn't hurt a fly."

"Well, the police have come up with some crazy theory that Sylvia Abbott was about to unmask him as gay, so he killed her to keep it quiet."

"Holy shit. Knowles is certifiable. That's the weirdest thing I've ever heard. But you know what, Allie? I do know Knowles has a thing about homosexuality. Remember when they released the list of donors who paid for that full-page ad in the Portland paper against the Vote Yes for Love campaign? He and his wife had given several thousand dollars. That's a big donation to make on a small-town police chief's salary."

"Hmmm. I didn't know that."

"Yeah, and there was a rumor he called Jimmy Wilson a 'flaming faggot' when he arrested him for drunk driving last summer."

"Lovely. Well, whatever it is, Knowles thinks my father is gay, and that's why he thinks he... he killed Dr. Abbott." Allie stopped for a sip of water.

"This totally sucks," said Luke. "We've got to prove your dad's innocence. Does he have a lawyer yet? My dad knows..."

"He's got Nat Roy."

"Whoa, impressive! Does Roy have any idea about how we can help?"

"Actually, he does. He asked me to find out if anyone saw Dad leave the kitchen after intermission and head for the parking lot. You were in the kitchen. Did you see Dad leave?"

"Crap. I left the kitchen before the intermission was over—when the first bell rang—because I spotted two full wine glasses on a tray in the hall and decided to polish them off. So, sorry, no help there."

Allie sighed. "Well, that's two of you who are no help at all."

"Who else?"

"George. He was already out of the kitchen when the second half of the concert started."

"Well, that ditsy woman, Mrs. Kelley, was in the kitchen. Maybe she saw something. And I think Kate Z. was there, too. Might have been some other folks, too. Let me think on it."

"God, I hope you think of something," said Allie.

"Are you going into work this morning?" asked Luke.

"No, George knows I'm wrapped up in this."

"Want me to come over?"

"No, thanks, Luke. You do have work to do. But I'll let you know if I find anything out."

"And I'll let you know if I remember anything else. Sorry, Allie. This really sucks. I'll think about what more I could do to help you."

"That'd be great, Luke. Talk later. Bye."

Sixty

"In order to compose, all you need to do is remember a tune that nobody else has thought of."
—*Robert Schumann*

Allie noticed that a half hour had passed. She dialed Kate's
number again. Kate picked up right away.

"Allie," Kate said. "What's going on? Why was David arrested?
What has he gotten himself into?"

"Nothing! But they think he killed Dr. Abbott."

Kate sat in shocked silence.

"Kate? Are you there?"

"That is absolutely ridiculous. How did they come up with that
idea?" Kate's inflection was practically hot enough to singe the
phone.

"It's a long story. Dad and Dr. Abbott went on some dates." Allie
felt like she was reciting a hated lesson by rote. "Dr. Abbott wanted
the relationship to develop into something more, but Dad wasn't
interested. So she wrote him some nasty emails."

"She wrote nasty emails to everyone."

"Well, he thinks that..."

"Who's 'he'?" interrupted Kate.

"Chief Knowles. He thinks Dr. Abbott decided Dad was gay, and
she was going to expose him. So, supposedly, he killed her to keep
that from happening."

"My God, she was not just evil, she was more idiotic than I thought."

"No, no, I don't think she believed that. I think the chief is reading something into her emails that isn't actually there. And, Dad's not gay, to begin with."

"So, what are you going to do? Does he have a lawyer?"

"Yes, Nat Roy saw Dad last night. He got him at the station and brought him home."

"What did Nat say to do?"

"He asked me to see if anyone at the concert noticed Dad leaving the kitchen and walking out to the parking lot when the second half of the concert started."

"Oh."

"You were in the kitchen, weren't you? Did you see Dad leave?"

There was a pause. Then Kate said, slowly, "You know, I think I did. I think I saw him go out the door. In fact, I'm sure of it."

"Really?" Allie was filled with hope. "You're completely sure?"

"I am. I'd swear to it."

"I should call Nat Roy right away. Thank you, Kate. You're a lifesaver. Thank you, thank you, thank you!"

⸺

"Nat, I think I already have found Dad an alibi," said Allie. "I spoke with Kate Zeller, who was in the kitchen during intermission. "She saw Dad walk out to the parking lot before the second half of the concert started. She said she'd swear to it."

"Excellent work, Allie. That is huge. Ok, sounds like we're not going to have much trouble getting David scratched off the suspect list. Listen, I've got a meeting about to start, but I'll be in touch soon. This is looking quite positive."

Allie heard Archie scramble down the stairs, followed by her father. David Brewster poured himself a cup of coffee and sat down.

"Dad, did you hear my conversation with Nat? Kate says she's certain she saw you leave the kitchen."

David stared at the coffee cup. He bit his lip in thought.

"You're awfully quiet, Dad," Allie said. "I guess you've had a pretty traumatic experience."

"True," replied her father, "but it's not that. I'm just thinking Kate had already left the kitchen by the time I headed outdoors. I don't see how she could have seen me."

"She said she'd swear to it."

"I must be wrong, then."

Allie searched her father's face. He shrugged.

"I'm bushed. I think I'd better take a nap before I do anything else."

Sixty-One

"I frequently hear music in the heart of noise."
—*George Gershwin*

W ith her father heading off to sleep, Allie decided she might as well go in to work. She stopped at the post office on her way in. Another huge bundle of mail was stuffed into the box. Allie was reminded of the decisions of the board yesterday evening, before the police hauled her father off to jail.

I wonder what George has done about all that, she thought. As she left the post office, she avoided looking at Mina Treat in the customer service window. No doubt, word of her father's arrest had already made the rounds in Kennimac. Mina was always one of the first to know any gossip, and she had no problem repeating it all day to anyone who would listen. I probably look guilty, thought Allie, slinking by her, but I can't face talking about it.

At the office, she carried in the mail and plopped it on her desk.

"Looks like another good haul of orders," said George. He got up from his desk and walked over. "So, you decided to come in? You didn't have to, you know. Has the situation improved?"

"Somewhat. Dad's out; he hasn't been charged. And there's been one positive thing—Kate Zeller says she saw Dad walk out of the kitchen and into the parking lot after intermission. So that establishes his alibi."

"Kate said that?" George flipped through the envelopes, pulling out the few that weren't ticket orders.

"What? Don't you think that's a big deal?" asked Allie.

"Oh, it is. Very good." George headed back to his desk. "I'm sure Nat Roy can work with that."

"Let's hope so," said Allie. "After Dad got home this morning, I remembered the board meeting last night. Have you contacted anyone? We definitely should let Karin know."

"I was waiting to see what would happen with David before sending out any announcements. But you're right, we should at least let the musicians know about the changes."

"And Tony. He'll be happy."

"Yes, he will. Why don't you go ahead and send each of them a quick email."

"What if Karin wants to tell the rest of the musicians?" Allie wondered why George seemed so preoccupied. "And should we work on a press release? Or...?"

George tapped a pencil on his desk absentmindedly. "I'm not sure what to do, with your father's situation..."

"I know. The other board members probably will know soon, if they haven't heard already."

As if on cue, George's mobile pealed. "Yes? Hi, Ken." George rolled his eyes at Allie. "Yes, but they've released him. And from what I hear, Nat Roy... Yes, Nat is representing him. Nat has established an alibi, so it's all going to blow over momentarily. ... No, I don't think this changes anything. ... Let's hold off on that, Ken. ...No, I don't think the press has got wind of it yet. ... Ok, we'll keep mum here. Bye."

George slammed his phone down on his desk. "Damn. As you probably gathered, that was Ken Henson. He wants to call another board meeting in light of your father's arrest, but I hope I scuttled that idea. Just what we need, Sylvia's henchmen coming back to life. Jesus!" George's vehemence surprised Allie.

"I still think you should inform Karin and Tony," George continued, calming down a bit. "The board approved those decisions. And, this business with your father is unfortunate, but it will blow over." George looked out the window. "I, for one, know he's innocent."

Allie was glad for George's vote of confidence, but she thought he was acting strange. What did he know?

George began thumbing through the pile of envelopes, pulling out things addressed to him. He opened a few things and piled them on his desk. He opened one envelope, stared at the contents, and then stuffed it into his pocket.

"I'm going to head out to grab some lunch. Back around two o'clock." George practically ran out the door.

Allie looked at the mass of envelopes George had been pawing through and groaned. Most of them were season ticket orders. Having such a big pile was fantastic in the long run, but meant a lot of tedious database entry in the short run. Well, it would keep her mind off her dad's predicament.

But first, Karin. And, maybe instead of an email to Karin, a phone call would be in order.

Allie's mobile lit up before she could dial Karin. "Luke, hi," she said, "I'm at the office. Yeah, they released Dad. Are you in the workshop? ... I'm just about to call Karin about what the board decided last night. Oh, wait! You don't know about that yet. Can you come up to the office? There was some good news, before..."

Sixty-Two

"To copy the truth can be a good thing, but
to invent the truth is better, much better."
—*Guiseppe Verdi*

L ike many people with a drab exterior, George Park had a
vibrant inner life. In gray sweaters, gray jackets, gray jeans
and even his hair starting to turn, he was a thin column of gray. Yet,
his social media updates showed a different person: a profile picture with an uncharacteristically jaunty smile and posts that were
exuberant and light-hearted, sometimes to the point of silliness.

Although he wasn't the most inspiring boss in the world, Allie enjoyed working for him. He had made her transition from
summer intern to assistant director go smoothly, treating her with
respect and encouragement. George's lack of a partner puzzled
her. He was certainly presentable and considerate; surely someone somewhere would recognize his value as a friend and lover?
He never talked about any sort of romantic relationship, gay or
straight.

The fact is, for much of his adulthood, George Park loved his
work more than he could love any person. An unfulfilled musician
himself (a self-described failure at becoming an operatic tenor), he
revered the ability of the musicians in the SummerFest Symphony
to rouse emotions deep inside him. He reveled in the cacophony
of violins, flutes, trumpets, bassoons, and other instruments that

floated during the summer from the windows of the converted chicken coop, now full of practice rooms. And he made sure that one or two concerts every summer featured a world-class vocalist.

—ele—

As Allie waited for Luke to appear, she thought about George. Like anyone, George had his secrets. It had surprised Allie to uncover an undercurrent of hostility between him and Sylvia Abbott. It was understandable; Dr. Abbott treated him with disdain. But she treated almost everyone that way, certainly all those she considered of a lesser status than herself. She wasn't singling George out for special abuse, at least as far as Allie could tell. He was always professional in his dealings with Dr. Abbott. He hardly ever spoke disparagingly about her to Allie or anyone else. But Allie had glimpsed real anger, or maybe even hatred, in looks that he'd shot at Dr. Abbott when he thought no one was looking. And she'd seen his lips tighten and his eyes narrow when Dr. Abbott was on the phone to him, though his voice never betrayed any emotion except for courteous respect. Had that hostility become unbearable? Was George capable of violence, even murder?

Luke flew in the door, upending her musings. "What a day!" he said. "In the mid-60s. I love spring. So, what's up, besides your dad getting sprung from the slammer?"

"That's not funny, Luke," protested Allie, suppressing a smile. "I'm so relieved we have an alibi for him. Thank God Kate saw him in the parking lot. Nat thinks the police will drop charges as soon as they talk to her."

"So Kate saw him. Wow, that really helps his case." Luke gave her a quick hug, then continued. "I thought she'd already left the kitchen, but I guess not. I know George was missing by then."

"It was pretty chaotic." Allie agreed as she took a step back. "What do you mean, 'George was missing'?"

"Well, I told you I was scarfing down those two leftover glasses of wine. I looked around to see if George wanted a glass, but I couldn't see him anywhere. So I just swilled them myself. He must have gone to take a leak or something."

"No, George said he went to sit in the last row of the audience for the second half of the concert."

Luke wagged his finger. "Don't think so. That's where he said he would be, so I scanned the back row. No George. At least, I didn't see him."

Allie was puzzled. What seemed so simple was more complicated than she thought. "I'm all confused." She counted on her fingers. "Dad went outside. Kate says she saw him leave. Dad and George say Kate had already left. George says he was sitting in the back row. You say you were sneaking two leftover glasses of wine, but you didn't see George in the back row." She spread her hands. "I don't know who or what to believe."

"Studies have shown that witnesses' memories are totally bogus," said Luke. "Except mine, of course. I mean, I'm absolutely positive George was not in the last row."

"I've read that, too, about memories. People will swear up and down they saw something when, in fact, they didn't." Allie sat down at her desk and started rearranging the stack of mail. "And your memory hasn't always been infallible, you know."

"What do you mean?"

"I think you know."

"Really? What are you talking about?"

Allie continued to shuffle through the envelopes. "Your recollection of our breakup is quite different from mine."

"Come on, Allie," Luke pounded his fist on her desk, making the envelopes scatter. "Will you give it up? You're not the Miss Perfect you think you are!"

Allie watched as he left the office, slamming the door behind him.

Sixty-Three

"The only truth is music."
—*Jack Kerouac*

from: Ken Henson
to: George Park
date: May 5 at 3:53 PM
subject: board decisions

George,

I've spoken with a majority of the board and there's a common feeling that we should revisit the decisions made at last night's meeting, particularly in light of subsequent events.

Due to the fact that David Brewster is now being questioned about the murder, we feel he should be removed from the board posthaste. The by-laws make it clear that board members must be citizens in good standing, which he, a suspected murderer, surely is not.

I would like to call a meeting to vote on reversing the decisions of last night. With the loss of Sylvia and the expulsion of David Brewster, we also need to nominate and ratify two new members. Finally, we must elect a new chair and vice chair. I will personally be campaigning to become the new chair, as I feel the organization is in need of tight management to insure its long-term viability.

Please contact me at your earliest convenience to schedule a meeting. I expect to hear from you before close of business today.

from: George Park
to: Ken Henson
date: May 5 at 4:45 PM
subject: re: board decisions

Hi, Ken,

Thank you for your email of this afternoon. I agree with you that David's arrest was
an upsetting development. However, I would ask you to hesitate before reversing
decisions made by the board last night. There are several considerations, one of
which is that those decisions have already been made public to interested parties
such as our music director and the union's representative. Karin Anders has
probably passed the news along to the musicians. I fear that to go back on that
decision now would have disastrous public relations consequences.

Regarding expelling David Brewster from the board, I believe the case against him
is weak and he will not be charged. In any case, he's innocent until found guilty. If
you think he should be given a leave of absence from the board, that is something
you could discuss with the other members. I ask you to hold off on scheduling a
meeting for several weeks. A possible date would be Monday evening of May 18th.
Let me know if that is acceptable to you.

from: Ken Henson
to: George Park
date: May 5 at 4:48 PM
subject: re: board decisions

George,

George,
If you insist on May 18th, I suppose we'll have to agree. We are not
happy that the board decisions have already been disseminated.
Please put that meeting on the calendar and have the notice of the
meeting mailed to board members.
One last question: do you think it is proper to keep David Brewster's
daughter on staff when he's suspected of murdering her boss?
Shouldn't she be let go?

from: George Park
to: Ken Henson
date: May 5 at 4:51 PM
subject: re: board decisions

No need to fire Allie Brewster. She is vital to the continuing operation of this
organization.

ele

George sighed as he hit "send." David Brewster hadn't killed anybody.

Sixty-Four

"Let me be clear about this: I don't have
a drug problem, I have a police problem."
—*Keith Richards*

Allie watched George out the corner of her eye as she opened the season ticket orders piled on her desk. He was obviously upset about something. He had returned to the office about four o'clock looking, well, frightened was the only word Allie could think of to describe it. Rattled. Shaken. Then he'd opened his laptop and evidently read something that bothered him, because he swore under his breath. Allie had never heard him say "fuck" before. He then began pounding something out on the laptop's keyboard, hitting each key as if it were the cause of his anger.

Now he was pacing around the office. Finally, he stopped and faced her.

"Your dad, Allie...," he began.

"Yes?"

"Uh, how optimistic was Nat that he could get them to drop the charges?"

"With the new support for his alibi, I think Nat was quite optimistic. Why?"

George pursed his lips, seeming to search for an answer. "Well, I wasn't sure I should mention this, but Ken Henson and his friends are thinking they should kick your dad off the board."

Allie didn't say anything. She wasn't all that surprised.

"You know how Ken called me earlier and said they wanted to have a board meeting? Well, they're still at it. They want to kick David off the board and they were hoping to rescind the board's actions from last night. Luckily, you've already told Tony and Karin. I said going back on the deci... what?"

"I didn't reach them yet. So they don't know." Allie didn't want to admit she hadn't wanted to tell them the police had formally accused her father of Dr. Abbott's murder.

"Let's keep that a secret between you and me. And let's contact them right away. I'll call Tony first."

George's mobile rang before he could dial. He spoke in clipped tones to someone who was asking a lot of questions. It must be a reporter, Allie realized.

George set his phone down. "The police held a press conference. I can't believe it. Chief Knowles admitted publicly that they have questioned your father. A reporter asked him if it was true David Brewster was his prime suspect and Knowles didn't deny it."

Allie felt the tears flood her eyes. Now everyone would know. "What should I do, George?" she asked.

George shook his head.

"I'll call Nat," she said. "He'll tell me what to do." Allie dialed the lawyer's number.

"I'm sorry," said Nat's receptionist. "Attorney Roy is meeting with a client right now."

"Is it David Brewster?"

"I'm sorry, miss, I'm not at liberty to say."

"I'm Allegra Brewster, David's daughter. If that's who Nat is meeting with, can you please put me through?"

"Hold on one minute." The receptionist returned in a moment. "Mr. Roy will be with you shortly."

"Allie!" The voice on the phone was her father's, not Nat's. "We just heard Chet held a press conference basically naming me. Nat and I are trying to figure out our next steps. I'm afraid all hell's going to break loose, press-wise."

Allie looked outside. "Dad, there's a WCSH-TV camera truck arriving as we speak. What should I do?"

David and Nat conferred briefly, then Nat spoke to Allie. "Don't talk to them, Allie. If you can, slip out the back. If not, if you have to walk by them, just say 'no comment.' But, if at all possible, try not to go near them. Ok?"

"Yeah, fine. There's a door in the back. I'll go out that way."

Nat had handed the phone back to David. "Allie, don't worry about this," said her father. "Nat and I are confident the police will soon lose interest in me. The evidence from Kate is helpful. I'm sorry you have to go through this, but it will be over shortly. Please try not to worry."

Allie swallowed. "I won't, Dad. I know you're in good hands. Love you."

"Love you, too. And I'll see you at home tonight." After they said goodbye, Allie turned to George. "Can you deal with the TV guys?" she asked him. "I'm going to try to slip out the back."

George looked uncertain, then seemed to gather himself together. "Yes, I'll go tell them we have no comment. I was about to go home, anyway." He straightened his jacket, checked his hair in the bathroom mirror, slipped the laptop in his briefcase, pulled his keys out of his pocket, and stepped out the door. Allie saw a group of people cluster around him, one with a huge camera and another thrusting a mike in his face.

She looked around the office. What a mess. When George had opened the door, some of the mail had fluttered to the floor in the draft. Allie picked up the pieces of paper in an attempt to bring some order to the chaos. One envelope had even made it almost as far as George's desk. As she picked it up, she noticed a crumpled piece of paper under it. This must have come from George's pocket, she thought. She idly pushed it into her own pocket, planning to give it back to him if it amounted to anything important.

Allie exited out the back door, then realized that the way to her car in the parking lot was still blocked by the television van. I'll have to take refuge in the wood shop, she thought. Maybe Luke has left. I really don't want to deal with him right now, either.

Sixty-Five

"Every great inspiration is but an experiment."
—*Charles Ives*

T he sound of hammering in the wood shop made it clear Luke hadn't gone home yet. He looked up as Allie entered, and set down his hammer.

"Sorry to bother you," she said. "But there are a ton of reporters in the parking lot who want to ask me about my father. The police held a press conference and named him."

"Oh, shit. I'm sorry to hear that, Allie." He walked toward her, but she shook her head.

"It's ok, I guess. I talked with Dad and Nat. They seem to think they'll get the charges dropped soon, anyway."

"I'm sure they will," Luke agreed.

"Kate's testimony about seeing Dad in the parking lot will help," Allie added.

"For sure."

Allie remembered the crumpled slip of paper she'd retrieved from the floor by George's desk. Pulling it out of her pocket, she set it on the worktable and smoothed it out.

"What the heck? Look at this," she said to Luke.

The note was lettered in shaky handwriting, as if the writer was highly emotional.

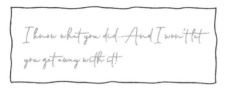

"Where did you get this?" Luke asked.

"It was on the floor by George's desk. I guess it fell out of his pocket. Do you think...?"

"Are you thinking what I'm thinking? We need to take this to the cops." Luke grabbed the paper.

"Wait a minute." Allie thought for a few seconds. "Do you think this means George did it?" Although she'd had some inklings, she still didn't feel convinced it was possible.

"Seems like it."

"But George? I don't know..."

"Look, Allie, if George is involved, then that needs to come out. And remember, every clue that leads to the murderer leads the police away from your father."

"True. Do you really think...?"

"Do I think George did it? Yah, kinda sounds like it." Luke banged his fist on the worktable. "That is so fucked up! I wouldn't have guessed..."

Allie nodded. "Whether or not he did it, someone is trying to blackmail him. Or threaten him."

Luke pulled out his phone. "I'm calling the police."

"Hold on. Let's think this through." Allie sighed. "At the moment, I don't have a lot of faith in the police to draw the right conclusion."

"I can understand that. Alright, what should we do?" They both sat down on the stools scattered by the bench.

"Here's an idea," said Luke. "What if I tail George? I'm bound to find out something incriminating."

"Come on, Luke," Allie said. "As if you know how to tail someone. He'll be on to you in a second."

"Ok, how about if we confront him with the note and we record what he says and then play that back for the cops?"

"What if he acts dumb? I mean, his name isn't anywhere on the paper. He could deny any knowledge of it and then he'd know we suspect him. That could be dangerous for us."

They both sat with slumped shoulders, temporarily stymied.

I know!" said Allie. She brushed her hair off her shoulder. "Let's have Chief Knowles meet with George and us tomorrow. We'll pull out the slip of paper then, and Chief Knowles will ask George to explain. George will be so shocked that he'll crumble. What do you think?"

"It might work. But where? We want there to be an element of surprise. If George knows Knowles is coming to the SummerFest office, he'll put his armor up."

They thought for another few moments.

"How about this?" said Luke. "You go to the cops and convince them to come to the SummerFest office." Luke ran his hand through his curls. "Meanwhile, I'll tell George there's something I'm working on that I need to talk over with him, or some excuse like that. We'll time it so the cops show up without warning George. That way, he won't have time to suspect anything before we hit him with the note."

"I think that might work." Allie wasn't a hundred percent sure George would fall for it but she couldn't think of a better plan. "I'll take the note with me," she said.

"Why not leave it here with me?"

She shot Luke a cool stare. "This is really important, getting my father out. I want to keep that note with me every second until we use it."

"Ok, fine. So you still don't trust me."

"It's not that." Allie shrugged her shoulders. "I just trust myself more. And if something should happen to the note, I'd have to be mad at myself instead of at you."

"Yeah, right." Luke said. "What are you going to do now? Do you want to grab some grub? And when do you think we should have this show-down with George and the cops?"

"Right now, I'm going home. Dad should be there. And how about tomorrow morning, around ten o'clock? I think that should work. As long as we can get Chief Knowles to come. I'll let you know from the police station when he's on his way. Then you can make sure George is in the office."

"Sounds good. Can I do anything else to help, Allie?" He reached for her sleeve.

She let him hold it for a second, then shook her arm. "No, Luke, this is enough," she said, stashing the note in her jacket pocket.

"Wait, let me at least make sure the reporters have gone," said Luke. He walked out of the wood shop and around toward the parking lot. "The coast is clear," he called out.

Allie gave him a quick kiss on the temple as she walked past him on her way to the car. "Thanks, Luke. I mean it."

—ell—

Realizing that there wasn't even any peanut butter at home, Allie reluctantly stopped at the grocery store. She was afraid she'd bump into someone she knew or, worse yet, someone who knew her and knew about the charges against her father. She quickly put a few things in her basket and strode to the cashiers, choosing one without a line.

"Allegra!" Mina Treat, just about the last person Allie wanted to see, joined her in line.

"Oh, hi, Mina," she said.

"So sorry to hear about your father. It's quite unbelievable. I mean, I always thought he was the sweetest guy around."

"He didn't do anything, Mina." Allie avoided the cashier's curious look and paid for the food. She grabbed the bag and walked quickly out of the store, while Mina proceeded to explain the story to the cashier. "Well, you know that murder case at the Summer-Fest Concert Barn two weeks ago? Her fath..." Mina's voice was cut off as the automatic doors closed behind Allie.

Music. Something to push Mina's voice out of her mind. Allie turned on the radio and *Somebody That I Used to Know* by Gotye[36] filled the car. The slightly menacing, angst-ridden vocals matched her dark mood. She turned it way up, lip-syncing to the words.

As Allie turned into the driveway, she saw the same television van parked in front of the house. She quickly reversed the car and sped away, gravel spitting out from under the wheels.

Sixty-Six

"Without craftsmanship, inspiration is a
mere reed shaken in the wind."
—*Johannes Brahms*

K ate opened the door. The mudroom was bright behind her
and Kate's smile was welcoming. "Allie! Come on in. This is
a nice surprise."

"Have you heard?" Allie asked her.

"Heard what?"

"Chief Knowles held a press conference this afternoon and
told the world that they'd brought Dad in for questioning about
Dr. Abbott's murder." Allie's voice cracked. "And now everyone
knows."

"Oh, Allie. I'm so sorry. Come on in."

"The television news van is now parked in front of our house.
That's why I came here."

"Where's your dad? Is he at home?"

"No, I didn't see his car." Allie checked her phone. She had
turned it off earlier to conserve the battery, which died quickly
these days. Turning it off had the added benefit of sending reporters' calls to voicemail. But she'd also missed the text from
her dad, saying he decided to have dinner with Nat so they could
continue their work on the case.

"Oh, thank god," Allie said. "He's still with Nat. I'll send him a text and warn him about the reporters." She typed in the message and got a quick reply, saying he'd be along in a couple of hours and they'd probably be gone by then. Allie let him know she was at Kate's for the time being.

"Have you eaten?" asked Kate, pulling her into the kitchen.

"No but I'm not hungry right now," said Allie. "These last few days..."

Kate gave her a hug. "I know it's been tough. But your dad should be exonerated soon, don't you think?"

"I hope so. Your testimony about seeing him in the parking lot will help, that's for sure."

Kate nodded. "Hey, come try some mac'n cheese. You know, my special recipe."

"The one with the hidden broccoli?" Allie smiled tiredly. "Ok, I'll try a little for old times' sake."

"So," Kate said, dishing out some macaroni. "Nat and your dad called me this afternoon and we talked about what I saw. They seemed to think that would help get the police off David's back."

Kate set a plate of food on the table in front of Allie, who picked at it. "Something else has come up, Kate, that I think will also help."

"Like what?" Kate pulled out a chair and sat down across from Allie.

"I found this blackmail note to George."

"What!" Kate leaned forward.

"Yeah. It's a note that says something like, 'I know what you did' written in a threatening-looking scrawl. Luke and I figure it must be from someone who knows something."

"Wow," Kate whispered. "So what are you going to do?"

"Well, we figure that if we showed the note to George ourselves, he'd just deny having anything to do with it. And if we take it to the cops, there's nothing on it to link it directly to George, and they'll be skeptical."

"So...?"

"So, we're trying to set up a situation where we surprise George with the note in front of the police. We're hoping the shock will lower his defenses and he'll confess."

"Sounds pretty iffy. I don't know, Allie." Kate shook her head.

"Well, what would you do?" asked Allie.

"I think I'd keep the note for backup, maybe, but try to find some other proof, too. Maybe he'll get another note from the blackmailer that's more incriminating."

"But I want to get this cleared up as soon as possible! Every day that the police don't know George is the killer is another day they think my father is." Allie pushed her plate away.

"Ok, ok. So, what's your plan. Did you and Luke cook something up?"

"Yes. Luke's going to keep George distracted in the office and meanwhile I'll go to the police station and get them to come back with me."

"And when is this all going to happen?"

"Tomorrow morning. Around ten, if all goes according to plan."

Kate looked worried. "I wish you weren't involved," she said.

"I've been involved right from the start, Kate. Remember," she added, "I found the body."

"I'm well aware of that," said Kate.

"Hey, Allie," said Harris from the doorway. "I thought I heard your voice. I saw some stuff online about your dad..."

"I know, I know," Allie said. "But he's innocent."

"I"m glad," said Harris. "It's so terrible. A murder in Kennimac. Who'd've thought?"

"Harris, did you finish your homework?" Kate jumped up from the table and shepherded him to the stairs.

"I'm going to try going home again, Kate. Good to see you, Harris. Keep the faith about my dad." Allie called to them as they headed upstairs.

"Bye, Allie. Be careful. Rethink those plans," Kate called back.

"What plans?" asked Harris.

Sixty-Seven

"There was no one near to confuse me,
so I was forced to become original."
—*Joseph Haydn*

"We thought you should see this. It came for George Park."
Standing in front of the police officer's desk, Allie held out the note for Officer Ouellette to see.

"And you came by this how?" she asked, getting some tweezers and a plastic bag. Carefully, she deposited the note in the bag without touching it.

"I think it came in the SummerFest mail yesterday."

"It was addressed to you?" Cheri Ouellette didn't seem impressed.

"Oh, no! George had it. It fell out of his pocket and I picked it up off the floor after he left. We thought it seemed pretty incriminating."

"Who's 'we'?"

"Lucas O'Donnell and I."

"Is the envelope still around?" Officer Ouellette turned the plastic bag this way and that, as if to find some additional secret message on the note.

"It's probably back in the office. I should have thought to look for it," added Allie.

"Let's hope we can find it." The officer looked at Allie. "I need to show this to the chief."

"Of course."

"Wait here." Ouellette turned and headed down the hallway.

In a few minutes, Chief Knowles lumbered out to the front desk. He motioned to Allie to follow him back to his office. Holding the baggie in his hand as he squeezed behind his desk, he said, "Here, sit down. Now tell me how you came by this, Allegra. From the beginning."

"It might have been in the mail when I picked it up on my way to work about 11:00 yesterday morning. There was a lot of mail. I didn't notice it." Allie stopped for a breath. "George looked through the mail and separated his mail out. He must have taken it."

"Uh-huh. And..."

"So then I found it later. He had dropped it. So I picked it up and read it. And we thought it was important."

"We?"

"I showed it to Luke O'Donnell."

"So you both put your fingers all over this note."

Allie was surprised the chief wasn't happier about the fact that she'd brought in the note. "Yeah, I guess we did."

"And George Park held it, too, right?"

"I guess so."

"Ok, I know we have your fingerprints on file from the investigation, and George's, but I'm not sure about O'Donnell's. Where is he? Why didn't he come with you?"

"We were afraid you might not take this seriously. So we've arranged for you to show the note to George—to surprise him with it—in hopes he'll break down and confess."

"Is he coming here?" Knowles looked rather disgusted with the whole idea.

"No, that would make him suspicious and he'd have a chance to concoct an excuse. Or a denial. We thought it would be better if you'd come to the SummerFest office and meet him there."

"For Pete's sake, this seems pretty harebrained." The chief turned his attention to some papers on his desk.

"Chief Knowles?"

"What?"

"Will you come?"

"In a moment. I want to finish up with this paperwork first."

"Do you think this will this change the case against my father?"

"It's too early to tell that, Allegra. I'm not at all convinced yet."

"And also, don't forget we found someone who saw Dad in the parking lot after intermission that afternoon. Kate Zeller."

"Well, we're going to talk to Kate again. Now go wait in the outer office while I finish up."

***

Allie sat on the hard wooden bench, the spindles digging into her back. First she texted Luke:

chief not excited. i'll wait. don't talk to george yet

He texted back:

fine I need to haul some lumber from behind the concert barn. I'll wait to hear from u

Then Allie checked her messages. Karin had sent her four texts, asking what had happened at the board meeting Monday night. Her father had sent her a text an hour ago, telling her he would be at Nat Roy's office again if she was looking for him.

The sounds of the busy municipal office swirled around her—phones ringing, people talking, dispatch radios blaring, doors opening and closing, copy machine whirring. She sat, engrossed in her email, after deciding not to respond immediately to Karin. Suddenly, Office Ouellette and Chief Knowles came barreling down the hall.

"Was it Lucas O'Donnell we were going to meet?" asked the chief.

Allie nodded.

"We just got a 911 call from him," said Officer Ouellette. "There's been some sort of incident at the SummerFest wood shop."

Sixty-Eight

"To some extent, I happily don't know
what I'm doing." —*David Byrne*

T he police car was already disappearing up the road by the
time Allie got into her car to follow. Her hands shook as she
turned the key and the engine sputtered and stopped. "Come on,
Pablo!" she shouted, banging on the steering wheel. As if on cue,
the radio blared on with the dauntingly thunderous chords from
the first movement of Schubert's *Symphony No. 8, Unfinished.*[37]
Allie switched off the radio and tried the key again. This time
the engine coughed but caught. Allie drove out of the parking lot
and headed down the road, her mind in a panic. Luke! What had
happened? Was he ok?

As she pulled into the driveway of the SummerFest campus,
an ambulance screamed in beside her. Oh my God, Allie thought,
Luke is hurt! She parked the ancient Volvo wagon and jumped out.
The ambulance continued down the driveway toward the wood
shop. Allie ran behind it.

"Luke!" He was standing just outside the door to the wood shop,
looking pale but unharmed. "What happened? Are you alright?"
Allie rushed to him and wrapped her arms around him. He didn't
respond.

"What happened?" she asked again, stepping back and looking
at his stricken expression.

"George..." Luke answered. "Geor... Ugh, I'm going to be sick again." He ran to the side of the building and vomited. Allie was right behind him.

"What about George? Luke?" She turned and looked at the wood shop. The EMTs were wheeling a stretcher into the doorway.

"George is... George is..." Luke struggled to regain composure. "I think he's dead."

"Dead! What? Was there an accident? What happened?"

"I went to get the lumber. I hadn't told George to come see me yet. When I carried the lumber into the wood shop I didn't notice anything. I dropped it and it fell on the floor with a loud noise. But then everything was quiet again and I heard something ... there was this sound, a sort of gurgling, coming from behind the workbench." He looked down at his feet. "It was George."

"Oh my God."

"He'd been stabbed. Like Abbott was. In the throat. He was barely alive. I went to him... I didn't know what to do, Allie!"

Allie held his trembling shoulder, trying to calm him.

"He was talking but I couldn't understand. All I got was something like 'Watch out. Ok.' At least, that's what it sounded like." Luke rubbed his face. "Then he made this horrible sound. He was dying!" Luke started crying.

"Oh, Luke!" Allie wrapped her arms around him. "Poor George. How awful!"

"I called 911," Luke croaked.

"I know. I know." Allie rubbed his back. Luke looked at her as she wiped the tears from his cheek. "The EMTs are here."

Chief Knowles walked over to the pair. "Lucas O'Donnell, right?" he said to Luke.

"Yes." Luke and Allie turned to face the large red-faced man.

"Is this yours?" The chief held up a baggie. Inside was a small metal tool with a sharp point, covered in blood. Recognizing it, Allie gasped.

"That's my spindle gouge!" Luke said in surprise. "How did you get it? Where was it?"

"I think you know, Luke," said Chief Knowles. "Officer Ouellette," he nodded to the young female officer, "Please bring this man to the station for questioning." He turned back to Luke. "Lucas O'Donnell, you're under suspicion for the attempted murder of George Park."

Luke looked as if he didn't understand what Chief Knowles had just said to him. But Allie knew. "No, Chief Knowles, that's not possible! Luke couldn't have done it. He called 911!"

"Wait!" Luke held up his hand. "Attempted murder? Are you saying George is still alive?"

"Barely," answered the police chief.

"Will he live? How bad is it?" asked Allie. She ran over as the EMTs wheeled the stretcher out of the wood shop. George was under a blanket. One of the EMTs, a young woman in a blood-spattered jumpsuit, was holding a bandage to George's neck. An oxygen mask had been placed over his nose and mouth. His skin was slack gray and his eyes were closed. "He's not conscious," said the EMT. "Please back away."

Allie whirled around to the chief. "Luke had nothing to do with this, Chief Knowles. Please believe me."

"The police will be the judge of that. Opportunity and weapon—we're only lacking the motive. And I'm sure that will become evident soon."

Officer Ouellette turned to Luke. "Will you come willingly?" she asked. Luke nodded and followed her to the police car. He got in the back seat and looked through the window at Allie, still not seeming to register what was happening.

"I'm coming, too," Allie said to the chief. "I'll meet you there." As she spoke, more cars arrived. The medical examiner, Dr. Green, got out of one.

"Chief Knowles," she said, "You're not doing a very good job of keeping your folks alive."

"That's not funny," said the chief. "And this one is still alive, at least for now. Allegra, you can go to the station. But you can't talk to your friend for quite a while. We have many questions for him." He stopped for a moment. "One thing, though. This may put your father in the clear." He signaled to one of the other police officers to give him a ride to the station.

Allie got into her car and sat. Her mind was in tumult. George, someone attempted to murder him? Why? And Luke, in custody? Accused of the attack?

Her phone buzzed with a text from her father:

Allie, I'm still with Nat Roy. Want me to pick anything up on the way home?

As if on automatic pilot, Allie texted back

something bad happened – i might be late

The old car started on the first try, and she headed toward town and the municipal building, this time driving more slowly. I need to talk to someone, she thought. I feel like I can't think clearly. Maybe Kate can help. When she got to the parking lot at the police station, she sent a text:

kate r u there? i need to talk

Allie waited a few minutes but Kate must have been busy. She locked the car and went inside.

Sixty-Nine

"We do not play the piano with our fingers but with
our mind." —*Glenn Gould*

At the police station, Allie was told to wait. She resumed her
seat on the same uncomfortable bench she had left about an
hour ago. Was it only an hour? It seemed like days had passed.

Allie sat miserably, watching the comings and goings of the
office. People paying parking tickets, making complaints about
neighbors' dogs. The medical examiner, Dr. Green, rushed past
the reception area, asking where the chief was, and followed
the hall toward his office. When Allie asked if she could make a
statement, she was told that all the on-duty officers were busy.

She got up and walked outside with her phone. Kate didn't pick
up. Allie had a moment of panic—what if Kate had been attacked,
too?—then calmed down. Kate was probably driving one of the
boys to an after-school activity. She left a voicemail. "Kate, I'm at
the police station. Something awful has happened. Give me a call
when you can."

Next she tried her father. Again, the call went immediately to
voicemail, but Allie decided to send a text. It was likely he would
see that before he listened to any phone messages:

dad, geo was attacked. don't kmow if he's alive. police think it was luke
– i don't believe it. i'm at the station waiting to be interviewed

He called back immediately. "Allie, what on earth? I'm still at Nat's." Allie could hear a voice in the background, then her father came back on. "Can I put you on speaker phone? Nat wants to hear this, too."

Allie's legs seemed weak; she wished she could sit down. She felt as though she was reliving the afternoon when she discovered Dr. Abbott's body. She took a shaky breath. "Luke and I had found a note we thought implicated George in the murder. It looked like someone was blackmailing him or something."

"A note? I thought you said George was attacked."

"Hold on. I'm getting to that." Allie tried to slow her breathing down, to help her get a handle on the sequence of events of the past few hours. "So, we found this note, and I took it to the police. We were going to get Chief Knowles to confront George with the note in the SummerFest office."

"Ok." Her father's calm voice reassured her.

"While I was waiting for the chief at the police station, a 911 call came in—it turned out to be from Luke—that something had already happened at the wood shop. So the police went running out and I followed. When I got there, I saw Luke." She paused to get control of herself.

"And..." This time Nat was the one urging her on.

"And when I got there, Luke told me he had gone to the wood shop and while he was there, he found George lying on the floor. George had been attacked the same way Dr. Abbott had been. Luke called 911 and tried to help George but he thought he was dying."

"That George was dying?"

"Right. The ambulance came and they took him to the hospital. He was still alive when they left. I don't know if he is now. And then, Chief Knowles told Luke he was under arrest for attempted murder."

"What did Luke say or do at that point?" asked Nat.

"Nothing! He seemed completely out of it. I think he was happy to hear George hadn't died yet, though." Allie stopped for a moment. "One thing. Chief Knowles showed us the tool George had been attacked with, and it was Luke's."

Allie could hear Nat and her father take a sharp intake of breath.

"And another thing. The chief told me this probably meant they would not think you were involved with Abbott's murder, Dad."

"Well, that's good news," said Nat.

"In the midst of terrible news," said David.

"Dad, I know Luke couldn't have done something like this. He just couldn't have." She had a thought. "Would you be able to defend Luke, Nat, if my dad isn't under suspicion anymore?"

"Luke does need legal representation," said Nat. "But who provides that is a decision for Luke and his family. My immediate concern is to make sure your father is off the suspect list."

"Then, what should I do to help Luke, Nat?"

"Give the police as complete and thorough a statement as you can," said Nat.

"And after that, Allie," her father added, "go home. I'll be home soon."

Seventy

"Don't only practice your art, but
force your way into its secrets."
—*Ludwig Van Beethoven*

E ventually, Allie had a chance to tell her version of the morning's events to Officer Thomas, who didn't seem overly impressed. He kept trying to get her to say there had been some
sort of nefarious connection between George and Luke, but Allie
remained steadfast in her denial of this.

She was sure Luke hadn't been the one to attack George. It
was his tool, though, that had been used. She remembered how
strange he had acted when she saw it a few weeks ago. He had
been mysteriously defensive. Why? And why was he working with
that tool, anyway? He didn't do any carving in his job in the shop.

Allie knew her father had said she should go home but she
wanted to head up to the SummerFest office before then. With
all the cataclysmic events of the last 24 hours, there was still some
office work that needed to be carried on. And with George out
(possibly permanently, she shuddered), she felt responsible for
keeping things going.

The wood shop was taped off with crime scene tape, and it
looked as if the crime scene investigators were still at work in
there. Allie parked and went into the office. A pile of mail still
covered her desk, eliciting a groan from her. Then she remem-

bered the missing envelope the fateful note had been delivered in. Maybe she could find it. The only thing in the wastebasket next to George's desk was a crumpled envelope. Eureka! Allie wrapped a kleenex around her fingers and gingerly lifted the envelope out. Yes, it looked like that was the envelope the message had been delivered in. Allie set it on George's desk, figuring that the police would come to pick it up soon.

Then she turned to her desk. Well, she couldn't start opening and processing the ticket orders; that would have to wait for another day. She opened her laptop and saw the number of text messages and emails had mounted during the day. Many were from Karin, who was frantic to find out the conclusion of the board meeting. Allie decided she should let Karin know the outlines of the board's decisions, at least. Someone deserved to hear some good news...

She first sent Karin a short text:

board mtg much better than expected. no pay cut. other stuff (not good) happening. more later

Karin quickly responded:

No pay cuts! HOORAY! I await further details. Sorry other stuff not good. Hope not serious.

Allie hoped that would hold Karin for a while. She didn't feel like explaining the whole mess right now. And she knew the news of the attack on George would upset Karin. Thinking of George, Allie decided to call the hospital to see if there was any information about his condition. She found out he was in intensive care in critical condition, but the nurse at the desk wouldn't tell her anything else. He was alive, at least, if barely.

There was a ping, another message coming in. From Kate:

Sorry, busy. Later.

Allie responded:

terrible attack on george — in ICU same method as abbott. BE CAREFUL. who is next???

Quickly, another message came in from Kate:

He's still alive? Is he conscious? Yes, be careful!

Allie typed her answer:

he's been unconscious and i don't think he'll make it. police think it was luke – not possible

After a few seconds, another message appeared:

You don't think Luke is guilty? Let's be careful. I'll call you later. Better yet, come by the house on your way home.

Allie typed a response:

thnks – if i'm not too late

She thought about who else should know about the attack. Tony, for one. Having George in the hospital was going to make getting the festival ready in time for the start of the season a challenge. She should let the board know, too. But every time she thought of telling people about George, she got stuck on the idea of having to tell them also that the police were blaming Luke. She didn't want to say those words out loud, or type them, or even think them.

But if it wasn't Luke, who was it? Allie decided to make a chart to clarify her thinking.

Who else would have wanted Dr. Abbott dead? Allie tapped her pen against the desk's surface. She needed some music to help her think. Hey, Mozart—wasn't that supposed to make you smarter? Allie smiled grimly to herself; that research had pretty much been discredited. But a bit of Mozart would still be stimulating. Nothing in a major key, though. The subject was too somber for a sunny piece. She found a YouTube recording of Mozart's *Symphony No. 40 in g minor*.[38] The repeated motive that started off the first movement seemed fitting, as if Mozart was asking an important question.

The office phone rang over the music and Allie let it go to voicemail. She noticed there were quite a few messages in the voicemail box. Groaning, she decided she'd better listen to a few, in case they were important. The recent calls were from reporters;

somehow they had already learned of the attempt on George's life. No way was she prepared to talk to the press. And if they were calling now, they were likely to be showing up in person soon. Allie thought she might as well go home. She'd stop at Kate's on the way. Maybe Kate would be able to help her figure out who the real culprit was.

As Allie walked to her car, she noticed an object on the ground reflecting the low sun's rays. Curious, she walked along the path that led behind the barn, to get close enough to examine the shiny object. At about ten feet, she stopped, dumbfounded. It was a distinctive silver hair comb, its geometric design created by a Native American artist. Allie knew that comb. She picked it up and put it in her pocket, fingerprints be damned.

Seventy-One

"To listen is an effort, and just to hear is no merit. A duck hears also." —*Igor Stravinsky*

Allie sat in the driver's seat for several minutes without starting the engine, turning the silver comb over and over, as if looking for a clue. How did Kate's New Mexico comb end up on the gravel path between the parking lot and the wood shop? It wasn't there yesterday; she hadn't seen it earlier, and it wasn't dusty or dirty as if it had been there for a long time. Besides, Kate wore it often. Allie thought she remembered it in Kate's hair the last time she saw her.

What was the meaning of this? Allie almost didn't dare to think. What connection did Kate have with Sylvia Abbott? They both were sailors? That wasn't a motive.

It was true, though, Kate had been acting weird lately. The woman who'd been Allie's confidante and supporter had been strangely distant. But it couldn't be what I'm thinking, Allie admonished herself. It's not possible. Kate's not a violent person. And whoever killed Dr. Abbott had tried to commit murder again. Certainly, that person was vicious and violent.

Allie talked herself out of considering that Kate might be that person. She put the comb in her pocket. Then she started up the Volvo and drove to Kate's house. Kate's car was in the driveway. Allie parked behind it.

The front door was ajar. As Allie pushed it open, she knocked, but no one seemed to hear her. A Bruce Springsteen song, *Brilliant Disguise*[39], was playing somewhere in the background.

"Hello?" Allie ventured. "Kate? Anybody home?" Allie stepped into the unlit mudroom. "Kate? Harris? Chris?"

"Chris and I are in the kitchen." Kate's voice floated down the hall. "He's just finishing up his homework."

Allie slipped off her shoes, one of Kate's rules, to protect the blond maple-floored home. Allie knew this house as well as she knew her own. After all, for many years, she'd practically lived here. This evening, though, it looked as if a cyclone had gone through. Allie was surprised; Kate was usually emphatic about the boys picking up their things. But today there were jackets on the floor instead of on hooks, and two backpacks were lying haphazardly in the middle of the floor. Several different sizes of sneakers were jumbled with the backpacks, and the rug underneath was bunched up, with school papers sticking out from under it. Allie stepped over the pile and walked on toward the kitchen.

Chris and Kate sat at the table in a circle of light. As Allie came into the room, Chris began gathering up his papers. "Chris has a science report due in a couple of days. We were just working on it." Kate turned to Chris. "Good work, honey. You head upstairs now and get ready for bed. I'll be up soon to say goodnight."

Kate seemed to be in good spirits. She didn't have that downtrodden expression she'd had since Toby's death, or the more frantic appearance she'd sometimes worn recently. She almost seemed like the Kate of old—calm and warmly happy, as she turned on more lights in the kitchen. "I love how long the sunlight stays these days," she said, running to the living room. "It seems like we can get a lot more done in a day. Hang on, I'm just going to turn off the stereo." On her way back in the kitchen, she picked up a plate of cookies. "Harris made these chocolate chip cookies this afternoon," Kate said. "Want one? They're delicious. He experimented with them and added coconut and chopped almonds. They came out really well."

Allie realized she was hungry and reached for a cookie. "Wow," she said, taking a bite, "these are good. I love the added ingredients. Where is Harris?"

"Oh, he's in his room, either studying or listening to music." Kate gathered her long dark hair into an unpinned French twist that uncoiled when she let go. "Allie, it sounds like your day has been wild. I mean, last night your dad and now Lucas being accused of Sylvia Abbott's murder. And George's death. How are you holding up through all this?"

Kate's hair. Allie looked at Kate's hair, normally held back by a silver comb, as it streamed around her shoulders.

"Um, Kate, did you lose your silver hair comb?" Allie wasn't sure how to broach the subject.

Kate reached back and gathered her hair again. "My silver comb? I guess I did. Why do you ask?"

"You usually wear it. Almost every day." Allie fingered the comb in her jacket pocket.

"I guess you're right. But not today." Kate said it lightly, but she looked wary.

"Oh." Allie didn't know what to say next. It would be awkward to now bring the comb out of her pocket and explain where she found it. "Um, Kate, George isn't dead. At least, he wasn't when I called the hospital about an hour ago."

"He's alive? Are you sure?"

"Well, he hasn't regained consciousness. But he was still alive then."

Kate sat down, frowning. "Where is he?"

"He's in the ICU."

Kate pushed away the plate of cookies. "I need to go see him. I need to go right now. Can you stay and make sure Chris gets to bed?" Kate pawed through the items on the counter, looking for her car keys.

"Kate." Allie didn't get a response. "Kate! You can't see him. He's in Intensive Care. No one can see him right now."

"I have to." Kate found her keys and started running toward the door. As soon as she saw her car was blocked by Allie's car, she ran back in.

"Allie, give me your keys. Now. I need them. I have to get to the hospital. Chris, go upstairs," she yelled at the confused boy, who did as he was told, looking back at his mother as he climbed the stairs.

Allie backed away. "Kate..."

"Allie, give them to me. Now!"

Allie reached into her pocket and pulled out the silver comb. Kate stopped as Allie held it up before her.

"Where did you get that?" Kate tried to grab it away from Allie, but Allie quickly drew her hand back.

"It was on the ground on the path to the wood shop."

"Give it to me!" Kate tried to wrench the comb out of Allie's hand. The comb's tines bit into Allie's palm as she held it tightly.

"Then give me your keys. I need your car keys!" Kate lunged at Allie.

"Stop!" Allie ran to the other side of the table. "What is going on, Kate? What have you done?"

"I did what someone had to do."

"Kate, you had something to do with Sylvia Abbott's death?"

Kate grabbed a chef's knife off the counter and pointed it at Allie. "I don't want to hurt you, Allie, but I will if I have to. Just do as I say. Give me your car keys. Now!"

Allie reluctantly tossed her keys on the table. Kate grabbed them and sped out the door, knife in hand. She dashed into the ancient Volvo without bothering to close the car door. Allie watched as Kate tried to get the car to start. Each time, it made a grinding noise without catching. Again and again, Kate turned the key, but to no avail.

In a state of shock, Allie took out her phone to call 911. It didn't respond. The battery was dead.

Crazed with frustration, Kate jumped out of the car and ran back to the house, still clutching the knife.

"Stay right there, Allie," she ordered. "Harris, Chris, get down here right now. We're going somewhere. Chris! Harris!"

The two came down the stairs, both looking scared.

"Hurry! Grab your jackets and shoes and jump in the car." Kate ran out to her car, which appeared to be blocked in the driveway by the Volvo. She started it up and rammed it over the hedge that separated the Zellers' driveway from their neighbors'. The car lurched forward with a loud crunching sound. Chris, dressed in pajamas and rubber boots and carrying his parka, ran out to the car, but Harris hung back.

Kate leapt out of the car. "Harris, get out here. Hurry!" She jumped back in the driver's seat.

Harris looked at his mother, bit his lip, and shook his head. Just then, a police siren wailed from up the street. Kate covered her eyes and slumped down.

Seventy-Two

"The most exciting rhythms seem
unexpected and complex,
the most beautiful melodies
simple and inevitable." — *W.H. Auden*

The squad car slid to a stop at the top of the Zellers' driveway
and Chief Knowles and Officer Ouelette quickly got out.

Allie pointed to Kate's car. "She has a knife," Allie shouted. "But
I don't think she'd use it."

The Chief and his officer approached the car with their guns
drawn. "Come out of the car with your hands up," Chief Knowles
said.

Chris ran out of the car, holding his arms high, and dashed to the
doorway, where Harris caught him. In a few seconds, Kate slowly
emerged. She threw the knife on the ground and held her hands
up. Officer Ouellette walked to her and patted her down. "She's
clean," she told the chief, as she clipped the handcuffs on Kate.

"Ok," said Chief Knowles, "let's all go in the house and figure out
what's going on."

"How did you know to come?" Allie quietly asked the chief, as
they trooped into the house. "I tried to call 911, but my phone was
dead."

"I did it," said Harris. His mother shot him a look of confusion.
"I knew things were dangerous. I called 911."

Kate was seated at the table. Harris stood behind his mother, his hands gently resting on her sagging shoulders. Kate looked defeated. Allie thought to herself, this is how Kate will look in twenty years.

"Well, ma'am," began Chief Knowles, "We understand that you have confessed to the killing of Sylvia Abbott." He held up his thick palm. "Before you say anything, let Officer Ouellette here read you your rights. Officer Ouellette?"

The young officer folded her hands in front of herself, cleared her throat, and began. "You have the right to remain silent. Anything you say can and will be used against you in a court of law. You have the right to an attorney. If you cannot afford an attorney, one will be provided for you. Do you understand the rights I have just read to you? With these rights in mind, do you wish to speak to me?" Kate didn't respond.

"Ma'am," said Officer Thomas, "I'm sorry but you need to say yes or no."

Kate barely nodded.

"You need to give an audible answer to the question, Mrs. Zeller," said the chief.

"Yes," Kate said in a muffled voice, still looking down.

"Did you... did you kill Dr. Abbott?" Allie couldn't believe what she was asking.

Kate nodded again and sank lower.

"Why, Kate?" she asked softly.

Kate shook her head. Her eyes were closed.

"Kate," Allie asked, "Did you try to kill George, too?"

Kate looked up at Allie, her eyes brimming with tears.

Allie stood, frozen. For a few moments, she was so overwhelmed with a feeling of revulsion that she couldn't look at her dear friend. She thought she was about to vomit.

"Allie." Kate whispered.

Allie forced herself to look at Kate.

"Allie. I had to. Because of what she did to Toby..."

Allie looked at her, not understanding. Kate stood up, gesturing.

"She egged him on, Allie. She told him he was being a wimp and a baby. She even hauled the dinghy out to the float for him. I knew he was scared. The wind was gusting and the waves were building. He was white as a sheet. But he was determined. So determined. And so brave. I didn't want to humiliate him by telling him not to go in front of his brothers and his friends—she had already done a good job of that. Humiliating him. So I didn't stop him. I should have, but I didn't." Kate started sobbing. "And that woman... that evil woman sent him out. She shoved the dinghy—with Toby in it—away from the float. She sent my baby to his death, Allie." Kate pulled her own hair. "I couldn't stand it that she was alive and he was gone. Because of her, my family disintegrated. I have been so angry..." Kate's voice shook.

"And George?" Allie asked. "Why did you attack George?"

"He saw me leave the kitchen after intermission. He started asking me questions. I was afraid he'd figure it out. I... I couldn't risk that. So I told him to meet me at the wood shop..." Kate twisted her hands. "I didn't want to kill him but I didn't know what else to do. I guess I failed at that."

"You're right. He's not dead," Allie said. "At least, not yet."

Kate slumped into a chair and hid her face in her hands. Her shoulders shook. "I'll lose my only two boys. They'll take them away from me! I can't... I can't... I can't"

Allie reached out toward her. "You're ill, Kate. You've been so sad for such a long time. You need help. And I know you wouldn't let an innocent man go to prison."

"I don't care about Luke!" Kate wheeled around, her face savage. "What does he know about love, about children? Little rich boy. He's had everything he ever wanted. What does his life matter? No one depends on him! No one would grow up without him!

No one would... grow up... without his being there..." Kate began weeping again.

"Mom." Harris's voice was eerily calm. "You haven't been here for us for two years, ever since Toby drowned. Look at me, Mom." Harris walked over to his mother and pulled her hands from her face. "When Toby died, it seemed like our mother died, too. You were gone." Tears tracked down his face. "And now you've... I can't believe it was you. You did this." He dropped her hands as if they were hot coals. "It's too much death. It's too much. It has to stop."

Kate grabbed him and hugged him in a tight grip. "But I can't lose you and Chris. I love you. I've lost Toby. I've lost your father."

Harris pulled himself away. "Mom, MOM!"

"Allie," cried Kate. "Help me! I can't lose them. I can't."

"Kate," said Allie. Her voice shook a little but she felt surprisingly calm. "Kate, Chief Knowles will take you to the station." You're a good person, she thought to herself, you've been like a second mother to me. And I love you for that. But what you did was horribly wrong.

"We're going to take you to the station now," explained the Chief. "Do you want to call your lawyer before we leave?"

Kate shook her head. "Wait!" she said. "Chris—my little boy. Where is he... I have to say good-bye. Will you let me do that?" She looked pleadingly at Chief Knowles.

Chris had fled to the stairs, where he sat, watching. His freckles stood out on his pale face and his eyes were wide with fright.

The chief thought for a moment. "We will allow that. But Officer Ouellette will go with you. Remember, you're under arrest."

Kate stood up and turned to Allie. "Will you stay here with the boys tonight? I'm sure Paul will come in the morning to pick them up..." she choked on the words.

"Sure, Kate, you know how much I love Harris and Chris. I'll be happy to stay the night."

"Thank you, Allie," Kate said softly.

Chris had crawled up the stairs and into his bed. His row of stuffed animals stretched along the crack between bed and wall; he clutched his favorite, a soft dolphin, in his arms. "Mom?" he whispered. "What's going on? Why do you have handcuffs? Where are the police going to take you?"

"Oh, Chris." Kate struggled to hold herself together. She took a deep breath. "I have to go away for awhile. But Allie's going to stay here with you and Harris, and Daddy will come in the morning." She forced a smile. "How does that sound?"

"He will? Will you come, too?"

"I'm not sure, honey." She sat on the side of his bed. "But even if I'm not here, you know I love you, right?" She bent down and kissed him.

Chris relaxed. "I love you, too," he said. "And Daddy."

"Goodnight, sweetheart." Kate stood up. "Sweet dreams." She turned away quickly, as tears swarmed into her eyes.

"Ok," she whispered to Officer Ouelette, bitterly. "Ok, you can take me now." Together they walked back down the stairs and to the mudroom, where the chief waited with Allie and Harris. Harris was stone-faced as his mother came near. She shut the door to the mudroom so the sound of their voices wouldn't carry to Chris's room. Absentmindedly, she began picking up the backpacks.

"We need to go now, Mrs. Zeller." Chief Knowles reached for her arm.

"Let go of me!" Kate said, pulling her arm away. "I will go peacefully. But I need to say goodbye to Harris."

Harris's face crumpled. "Mom," he croaked, as she put her arms around him.

"Harris, take good care of your little brother," she said into his hair. "He's going to need you. I'm so sorry..." For a moment she couldn't speak, and kissed his head instead. Then she regained her composure. "You know how much I love you. I'm so sorry about this. I'm so sorry..."

Chief Knowles gently tugged on Kate's arm, and this time she let him lead her away. As they walked out the door, Kate's sobs became heartrending wails, cut off as the door to the police car slammed shut.

Allie thought Harris had the saddest expression she'd ever seen. Lost, hopeless, confused.

"Oh, Harris," she said. "I'm going to call your dad and you can speak with him after."

"No," said Harris, "I'll talk to him first. I want to tell him myself. You can talk afterwards."

Seventy-Three

"Without music, life would be a blank to me."
—*Jane Austen, Emma*

A llie stayed at the house. She didn't sleep very well. Her father had come over for a short while, bringing Thai food he had picked up for their dinner. Allie left the white bag on the counter. It didn't matter that her father had forgotten half the takeout order; neither of them was interested in eating.

Harris finally went to bed, but when Allie looked in, he was lying with his headphones on, his eyes wide open staring at the ceiling. He noticed her in the doorway. She didn't say anything, just nodded, and closed the door.

After her dad left, there was another knock at the door. Luke stood there, disheveled, his glasses crooked on his nose. He didn't smile. Allie opened the door and motioned him to enter.

They sat in silence at the kitchen table for a few minutes, each drinking a glass of water.

Finally, Allie spoke. "What do you know about what happened?"

"I know they brought Kate in. I didn't see her but I could hear talking. They were just about to transport me to the county jail." He paused. "I can't believe it."

"I know," agreed Allie. "This whole thing has been such a nightmare. But this is unreal. I mean, Kate!" She put her face in her hands and began to cry silently.

"Oh, Allie, Allie," said Luke, rubbing her back. "It's over."

"It's not over, not for Kate and the rest of the Zellers." Allie wiped her eyes. "And I thought you were going to go to jail. I knew my father wasn't guilty, but I knew you couldn't have done it, either. I was so worried... Oh, Luke..." She turned to him and he enfolded her in his arms. His neck was warm, his chest felt broad and strong, and his shirt still smelled like sawdust and sweat. Luke began running his hands through her hair. Allie leaned into him, relaxing all her tense muscles. Luke bent down to kiss her and his stomach rumbled. They both laughed ruefully.

"I guess I haven't had much to eat today," he said.

"Dad brought some takeout earlier," Allie said. "It's still sitting on the counter. And Harris made some good cookies this afternoon." Suddenly they were both ravenous.

ele

They decided Luke wouldn't stay the night, since Harris and Chris didn't know he was there. Allie wanted things to be as calm and normal as possible. As if they could be anything close to normal... When Paul Zeller arrived from Boston early the next morning, the boys were clearly relieved to see him.

Allie had helped Chris pack his duffle bag and Harris had packed his. Both boys were mostly silent. Paul stayed for about 30 minutes with the boys, then he said he had to go to the police station to see Kate. And he wanted to find out if Nat Roy would agree to be her defense attorney.

While Paul was still with the boys, Allie called the hospital to see how George was faring. He was still unconscious but now listed in serious condition, an upgrade from critical condition. The nurse at the desk told Allie, "signs look hopeful, although it's still early to tell."

"Will I be able to visit him when he regains consciousness?" Allie asked.

"That will depend. But if he improves substantially, he'll be moved to a regular bed where visitors are welcome. That may be several days away, though."

Allie texted Luke:

geo better but still out – want to come w me to office?

Luke answered in a flash:

good news re Geo! i bet i cant use the wood shop but ill come with u anyway. XO

Allie looked at that "XO" and felt a warm feeling spread throughout her exhausted body.

XO 2 u too

Seventy-Four

"If I were not a physicist, I would probably be a
musician. I often think in music.
I live my daydreams in music.
I see my life in terms of music."
—*Albert Einstein*

A pile of envelopes still covered Allie's desk. She dumped
even more on the pile after stopping at the post office. Since
he couldn't use the wood shop, Luke volunteered to open the
season ticket orders and staple the checks to the forms. He started
to gather up the envelopes and stapler and came upon the chart
of suspects on her desk.

"I'm glad you rated the likelihood of my being the perpetrator
as 'none,'" he laughed.

"Yeah, well look at how I rated Kate. The same as you. Shows
how wrong I was!"

Luke came over and put his arms around her. "Hey, Miss Perfect. You may have been wrong about several things."

"Don't rub it in!" Their kiss heated up, until Allie pulled away.
"Let's hold off on that for now, Luke. There's too much to do."

"Can I take a rain check?"

"I suppose so." She smiled.

Allie returned to making a list of tasks that needed to be done.
Without George to direct her, Allie knew she would have to get

some help besides Luke if the festival were to go on as planned—in just eight weeks.

There was so much to do! The list was endless; it ranged from big responsibilities to minor tasks, but all of them needed tending to. Allie looked through her iTunes library for something to play that would energize her and Luke as they waded through the work in front of them. It couldn't have English lyrics because those would interfere with her thinking. *Cantos de Amor* by the Gipsy Kings[40]—perfect. It was passionate and rhythmic. Allie admired the virtuosic guitar playing and the sense of space the recording created, as if being performed in the midst of a cathedral's beautiful ruins, the guitars and wandering bass echoing around the crumbling stone walls.

She called her father who suggested she look at the list of volunteers and board members and see if she could put an ad hoc emergency crew together.

"Assign us to particular jobs and create check-in points so you can be sure we're following through," he advised. "But don't be afraid to take charge. Right now there's a vacuum waiting to be filled. If and when George comes back, he can make adjustments. But for now, it's up to you, Allie, my girl."

That was all Allie needed to start formulating a plan. She started putting names next to the tasks she'd listed. But what was missing? She had never been near the helm of the festival during the summer. No doubt there were many details that she didn't know of. She thought of Tony. He might know about some of the things she'd left off her list. She put in a call to him and to her surprise, he picked up.

"Allie, what's up?" he asked.

"Hi, Tony. I wanted to bring you up to date on what's been happening here."

"Good or bad?"

"Both, I think. First of all, the murderer has confessed." Allie paused for a second, and inhaled.

"Good God, love, don't keep me in suspense! Who is it?"

"No one we thought. Kate Zeller. She was a volunteer at the fundraiser. Her son, Toby, drowned in a sailing accident two years ago and she blamed Dr. Abbott. I guess she became obsessed..."

"And not a little deranged," added Tony. "How did the police catch her?"

"She tried to kill George in the wood shop at the festival. She thought he suspected her. But that finally led to her exposure as the killer."

"Bloody hell! Who figured it out?" Allie thought Tony seemed a little too wrapped up in the drama of it all.

"I did. I found something of hers near the wood shop." Allie stopped for a moment. "Tony, she was a close friend of mine. She has two sons. It's a tragedy all around." Allie was afraid she was going to start crying again. Luke came over and put him arm around her, hugged her to his side, and kissed her closed eyelids. Inhaling deeply again, Allie went on, "It still doesn't seem real, the whole thing. It seems like a fictional murder mystery or something. I can't believe it happened..."

"Allie, I'm terribly sorry," Tony said. "I know this whole thing's been difficult for you and George. You said some of the news was good? Tell me the good stuff. Is George ok?"

Allie extricated herself from Luke's embrace, giving him a reassuring smile. "He's in serious condition in the intensive care unit at the hospital. I don't know if he'll be ok but his condition is improving. He's still unconscious, though."

"What happened?"

"She tried to... to do the same thing to George she did to Dr. Abbott." Allie had a hard time getting the words out. "She thought he was going to expose her."

"I'm coming to Maine," Tony blurted out. "You'll need help if we're to get the festival going this summer, and I want to be there when George wakes up." Tony tried to put a light touch on it. "I want my ugly mug to be the first thing he sees!"

Allie laughed a bit. "Tony, that would be fantastic. Do you want me to find you a place to stay?"

"Oh, heavens no. That's what I pay Ted for. I'll ask him to book me into that chatty woman's B&B; the house I usually rent in the summer won't be available yet."

"The Kennimac Inn. RuthEllen Cox will be thrilled to have you as a guest. Do you want to hear the good news I mentioned?"

"By all means."

"Two nights before George was attacked... Holy crap, that was just a few nights ago... The board met on Monday and decided to forget the earlier offer to the musicians and revert to the former contract."

"Marvelous!"

"Wait, it gets better—they voted to offer a three-percent raise!"

"That's incredible. Who do we have to thank for that?"

Allie was momentarily distracted as Luke signaled he was leaving for a short time. "Dad and Esther Swift."

"She's a darling. And your father's a pip. I'll have to thank them by taking them out to dinner while I'm in Maine. How did the rest of the board react?"

"It was almost unanimous! And another thing, Tony, you wouldn't believe how many season tickets we've sold. I'm getting worried that we won't have any open seats for people to buy. You know, for people who can only attend one or two concerts on the spur of the moment."

"That's a fine problem to have, indeed! Look, when I get there, you and I will do a bit of strategizing. We'll make sure we have full houses and happy patrons. Allegra, I think we've got a huge success on our hands. Hard to believe where we were a short time ago. Listen, love, I want you to join the cello section this summer. I've been meaning to mention it but haven't had a chance with all the bloody chaos. Would that suit you?"

"I'd love to. I'd better get practicing—I have to confess I haven't been putting in the time..."

"No worries. You'll be back in fine shape by the time we start. That's settled, then. Look, I'll have Ted let you know about my travel plans. So, next time we talk, it will be in person."

"That's so great, Tony. I really appreciate it. I know Dad and George will, too. Thanks."

As she hung up, Luke slipped back in the door, one hand behind his back.

Seventy-Five

"Music is the divine way to tell
beautiful, poetic things to the heart."
—*Pablo Casals*

"Tony is coming to Maine." Allie shared the news. "And he asked me to play in the orchestra this summer!"

"So I gathered." Luke walked toward her, one hand still hidden. "I was going to give this to you for your birthday, but I decided now would be a better time. I had to sneak past the yellow crime scene tape to get it."

"What?"

Luke held out the object he'd been hiding. It was a small block of wood with an indentation on the top and a piece of sticky rubber covering the bottom. He had carved waves, fish, sailboats, and musical notation along the sides of the block.

"It's an endpin rest for my cello!" Allie turned the block of wood around and around in her hands, tracing the carvings with her finger. "Luke, it's beautiful! I didn't know you could carve like this. It's so detailed." She stopped for a moment and looked up. "That's what you were using the spindle gouge for."

"Yes. I hope you won't hold that against my creation. I mean, the fact that its tool was turned into a murderous weapon."

Allie thought, then answered. "You know, Kate used her marlin spike the first time, but that won't put me off sailing. So I won't blame this piece of art for what happened to George."

She gave Luke a hug. "It's so perfect, Luke. I can't wait to use it. This means so much to me. I know, it's lunchtime. Let's go to my house. I'll try it out and you can see how well it works."

— ele —

Allie was glad her father wasn't home. She took out her cello and set the endpin into the indentation on the top of the block. It fit perfectly. She thought for a second then picked up her bow and started to play a fews bars of the sexiest song she could think of, Jeremy Messersmith's "I Want to Be Your One Night Stand."[41] As soon as Luke caught on, he sang with her, *I'm not worried, no, I've got it planned, I want to be your one night stand.*

— ele —

Shortly thereafter, the music stopped and the cello leaned silently against its case, abandoned for the time being.

Seventy-Six

"Simplicity is the final achievement. After one has
played a vast quantity of notes and more notes, it is
simplicity that emerges as the crowning
reward of art." —*Frederic Chopin*

George's faded gray Prius was back in the parking lot. Allie
hefted her cello case and headed toward the concert barn
for rehearsal. The office door was open and Allie peeked in as
she walked by. There was George, pacing around the office as
usual, rearranging the items on the bookshelves as he talked on
the phone. He was wearing a colorful madras plaid short-sleeve
shirt with a paisley neckerchief hiding his partially healed scar.
Allie caught his eye and waved, mouthing the words "It's starting!"
George returned her smile and made a thumbs-up motion with his
free hand.

Allie wondered if George would ever get his full voice back.
George had confessed he was the person who serenaded the
peepers on the night of Sylvia Abbott's murder. "My only solo
engagement," he'd said with his newly croaky voice, "but what a
backup chorus! Of course, now I sound more like one of them."
Allie shook her head, wondering how she ever could have thought
George was guilty of murder. The mysterious—but not actually
incriminating—note she'd found was from his boyfriend, Grant,
whom George had been keeping secret. Grant wrote the note

because he was angry George once again backed away from their relationship. After the attack, George found the courage to say yes to love. They planned to marry in the fall, after the SummerFest ended.

Walking down the hill to the barn, Allie could hear the faint sounds of the orchestra warming up. Random musical sounds came from the practice rooms in the renovated chicken coop as she passed by. Allie practically danced as she approached the barn's open doors. Beyond the barn in the distance, the bay glimmered. It was a sunny day but not too warm, and she would be playing Dvorak's New World Symphony[42] with the SummerFest Symphony. What could be better? She waved to Thomas as he sped into the parking lot, a glamorous blonde in his passenger seat. She looks more like L.A. than Kennimac, Allie thought. Wonder how long she'll last here.

As she passed through the doorway, Luke joined her. "That's a big smile," he said, smiling back. "Something tells me you're feeling better about things, Al."

"Much. Although..." Allie frowned as a thought of Kate flashed through her mind. Then, quickly, she returned to the day at hand.

"Luke, it's the New World," she said, laughing.

"Hallelujah," he responded. "Both for the music and the end of uncertainty. All uncertainty," he added, with a significant look at Allie.

"Fine," she agreed. "All uncertainty."

She gave him a quick kiss and turned toward the stage, eager to join the other cellos. Setting her case down, she opened it and located the intricately carved piece of wood, setting it down before her chair at the end of the cello section. Luke watched from the back of the hall as Allie carefully fitted her cello's peg into the wooden stop and lifted the honey-colored instrument to her cradling arms. Above the random snatches of scales and Dvorak excerpts ricocheting around the stage, he was sure he could hear the singular soulful timbre of Allie's cello rising to meet the rafters of the old barn.

THE END

1. Music listed in the book is available as a Spotify Playlist, "DISSONANCE, the Novel": https://open.spotify.com/playli st/0zncQBBFV9d2xYp89ZTXFO
2. Tchaikovsky, Peter Illyich, Serenade for Strings in C Major, Op. 48
3. Stravinsky, Igor, Firebird Suite
4. Handel, George Frideric, Water Music
5. Elgar, Edward, Cello Concerto in E minor, Op. 85.
6. Holst, Gustav, "Mars, the Bringer of War," from The Planets, Op. 32 (James Levine conducting the Chicago Symphony)
7. 2Cellos, Let There Be Cello, "Imagine" (John Lennon)
8. Bach, J.S., Cello Suites (Yo-Yo Ma, soloist)
9. Dvořák, Antonin, Cello Concerto (Rostropovich, soloist)
10. Tchaikovsky, Pyotr Ilyich. Variations on a Rococo Theme, Op. 33
11. Satie, Erik, Gymnopédie No.1
12. Mahler, Gustav. Symphony 5 in C-sharp Minor
13. Arcade Fire, "The Suburbs"
14. Davies, Peter Maxwell, "Farewell to Stromness"
15. Mozart, Wolfgang Amadeus. "Requiem"
16. Mitchell, Joni. "Blue"
17. van Beethoven, Ludwig. Symphony #7, "Allegretto"
18. Vivaldi, Antonio. Concerto for Two Cellos in G minor, RV 531.
19. Dire Straits, Brothers in Arms, "So Far Away"
20. Michaud, Darius, "La Cheminée du Roi René"
21. Ewazen, Eric. "The Roaring Fork Woodwind Quintet"
22. Nielsen, Carl, "Wind Quintet, op. 43"
23. Mozart, W.A., "Clarinet Concerto," K. 622
24. Respighi, Ottorino, "Ancient Airs and Dances, Suite 1"
25. "Cello Submarine"
26. Ravel, Maurice, "Sonata for Cello and Violin"

27. "Going Home" traditional theme. Also appears in Dvorak's Symphony No. 9, the "New World"

28. Tchaikovsky, 1812 Overture

29. a-ha, "Take on Me"

30. Fauré, Gabriel, "Sicilienne"

31. Haydn, Josef, "Trumpet Concerto in E-flat Major"

32. Bach, J.S., "Concerto #5 in F minor for Harpsichord and Strings," BWV 1056

33. Krishna Das, "My Foolish Heart"

34. Tchaikovsky, Pyotr Ilyich, "Symphony No. 4"

35. Borodin, Alexander, String Quartet No. 2, the third movement, "Notturno"

36. Gotye, "Somebody That I Used to Know"

37. Schubert, Franz Peter. "Symphony No. 8 in B minor," D. 759

38. Mozart, W.A. Symphony No. 40 in G minor, K. 550

39. Bruce Springsteen, "Brilliant Disguise"

40. Gypsy Kings, "Cantos de Amor"

41. Messersmith, Jeremy. "I Want to Be Your One Night Stand"

42. Dvorak, Antonin. "Symphony No. 9 in E minor, "From the New World"

Acknowledgments

I stand in perpetual awe of musicians and writers who give our lives meaning and make our hearts dance. I was lucky to have a grandmother who was a book-loving librarian and a father who was a talented musician, so in a way this book was genetically programmed. The first readers of DISSONANCE were immensely helpful—Kathy McCreary, Chelsea Hedquist, and Laurie Tremain—and each in her own unique way set me on the right path. Of my many writing friends in Maine and elsewhere, I'd especially like to recognize Carole Zalucky, whose close reading saved me from many embarrassments. The enthusiasm of Julia O'Brien-Merrill, Chris Chapman, Sarah Schmalenberger, and Jane Margolis buoyed me, and their comments informed me. To my Memory2Memoir workshop friends—every time we met over the years, your brave, honest stories dazzled and inspired me. Finally, I am grateful for the support of my family: Jenna, Nita, and Maddie, who held down the fort while I was holed up in my study; and Rick, whose patience and faith in my ability to finish this project kept me going.

Most of all, I owe a huge hug and heartfelt thanks
to you, dear reader.

About the Author

A musician, writer, sailor, editor, educator, nonprofit executive and board member, and long-time New Englander, Barbara Burt now lives in Georgia with her husband, two daughters, one granddaughter, and two dogs. You can reach her at barbwriter@proton.me.

Also by the Author

For Young Readers
Burn Each Page
(unpublished winner of a PEN-New England YA award)
Stepping Back in Time
The Eve of the Revolution
Science in the Snow
Colonial Life: The Adventures of Benjamin Wilcox

Anthologies from Memoir2Memory Workshops
(Barbara Burt, editor)
Stories That Connect Us
Things We Know
Writing Our Secrets

Made in the USA
Monee, IL
23 August 2023

41502310R00174